# The Diary of
# ESSIE
# LASSITER

BOOK 1 *of the* ESSIE LASSITER TRILOGY

# SAM
# POLAKOFF

THE DIARY OF ESSIE LASSITER
BOOK 1 of the ESSIE LASSITER TRILOGY

Published by Komodo Dragon, LLC
Forest Hill, Maryland

Book design by GKS Creative

Cover image used under license from Alamy

ISBN (print): 978-1-7338898-6-5
ISBN (e-book): 978-1-7338898-7-2

Library of Congress Control Number: 2024919800

FIRST EDITION
Printed in the United States of America

www.sampolakoff.com

ALSO BY SAM POLAKOFF

*Hiatus*

*Shaman*

*Escaping Mercy*

*An Inch from Oblivion*

*A Christmas Tale (for children)*

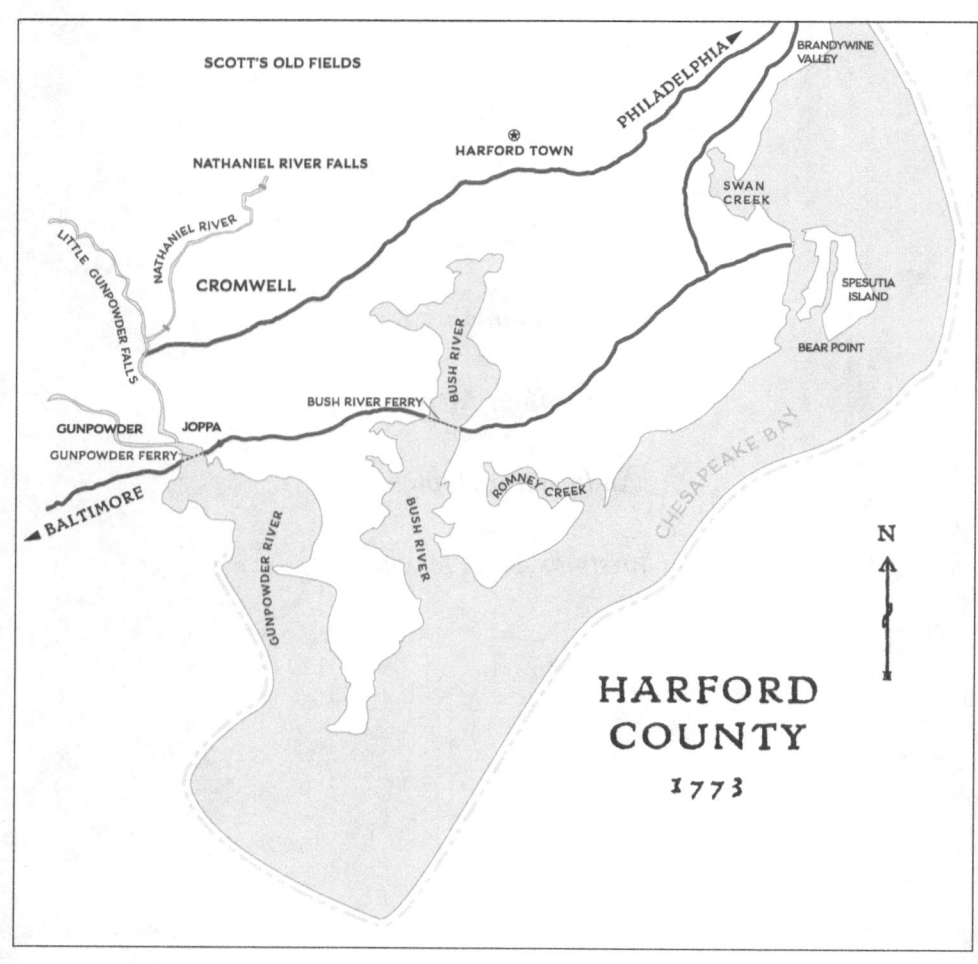

SCOTT'S OLD FIELDS

PHILADELPHIA

BRANDYWINE VALLEY

NATHANIEL RIVER FALLS

HARFORD TOWN

SWAN CREEK

NATHANIEL RIVER

LITTLE GUNPOWDER FALLS

CROMWELL

SPESUTIA ISLAND

BEAR POINT

BUSH RIVER

BUSH RIVER FERRY

GUNPOWDER

JOPPA

GUNPOWDER FERRY

BALTIMORE

GUNPOWDER RIVER

BUSH RIVER

ROMNEY CREEK

CHESAPEAKE BAY

N

HARFORD
COUNTY

1773

*Remember, all men would be tyrants*

*if they could. If particular care and attention is*

*not paid to the ladies, we are determined*

*to foment a rebellion, and will not hold*

*ourselves bound by any laws in which*

*we have no voice, or representation.*

—ABIGAIL ADAMS, 31 MARCH 1776

# CHAPTER ONE

## The Village of
## Wickhamshire, England

### 9 MAY 1773

Ugly lesions of smallpox marred Thomas's flesh. He coughed violently. In his final moments, a loud snapping sound abruptly shattered the peaceful aura I attempted to create. A broken string! The harp had been in my family for generations. The music gently caressing my husband's forlorn soul perished like Thomas's ability to incur a simple breath. His body ceased with a shallow intake of air strained by a wheeze. Smallpox ravaged our village. So many good people had died. And now, my Thomas.

Hours passed. Alone I sat in our cottage when a gentle knock befell my door. Reverend Pelt, a portly, older man with a kind manner, greeted me.

"My heartfelt condolences go out to you on Thomas's passing. I intended to come earlier, but as you know, so many have taken ill. Without Thomas here to tend to the sick, I am making the rounds and doing what I can."

"I know the people of the village appreciate anything you can do." I paused and then shifted from feeling sorry for myself to needing the Reverend's help in planning a proper funeral. "We have a small plot in back. I was hoping you could find two young men to dig a grave for Thomas, and maybe you could say a prayer, or a few words, or something."

Reverend Pelt looked at me with sad eyes. He placed an arm around my shoulder. "I know you aren't religious and have no family nearby. We will speak at church this Sunday of Thomas and the other villagers who have succumbed. I hope you will attend. It will bring you peace."

He was right. Thomas and I were not religious, although we believed in God. We arrived in Wickhamshire five years ago, just after Thomas was credentialed. He'd seen a post for a town doctor. The pay was meager, but the chance for a young couple to start fresh somewhere new felt like an adventure. Now, life was an angry wave exerting its temper against a rocky cliff. The reverend's next words cast stones upon my weakened spirits.

"I'm afraid the local ordinance stipulates we must burn the bodies of all smallpox victims."

Of course, I knew this already. My husband was the town doctor. I, the midwife, assisted him in many medical procedures. We worked together often, and I learned much beyond my designated station. "I understand," was all I could stammer out.

Reverend Pelt embraced me. He reminded me of my grandfather, an enormous bear of a man who said little but from whom love emanated. "We will burn Thomas's body this evening, along with the others. I recommend you stay home. I do not find it to be a pleasant experience."

I nodded but remained uncertain of my attendance. Being absent didn't feel like the right thing to do. Reverend Pelt left and returned within the hour. He brought two young men wearing neckerchiefs who wrapped Thomas's body in a bedsheet. I observed as they gently placed the body in a horse-drawn cart. Once they left, I sat alone on my favorite chair. It was from that position by the window that I usually worked on my quilts and enjoyed the late afternoon sun. Feeling more alone than at any point in my life, I cried. Thomas had been so sick I didn't realize how deprived I was of sleep. I napped on the hardwood chair until a rapping on the door sprung me to my feet.

"Mrs. Lassiter, open the door at once!"

I opened the door but only partially, poking my head through to see a stranger who bore a black handlebar mustache and an evil grin. I was not in the mood for visitors. Didn't he know my husband died only hours ago? "May I help you?" I asked.

He pushed his way past me into the house. "My name is Elias Carmichael. I hold your husband's debt. I understand he passed away earlier today. May I ask when you will make good on the amount owed?"

I shook my head in disbelief. "My husband's body has barely turned cold. You have some nerve showing up now and demanding money. How dare you! I would thank you to leave."

The evil man shrugged. His burly shoulders rolled backward in temporary defeat. "Fine, fine. Take a day or two to mourn. I'll be back to collect the two hundred pounds that is owed."

"Two hundred pounds?" I exclaimed. "Well, you may as well say one thousand pounds. I have no such fortune to give."

"You have a deadline of two days to figure it out. Otherwise, I will take possession of all your belongings, including this house, and throw you into the London Debtor's Prison."

"Good day to you, you wretched man."

With that, I slammed the door and contemplated my predicament. Thomas and I had worked steadily. We had no family about. The people in the village were appreciative constituents. There were no close friends from whom I might borrow this grand sum. I supposed I could run, but my family never condoned cowardice.

The hour for supper was drawing near. I wasn't hungry but, as was my habit, I went to the kitchen and prepared a meal, a bowl of chicken broth. I took a spoonful to my mouth and discarded the notion of eating. My will to live evaporated with Thomas's last breath. Eating was superfluous. I needed to leave the house. It smelled of illness and felt confining. As I hurried toward town, I detected an enormous plume of smoke filling the early evening air. Several of the men from town had dug a trench. Bodies wrapped in bed sheets were carelessly flung into a fire. My Thomas was one of them. These men showed no respect for the dead. Thomas deserved a proper funeral. He gave everything, including his life, to help the people of Wickhamshire. Is this how they repay him? The acrid smell of the event turned my stomach and lowered my spirits to depths previously unseen. Scared and alone, I returned to my cottage to face the murky future.

## CHAPTER TWO

# The Village of
# Wickhamshire, England

## 11 MAY 1773

Despondent when I awoke, I thought I might write a letter. Sadly, my parents had passed on. Since I had no siblings and no close friends to speak of, I settled on the only person who came to mind, Thomas's older sister, Charlotte. Three years Thomas's senior, Charlotte was the first to leave home upon marrying a teacher who was enchanted by the growing population of Wales. I dipped my quill in the ink jar and realized my letter held a true purpose. I did not intend to exploit my feelings and seek personal solace but to inform Charlotte about her younger brother's passing. How did I not think of this? What kind of person was I?

I could not complete the salutation before the angry rapping darkened my doorstep.

"It is Mr. Carmichael. I have returned to settle your debt."

I cautiously opened the door and was crestfallen to observe a small army complete with horses and covered wagons. Why did they need to send so many men to confront a grieving widow with her husband's debt?

"Do you have the two hundred pounds?" he barked, as if he already knew the answer.

Drawing breath deep into my lungs, I replied, "I do not, but if you grant me some time, I will find a way to repay the debt."

Mr. Carmichael snarled. "Mrs. Lassiter. It is not within my purview to grant extensions. The fact of the matter is your husband was already severely delinquent." Then, as if to add insult to injury, he said, "After we sell your meager abode, your husband's medical supplies and whatever else you may own, your remaining debt will still be substantial."

He paused and then, as if inconvenienced, went on. "I am required by law to ask if you have anyone who might stand in for you?"

"I don't understand."

"To retire your debt, my lady."

There was no one. I shook my head side to side while my eyes drilled into the wooden floor of the cottage.

"Fine." He nodded to a much older man with rounded spectacles and a kind disposition. "The town sheriff will read a proclamation."

The sheriff reluctantly read from a piece of parchment. "We hereby order the repossession and sale at auction of this home and all its possessions to partially retire the debt of Dr. Thomas Lassiter. His widow, Esther Lassiter, known by the name of Essie, shall be immediately remanded to the London Debtor's Prison where she will remain and pay rent until such time as the residual debt can be retired. Let all men here with me today bear witness."

An army of men invaded my home and began removing all that we owned, including my prized harp with the broken string. I recognized two of the men and spoke to them with fervor.

"Mr. Lindsworth! I delivered your son three months ago. Mr. Sammons! My husband cured your wife's fever just last week. Have you no shame?"

Memories waltzed past me as the men whom Thomas and I served faithfully refused to look me in the eye. When the last of our possessions was gone, I stood in the barren space, trying to suppress the tears, as two lawmen approached. They each grabbed an arm and escorted me to their carriage. I looked over my shoulder at the little home where Thomas and I had been so happy and wondered if life would ever be normal again.

# CHAPTER THREE

## London Debtor's Prison

## London, England

### 12 MAY 1773

For all intents and purposes, my life ended once Thomas died. We lived joyfully outside London in the quaint village of Wickhamshire. Even though we could not have children of our own, my heart filled with joy each time I assisted a young woman in bringing a babe into this world. Married seven years, debt, and hard times befell us. Thomas would not charge a fee to the indigent. Those who could, made installments for care and elixirs. The debts Thomas owed for medical supplies and training overwhelmed us. Somehow, Thomas kept the creditors at bay.

Days after my husband's passing, I experienced the distressing event of being removed from my home and taken to this horrid place with nothing but the clothes on my back. Here, I was expected to retire Thomas's remaining debt and pay rent for the privilege of residing in this place of incarceration. The jailers offered prisoners meager sums as offsets to debt for completing simple tasks. Certainly, I could cook, mend garments, and clean their quarters, but since I had no means of significant income, retiring the debt would be impossible.

A quarter century has passed since my birth. I draw breath, but I am no longer alive. Too afraid to speak, I sat against the wall on the cold stone floor.

Thirty or more women—I can't be sure—live in a space suited for a third that number. Some had been here for months. I had just arrived and wondered how I might survive a single night in this dreadful building. There were no beds. In a corner sat the unattended lone wooden bucket used for relieving oneself. The odor was ten times more pungent than any stable I'd mucked. The noise sounded like a vulture's screech upon discovering a dead animal on a country path. The room felt oppressively hot. No one could bathe, and the sweat poured from us like moisture sprouting from a rotten plum. I glanced to my right. A young woman, a girl really, perhaps fifteen or sixteen, sat sullenly, and I slid over to her, never rising to my feet. I feared drawing unwanted attention. When I reached the young girl, she was sitting up, her knees pulled to her chest and her head hanging low.

"I am Essie," I said, as I placed one arm around her shoulder for comfort.

Her head lifted gradually, acknowledging the gesture. I could see the young, freckled face was more frightened than I. Her blue eyes radiated the unabashed innocence of youth.

"What is your name?" I asked.

Speaking in broken English with a French accent, she replied, "I am called Marie." She stated her name in two long drawn syllables: Ma-ree.

Marie possessed a cold sweat across her forehead and was pale, like a faint yellow moon. When she spoke, her tongue appeared pasty, as if she had had no water for days.

"How long have you been here?" I asked.

Marie sat up. It was then I could see she was with child. "Two days," she said. Marie shivered, showing her sweat was from fever and not the warm spring day in the overcrowded room with only one barred window.

"You are unwell," I proclaimed. "How far along are you?"

She shrugged. "I cannot be sure. Seven or eight months, I think. I am so scared. I do not wish my child to be born in this place."

I softly swept her strawberry blond hair from her eyes and felt her forehead. For sure, Marie was feverish. I worried her illness would endanger her child.

"I am a midwife. I could help you, but I have no supplies. We must let the guard know you are ill and require a doctor."

Marie let go a nervous sort of laugh. "It is frivolous to try. When they found me in an alley and tossed me in here, my condition was obvious. They are unsympathetic."

Alarmed, I boldly asked if she were prepared to lose her child to cowardice. "You have nothing to lose," I proclaimed.

Marie smirked in a manner I thought immature. "The primary guard assigned to this cell is called *the Ruffian*. He is a large, round man with bulging eyes and a sagging jowl. I have watched him come into this hell hole, pull out prisoners by the hair, and then from the shrieks, I know he has his way with them in the next room. Do not fool yourself that a man like this will pay any mind to our medical needs. They'd sooner see us die than offer proper care."

The argument proved difficult to counter.

"If you let me look between your legs, I can tell when the baby might arrive."

Marie nodded and lifted her soiled skirt and pulled down her undergarment.

As I prepared to examine her, a powerful hand landed on my shoulder and a deep, throaty voice barked, "I got me first rights on that young lass." Her lurid breath swooped down on me like an approaching storm kicking up the road's unwelcome dust.

"You have mistaken the situation," I replied. "This girl is with child. I am a midwife."

Her large hand curled into a fist and struck on the right side of my jaw. I fell back, dazed, barely aware of my surroundings. My vision blurred, and the sudden pain obscured my thoughts. I could hear the ogre speaking haughtily as she forcefully inserted her filthy hand between the legs of young Marie.

"I'll show you a good time," she said. Wracked with fever, Marie writhed in agony on the unsanitary floor until the last breath left her body. The disgusting ogre who murdered Marie and her unborn child exhibited no remorse, returning to her clan and seeking some other way to exert her dominance.

I lay on the floor longer than I needed. There was hardly any space for movement. I admit I felt guilty for not rising to Marie's aid. Being scared, I didn't feel strong enough to stand up to the larger woman. I pulled myself to a sitting position and slid on my buttocks across the small expanse, trying to get close to Marie. I don't even know why. She was gone. I felt like someone should pay some respect to her short-lived existence. I knew precious little about her, but I determined that no one should leave this world in the manner Marie did. No one should have to live in the deplorable conditions of the debtor's prison. I could only hope that something might arise from the tragedy of my current plight.

# CHAPTER FOUR

## *London Debtor's Prison*

## London, England

## 26 MAY 1773

I had endured this hell for fourteen days. The food supply was limited, and the living conditions were appalling. Tiny spiders were everywhere. One ran up my leg while I slept. My lack of hygiene made me unworthy of being a human.

I had Thomas's debt, and I accumulated even more as they levied daily rates to simply exist. As I rested on the stone floor, my back was pressed against the wall. I learned to always be watching. Even though they took away the ogre who murdered young Marie, I still couldn't feel safe. I didn't know where the ogre went. I suspected they put her down like a rabid animal. For me, I saw no way out. My dark cloud had no silver lining. Death would have been a welcome respite.

A guard deposited a pail of warm water and two loaves of stale bread into our room. Parched women attacked the pail and each other to get a drink. I didn't bother. Loathing violence, I prefer to wither and perish. An older woman rescued a small portion of the bread and was kind enough to offer me some. Not eating for so long twists your stomach in knots. After a while, you cease to feel hungry. Concluding that the irritation would likely pass, I tucked the tiny morsel into a pocket of my dress. I sat, yearning to get a turn at the recently emptied waste bucket. I closed my eyes and felt myself doze off when a loud, threatening voice startled me.

"You! You over there against the wall. Come with me."

The older woman who shared her bread looked at me. "My dear, I fear the Ruffian is calling for you. Be still, and it will pass quickly."

I swiftly comprehended her warning. The Ruffian had been working his way through the younger women in our cell. I became adept at blending in along the back wall. Apparently, I hadn't escaped his notice, nor could I stave off the unwanted advance.

I rose gradually. "Me, sir? I am feeling unwell. I have come down with dysentery."

He grumbled something undiscernible in reply. The raucous women of our cell were too loud for me to hear. He finally motioned with one finger for me to approach. I inched across the room to the accompaniment of jeers. As I was just mere steps from his putrid stench, I decided to faint. I rolled my eyes toward the top of my head and let my knees buckle. I fell in a heap on the pestilent floor and lay motionless with my eyes closed. The Ruffian grumbled again before choosing another and departing.

My heart ached for the woman chosen to take my place. I snuck a peek through a squinted eye. She looked to be about my age and was, if I may say so, a homely type. However, maintaining any appearance of beauty in a place like this was difficult. In this situation, the only option was to survive at any cost or face certain death. Once I felt it safe to do so, I rose, hunched over for effect, and retreated to my spot on the back wall. On the way, I used the waste bucket and thought about how refreshing it might be to take a simple bath. My skin crawled and itched so. I wanted to scratch the flesh right from my bones. I fell asleep and was again interrupted by the calling of my name.

"Mrs. Lassiter, come to the front."

The guard calling my name was a young man, tall with chestnut hair. "The governor of this prison would like to see you. You shall address him as Lord Hall."

I nodded. As if he sensed my fear, he offered, "Do not despair, madam. Lord Hall is an elderly man serving his final post. He looks the other way with guards like the Ruffian, but he is not like that himself."

We walked from the cell along a cobblestone path to a large red brick house serving as the governor's residence. The air was cool, and the smell of blooming honeysuckle made me feel alive. I had almost forgotten the pleasing sensation of the sun on my face. "What does Lord Hall require of me?"

"First, that you become sanitary. Lord Hall won't tolerate filth in his presence. We have prepared a warm bath in the entry level drawing room for you to get cleaned up. There you will have privacy and a clean dress to wear. Once you are presentable, Lord Hall requires your service to mend his favorite quilt."

"To mend a quilt? I am sure there are many here who could accomplish such a simple task. Why was it that he chose me?"

"I am told that Lord Hall had a chance encounter with a woman from Wickhamshire who swore to him you were the best quilter in England."

The coincidence of it all struck me. I could not fathom who from my village could have met Lord Hall and what would have caused her to speak of me and my quilts. Of all things! They gave me fifteen minutes to take a bath, brush my hair, and dress. The new dress was a basic gray cotton gown and proved too big for my petite frame. But having clean clothes and feeling dignified was a comforting experience.

I opened the door and found the young guard waiting diligently to take me to Lord Hall. We climbed two flights of a wide, circular staircase, adorned with the most exquisite wood carving. I imagined it as one ascended by a fairy princess. When we arrived at the top, two matching doors blocked the path to Lord Hall's chambers.

The young guard tapped on the door and stated his purpose. "Lord Hall, I am accompanied by Mrs. Esther Lassiter, by your request, sir."

"You may enter," came the reply.

My first impression was one of relief. Lord Hall was a tall but elderly man, clearly in his seventies. His midsection held a slight paunch, and he wore his powdered wig on a head held high. This man saw himself as a gentleman, despite his willful ignorance of the operation of his prison. He was like a king, oblivious to the actions of his knights. Lord Hall wanted to hear what pleased him and just coast until retirement or death, whichever came first.

"I am Jonas Hall," he stated regally befitting his station. "I understand you are a gifted quilter. I fear that in my older years, I am always cold. My favorite quilt has come undone and requires mending."

I spotted the quilt on his large four-poster bed and immediately noticed a tear in the well-worn material. "I could certainly mend the old one, or if you prefer, I could make a new one."

"Oh, that would be divine," he replied. His smile revealed yellow teeth, likely from a lifetime of tobacco. A pipe sat in a holder on the round table situated beside Lord Hall's stuffed armchair. "How long do you need to complete the task?"

I didn't offer an immediate reply. I reasoned I could spend more time away from the cell if I prolonged my effort. "It depends. Would you want a similar pattern or perhaps something more elaborate?"

Lord Hall clenched his thin lips as a smile broadened his creased face. "I believe the Hall family crest would do just fine."

"A complex design could certainly take more time. I would think the task might be complete over the course of six weeks if I may work on it for the duration of each day." I would do almost anything to stay out of the prison cell. Since this institution charged daily rent for its corrupt operation, I calculated an opportunity to perhaps mitigate my growing indebtedness. "Lord Hall, if I may be so bold, would you consider letting my work on your new quilt pay down some of my debt?"

He cleared his throat and said rather directly, "I will pay you six pence per day, no more. My valet will provide you with everything you need. While this effort is ongoing, you will be taken to the main house to do your work. Returning each evening to the cell will place you in danger. The other prisoners will resent your being favored. You will have a cot set up in the stable. Each morning, you will bathe before entering the main house, and we will provide meals for you. Is this understood?"

No benefit remained from further negotiation. Sleeping in the stable, meals, and a regular bath were payment enough. Thomas's debt and the new daily assessments could never be overcome. I nodded and merely replied, "Yes, milord."

# CHAPTER FIVE

## *London Debtor's Prison*

## London, England

### 16 JUNE 1773

As the quilt neared its completion, Lord Hall took ill. I requested to see him, and the same chestnut-haired soldier who first brought me to the big house escorted me to his chamber. The truth was that Lord Hall and I developed a friendship of sorts. He was lonely and favored me for my compassionate listening and optimistic point of view. Despite being my captor, I didn't overlook the fact that Thomas once valued those same qualities.

As I entered the expansive quarters, the air held the scent of illness. It wasn't as severe as Thomas and smallpox, but it was still apparent. The room felt stuffy, and Lord Hall lay underneath the old, worn quilt, coughing. His cheeks turned crimson with each hack. It reminded me of the many pleurisy patients I worked with when I assisted Thomas. He would prescribe remedies to reduce inflammation of the lungs and promote free flow of the blood. Honey and milk might ease the symptomatic cough.

"Lord Hall, might I suggest you try barley water, linseed oil, or sarsaparilla?"

Before he could answer, I went to his bedside and helped him to prop his upper torso against the headboard. I placed two down pillows behind his back and head. That would keep the blood from stagnating and mucus from collecting in the lungs.

Once he was comfortable, he replied to my question with a decided huff. "The doctor attending me spoke of bloodletting as a means to recovery. I much prefer your suggestion."

"With your permission, milord, I will take my leave and visit the kitchen to see what I might find."

"Of course. Thank you, Essie."

That he called me by my first name, a nickname at that, was a comfort. Lord Hall viewed me as the daughter he never had. I walked unescorted to the kitchen and found the storage cabinet. I surveyed its contents and discovered a small burlap bag with barley roots. That would do just fine. I took the bag and turned to go when a sharp voice commanded my attention.

"What, pray tell, do you think you are doing?" The chestnut-hair soldier appeared angry and in no mood for interruption to his mundane patrol.

"If you will pardon me, kind sir, Lord Hall sent me to fetch a remedy for his illness."

"You are not a doctor," he proclaimed. "You are a quilter, and a prisoner at that. Do you know what the penalty is for stealing?"

If they would throw a widow in prison for her late husband's debt, I could only imagine what they might do to a thief. I chose not to debate the irritable soldier but to appeal to his sense of reason.

"If you speak to Lord Hall, he will surely validate what I have told you."

He grabbed my wrist, hurting me and causing the pain to travel through my forearm. The barley roots fell to the floor.

"Why don't we do that?" he snarled. The soldier dragged me up the stairs to Lord Hall's chamber, only to find the old man sound asleep. "I dare not disturb Lord Hall to corroborate your lie. Back to the cell with you."

"But I reside in the stable now," I pleaded.

"Not anymore," he remarked with disdain.

"But the new quilt. Lord Hall anxiously awaits its completion."

He paused at this notion. I appealed to his sense of responsibility—or rather, that he didn't wish to be held responsible for the delay in the quilt's completion. Maybe he realized the possibility of making an error in judgment was not beyond the realm. Never releasing his grip on my wrist, the soldier looked at the sky, as if in prayer, and exhaled forcefully. "It is clear what my responsibilities are. I caught you red-handed. You are a thief. I'm sure one of your other cellmates can finish the quilt."

And he threw me back to the wolves.

# CHAPTER SIX

## *London Debtor's Prison*

## London, England

### 30 JUNE 1773

Lord Hall passed away in his sleep last night. After suggesting barley water and other remedies two weeks prior, I never saw him again. The scuttlebutt was already ablaze concerning who London may send to replace Lord Hall. No doubt it would be someone less accommodating and undeniably stricter.

Since being tossed back into the hell of the large cell, I have had to fight for morsels of food and an occasional sip of water. Four days ago, I abandoned all hope. My strength started to wane, and without a purpose, I lost my will to live, just like the last flicker of an overused candle. My stomach churned. As I placed my hand on its surface to ease the discomfort, I felt my ribs protruding. I lay on the filthy floor and yearned for the days of a short while ago. Tending to Lord Hall and making his quilt provided a purpose, meager as it was. This existence offered nothing but misery and eventual death.

How quickly tables turn. Only two months ago, Thomas and I were content in our daily routines in Wickhamshire. We'd not a care in the world, and the future was bright. We shared dreams of traveling. Thomas longed to visit the New World. He theorized that individuals with medical training could find opportunities. The lands were abundant and fertile. The money we could make from farming was far greater than Thomas's minuscule pay as a doctor or the pittance I earned for delivering babies. These things we did from the goodness of our hearts. Still, we both had ambitions we would never realize. Driving these now fruitless thoughts from my head was no small task.

I breathed in the tepid air of the cell while doing my best to ignore the unsanitary stench of confinement, with dozens of women denied the tiniest aspects of humanity and self-preservation. The rusty creaking noise of the cell door distracted me from wallowing. A boisterous voice bellowed throughout the cell.

"Ladies, your attention is required." The noise did not subside, and the soldier raised his voice. "Ladies, the new governor of this prison is here with an announcement." Although the noise level decreased, it didn't vanish completely. The soldier trumpeted into a ram's horn to seize the attention of the inmates. The next thing I knew, a man much younger than Lord Hall took command of the gathering.

"I am Lord William Tomlin. The temporary governor of this prison. London has ordered the closure of this place, and it is my responsibility to see the task completed in an orderly manner."

"What is to become of us?" asked an elderly woman in the room's front.

"We have arranged your passage to the colonies in two weeks' time. Each of you will be responsible for the cost of said passage to be added to your existing debt."

"It's outrageous," another woman yelled. "These debts can never be retired."

"To the contrary," Lord Tomlin responded. "Wealthy colonists have assumed your debts. Each of you will be indentured to a colonist and held liable to that gentleman for the debt you entered the prison with, as well as the costs of lodging, food, and passage to the New World."

The older woman reared up and screamed, "Paying for food and lodging? We barely have a scrap to ourselves. Look around. You see what you've done? And you mean to charge us for the pleasure of starving?"

A soldier produced a whip and scowled at the old woman. "I advise you to remain quiet, or I will be forced to assist you in this matter."

The older woman quieted down, and yet another spoke up. "Where are they taking us, exactly?"

Lord Tomlin assumed control of the gathering once again and stated, "You will journey to Annapolis in the British colony of Maryland." After pausing for a moment to collect his thoughts, Lord Tomlin continued. "You will travel across the ocean on a ship called the *Odyssey*. The journey will take a month or more, depending on seafaring conditions."

Wouldn't Thomas be surprised? I was going to the New World after all. I'd no idea what would come next. All I knew was that it must be better than the hell they called the London Debtor's Prison.

# CHAPTER SEVEN

## The *Odyssey*

## 16 JULY 1773

Until today, the only boat I'd ever been on was my father's small paddleboat. He kept it by a pond on the back end of the land where I was born. That paddleboat never felt seaworthy to the young girl I was. I remember the small craft rocking perilously as I held firm to the side, hoping the brief trips Papa deemed fun would not cause my stomach to turn.

The *Odyssey* was much larger than Papa's tiny boat, but it looked just as rickety to me. I turned queasy at the thought of spending a month or more on this ship. As I grew older, I shunned Papa's overtures to join him on the pond, hoping beyond hope I would keep my two feet on God's green earth for the remainder of my days. Dozens of frightened women gathered on the London dock, waiting for embarkment. Judging from their expressions, many shared my sentiment. As we stood there, the early morning sun caused sweat to break out across my back. A whistle blew, and a uniformed man with a bushy mustache ordered us to proceed up a gangway. None of us could carry belongings of any kind. All we owned was taken from us when we had entered the London Debtor's Prison. The threadbare clothes on our backs represented the current state of our existence. I ambled in the middle of a pack that crawled at a snail's pace. When I reached the foot of the gangway, I stepped on to the first weathered board and grabbed hold of the rope on both sides. The enormous strain of the group caused the gangway to feel as though it would fail and plunge us into the harbor. My stomach rattled with the cracking sound of each tired board on the gangway. I imagined the boards giving way and my body lodged in the wreckage, with my lower half wet and uncomfortable, my midsection in pain from the jagged edges of the broken boards, and my face succumbing to tears.

Despite my inner turmoil, I boarded the *Odyssey* without incident, and the crew herded us below deck into a dark, damp space that smelled of journeys past. The tiny quarters reeked of the sea and its rotten aftermath. At first glance, the quarters held a few small wooden tables of the most basic construction, and a handful of beds, if one could call them that. I approached one of these beds and realized it was simply a shoddy handsewn mattress stuffed with an inadequate number of feathers and tied to a collection of small barrels using a thick rope.

The uniformed man with the bushy mustache abruptly appeared at the stairs from the top deck and addressed the group. "Ladies, I am Captain Quarles. This is home for the next several weeks. The beds are to be shared. You will receive two meals each day, and there are two chamber pots on either side of the deck. You are to stay below in this space until we arrive in the New World. I expect there'll be no trouble from you. We deal with insolence swiftly." He paused, stroked his mustache, and appeared to grin as he concluded, "If you cause trouble in any way, we will take you up to the top deck and throw your arse to the sharks."

Sadly, I understood Captain Quarles's threat to be hollow. We were to become indentured servants, meaning we were to be no more than property to a well-to-do colonist for an undetermined number of years.

# CHAPTER EIGHT

# The

# Atlantic Ocean

## 2 AUGUST 1773

I remembered why I hated Papa's paddleboat. The nausea from the still pond was one thing. But two weeks at sea wreaked havoc with my insides and my balance. The heat from the summer sun coupled with the dark, moist hold, and the inability for anyone to bathe, made our quarters untenable. They infrequently emptied the two chamber pots. I could hardly bear the odor of my own being. Many of the women had become weak, I among them. I got the chance to sleep on one of the barrel beds for a night, something I had never done before. It wasn't any better than sleeping on the wooden floor. I moved back to the floor but was so weak that I'd nary the strength to arise from my spot against the wall. I turned to my right and dry-heaved before lifting my head to witness the unthinkable.

One woman simply lost her mind.

I'd heard of people becoming mad from illness. Seeing it was something else.

The woman, who looked to be about my age, ran up the stairs to the main deck and began pounding on the hatch. "Let me out!" she bellowed. "Let me out now, or I'll claw your eyes from your heads, you mealy-mouthed, flea-bitten dogs!" She pounded and pounded.

Finally, a crewman opened the hatch, and the madwoman fell backwards off the steps. The crewman descended the short flight of stairs and picked her up from the front of her tattered dress. The garment ripped as he lifted her tiny body from the floor. "Causing a fuss, are we? Want to go up top? Be careful what you wish for."

Suddenly, my head filled with visions of young Marie in the debtor's prison. The pangs of guilt struck me like lightning bolts in the evening sky. While Marie was being viciously attacked, I sat idle, devoid of strength but more so lacking courage. This time, while weak, I discovered the wherewithal to stand and speak. I couldn't watch them abuse this woman, or worse, kill her.

"Leave her be," I yelled at the crewman. My throat was so dry I thought my voice sounded pathetic, as if I had cotton in my mouth.

He regarded me as if I were a gnat, nothing more than an annoyance. A presence to easily be swatted away. "What did you say?" he inquired with disgust.

I swallowed hard as he dropped the madwoman on the deck and came toward me. "I . . . I said you should leave her be. She's not in her right mind. She needs food and water to recover."

"And how would the likes of you know what she needs to recover?" he snarled.

Gathering my courage, I replied. "My husband was a doctor. I assisted him, and I am also a midwife."

"Oh, a medic, are you? Our medic has taken ill. You come with me."

He picked up the madwoman from the floor and threw her over his shoulder. She continued to berate him and pounded her fists into his back as he hauled her up to the top deck.

Obediently, I followed. When I reached the top of the stairs, the sunlight stung my eyes. After all, we had endured near darkness for two weeks.

The crewman took the madwoman to the edge and acted as if he would toss her over the side for her insolence. "You know the punishment for misbehavin', now, don't you?"

"You filthy vermin. Let me go."

Again, I recalled Marie's attack and my cowardice. I found my voice and addressed the crewman. "That woman is the property of a wealthy colonist who retired her debt. If you kill her, you will find yourself in a predicament similar to ours . . . saddled with a debt you cannot pay and imprisoned for years."

He looked dumbfounded, as if the thought had never occurred to him.

"All right, missy. I guess you have a point." He set her down against the top deck wall and handed her a flask. "This here is filled with water. Go drink up. I'll fetch you some bread in a minute."

I felt a hint of exhilaration. When the crewman retreated to the galley for the bread, I sat down next to the woman and tried to calm her.

"Sip the water. Don't drink too fast. It will turn your stomach."

She returned my gesture with the smallest of grins. She wasn't herself, but looking into her eyes, I could tell she possessed a good heart.

"I am Essie. What is your name?"

"Hazel," she replied. "Hazel Giddings. Glad to make your acquaintance." Her Cockney accent revealed her London origins.

"I don't know what will happen after you finish eating and drinking, but get what you can, gather your strength, and for God's sake, hold your tongue. These men are dangerous."

Hazel took my hand and squeezed it. The crewman came back with a bread crust and tossed it near Hazel. She picked it up and promptly offered it to me. I appreciated her attempt to repay my kindness, but eating anything would have disagreed with my sea sickness. I motioned for her to eat the bread, and the crewman, having exhausted his benevolence, growled at me to follow him.

He led me to the crew's quarters on the rear of the ship. A set of small steps resembled those in the hold where I had been confined. The space had beds and mattresses built into the side of the ship's inner wall, unlike our space, which was designed solely for stowing cargo. All the bunks were empty except for one. The medic lay still on his back, eyes closed, and at first, I thought he was sleeping. I leaned my head toward the medic's face and waited to feel a breath. When there was none, I placed three fingers on the medic's wrist in search of a pulse.

"I am afraid this man has expired," I declared to the shock of the crewman.

"The captain will be most unhappy with this news."

Before I could utter another word, the crewman whistled, and two men appeared from the hatch opening. They lifted the deceased medic from his bunk and carried him to the top deck. I followed to see them explaining to the captain, who quickly ordered that his body be wrapped in a bedsheet and bound. The captain summoned the crew to the center of the top deck, and they placed the body on a plank with two low-rise guardrails. The captain removed his hat, bowed his head, and said, "We mourn the passing of our medic and friend, James Greavey. May God bless his soul."

With that, the plank was lifted, and the body of James Greavey slid gently into the sea.

Moments later, Captain Quarles addressed me directly. I feared he would somehow blame me for Mr. Greavey's death, and I recoiled. I am sure my expression did little to hide the concern.

"You are the midwife?" he asked. His manner was direct but not blatantly aggressive.

"Yes," I replied. "I did not receive medical training, although my late husband was the town doctor and I learned quite a lot from assisting him."

He stared at me, intrigued. His bushy mustache bounced up and down as he spoke. "Our journey is only halfway through. You will have to serve as the medic for the remainder. Can you manage that?"

I felt taken aback and unsure of what to say. I mustered only a meek "I can try."

Captain Quarles answered resolutely. "On a voyage like this, men become ill. Some drink too much, some get seasick, some get the scurvy, and like poor Greavey, some die. All you can do is what you can do."

I nodded slowly. "Are there medical supplies at my disposal?"

He looked at the crewman who accompanied me from the medic's bunk.

"Show her Greavey's medical gear." He then turned back to me and said, "We have no quarters for a female. You will need to remain in the hold with the other ladies, and we will call you if we need you. What is your name?"

"I am Esther Lassiter," I replied. "Everyone calls me Essie."

"Fine, fine," grumbled Captain Quarles. He again spoke to the crewman. "Give young Essie Mr. Greavey's rations before returning her to the hold."

# CHAPTER NINE

## Port of Annapolis

## the Maryland Colony

## 12 SEPTEMBER 1773

My stomach and my mind were both relieved. Through the small porthole in our cargo hold, the sight of land was clear in the distance. Soon, we would dock in the port of Annapolis in the Maryland Colony. The balance of our journey, from a medical standpoint, was quiet. Shy of one drunken sailor and a broken arm, my responsibilities as the ship's medic were minimal. I did, however, get called up once daily for Mr. Greavey's food ration, and where I could, I would smuggle half to the cargo hold and share it with Hazel.

I could only imagine what I looked like. A mirror would have produced a frightful response. Despite being afforded Mr. Greavey's daily ration, I could not bathe, and my dress was terribly soiled. Uncontained hair and skin as dry as parchment caused my self-loathing. What would my new benefactor think of me? I spent the next several hours conjuring up images of my new master and how brutally tyrannical he might be. I pictured an older man, a cross between the slovenly Captain Quarles and the aged Lord Hall. After surviving the London Debtor's Prison and the deplorable conditions at sea, I was sure I could survive most anywhere. Although truth be told, my heart ached for Thomas and our quaint Wickhamshire cottage. My heart was heavy. These were now mere memories to be cherished, vanishing with each passing day, as distant as I was from England.

We were approaching the docks in the Annapolis harbor. Through the tiny porthole, I could hear the commotion. Their voices were clear. I angled my head just so to get a glimpse. Bedlam reigned as an angry mob paraded around a man elevated by a simple wooden podium. In a state of frenzy, the mob leader, Williams, speculated whether the incoming ship—the one I was on—carried a consignment of tea. The other irate men were there to inquire about the same thing. The poor sod at the podium appeared exhausted in his attempt to allay their concerns.

Through a crackle in his voice, he yelled, "The colony of Maryland honors the importation of tea from any reputable English source! The tea shall be assessed the king's tax as prescribed by his majesty's government. All those who interfere with the importation or taxation of British tea shall be imprisoned."

The lead man, Williams, jumped forward and yelled, "If we find tea in that cargo hold, we'll set the ship aflame right here in the bloody harbor!"

More shouting ensued, making the conversation all but impossible to hear. As the ship slowed to a crawl, crewmen dropped anchor, and Mr. Williams approached.

"Where's the captain? I want to see the ship's manifest. In fact, we demand to search this ship."

Captain Quarles was an experienced man. He did not take kindly to the intrusion. "And who might you be? Are you the governor?"

Williams growled back, "No, just an honest businessman who doesn't take kindly to British rule."

Quarles scoffed and said, "You'll have no need to search this ship. We are transporting women from the debtor's prison. They have been consigned to a Mr. Benjamin Carver, the local magistrate."

Williams backed down, and Captain Quarles barked at his crew. "Secure the lines and open the hatch. Get these women on to the dock and in a straight-line formation."

A moment later, the bright sunlight penetrated the hatch's opening, and I, along with the other women, rubbed our eyes. We were tired and weak. Ascending the small flight of stairs to the top deck was difficult, as our bodies had succumbed to atrophy over the course of the long journey.

While waiting in line on the dock, there appeared a tall man with a powdered wig and a blue coat matching his patriot's hat. He was clean-shaven and spoke in a deep voice.

"Ahoy, Captain. I am Benjamin Carver. I have come to collect the consignment you have brought."

I bristled at being called a consignment. My life was no longer worth anything. They regarded me as a commodity, something to be bought and sold.

Captain Quarles presented Mr. Carver with a sheaf of documents and a quill and asked for his signature. Once procured, Quarles offered Mr. Carver his hand to consummate the transaction and said, "They're all yours now." With a laugh, he added, "Don't mind the smell." Quarles walked toward a tavern with his first mate.

Mr. Carver turned and addressed the hapless group of scared and emaciated women. "Hear ye, hear ye. Be it known that I am Benjamin Carver, the local magistrate in the town of Annapolis, the capital of the Maryland Colony. You are hereby indentured to colonists who have retired your English debt. You will work for your master in any way he deems appropriate until such time as a fair calculation of your efforts equals or exceeds the amount of your debt."

Even though I was already aware of these facts, hearing them proclaimed caused a shiver. What did "any way he deemed appropriate" truly mean? Was I to be conscribed as a prostitute for some elderly brute?

Pointing to a matronly woman with a kind disposition, Mr. Carver continued. "Mrs. Shelly Allen will be your guide until sunrise tomorrow, when your new masters will be here to claim you. There is a women's bathhouse where you will clean up and receive a new garment to wear. Two local inns will house you for the night. It will be four to a room and one meal at sundown."

He paused as if to consider his thoughts and then finished by stating, "Do not contemplate escape. Local militia will guard the inns. They will not hesitate to shoot if you run or otherwise cause trouble."

I poked Hazel, who was standing next to me. I didn't want her to speak out. Her expression told me my instinct was right, but she took my meaning and remained quiet.

## CHAPTER TEN

## *Port of Annapolis*
## the Maryland Colony

### 13 SEPTEMBER 1773

The night passed without incident. The inn was sufficient if not cramped, but even sharing a bed with Hazel proved to be the best night's sleep since being whisked away to the debtor's prison. Before bed, they gave us each a bowl of red fish stew. It was a completely unique taste. Someone heard the word *crab* mentioned. It delighted my senses and proved a welcome respite from the occasional morsels of stale bread to which I'd sadly become accustomed. Prior to the meal, Mrs. Allen led us to the bathhouse, where we undressed and washed with warm water from a stained basin. They gave us a soap cake of fragrant lilac. While a proper bath would have been appreciated, cleansing my body and donning a new dress, even if it was a drab, gray pauper's garment, still brought relief. Mrs. Allen ordered a junior aide to gather our old clothes and take them out back to be burned.

I stretched and sat up on the edge of the bed, poking Hazel's shoulder to awaken her.

"Today is the day," I proclaimed. "We shall find out to whom we are indentured. I hope we will be together."

Through sleep-filled eyes, Hazel yawned and matter-of-factly replied, "It doesn't much matter, now does it? Being close would be a joy, but it is likely not to be. Our lives are without hope."

"Don't be so melancholy. We won't remain indentured forever."

"I wish I had your sense of optimism," said Hazel.

The sun had risen, and the early morning was warm and sticky. A slight breeze off the harbor kept the air palatable. Mrs. Allen sang her good morning call summoning us to meet on the square outside. Ten minutes later, Hazel and I stood with the others while two men brought a podium. Mr. Carver, the town magistrate, assumed his position at the lectern and, holding a sheaf of documents, began to speak. Behind the podium, a crowd of well-heeled men waited patiently. I believed that these were the wealthy colonists to whom we would be indentured. Mr. Carver commanded attention.

"This morning, we shall begin the handoff of indentured servants to their new masters. As the magistrate, I have certified that each colonist has properly retired the debt of the servants that he will be granted possession of forthwith. I shall now recite the debtor-in-possession and the names of their servants. Ladies, once your name is called, please raise your hand and leave with your master."

Those words, *master* and *possession*, filled me with horror once more. Was I ever to feel human again? I listened as Mr. Carver droned on.

"We begin with Alice Bremington. You are indentured to Mr. Elijah Stonewall of Charles County." A girl of perhaps seventeen years of age timidly raised her hand, and a small, middle-aged man with a mousy demeanor approached her. I couldn't imagine how this young girl found herself in such a position, but then again, I questioned my own predicament.

Two quarters of an hour passed. Mr. Carver called the name of a woman, and the process repeated itself. Finally, I perked up when Hazel's name was called.

"Hazel Giddings. You are indentured to Mr. Charles Greene of Harford County."

Hazel left with Mr. Greene. I flashed her a smile and mouthed the words *Good luck*. I so hoped I would see her again. I was unfamiliar with the geography of the Maryland Colony and did not know where the county of Harford might be. Alongside the remaining women, I stood impatiently in the square, waiting for my name to be called. Finally, as there were only two of us left, Mr. Carver called my name. Two colonists remained behind the podium. One was younger, tall, and somewhat dashing, while the other was the ogre I feared when told we would come to the New World.

"Esther Lassiter. You are indentured to Mr. Aquila Wright of Harford County."

Which of these men was Aquila Wright? I raised my hand and ambled toward the podium. The younger of the two colonists proceeded forward and offered a warm smile. I was fortunate, I felt, that perhaps the future might be less tortuous than I expected, although back in England I'd known my share of young, handsome men who were only mean drunks. I tried to maintain my natural sense of optimism and thought about my new home in Harford County. That's where they had sent Hazel. I held onto the smallest glimmer of hope that we would somehow be reunited.

The brown eyes were kind in appearance. Before Mr. Wright spoke a single word, I came to appreciate this man's nature. He extended his hand and introduced himself. His voice struck me. It bore not a trace of British heritage. How long had he been in the Maryland Colony?

"Where are your belongings? I shall load them on the wagon."

Feeling ashamed, I blushed. "Thank you, sir, but I have nothing."

He shook his head, and I found myself bewildered that this man of affluence would have so little experience with indentured servants. He guided me to a horse-drawn carriage with a wooden cart. Up front sat a young girl wearing a dark blue dress and a white bonnet made of lace. Her hair had the same brown sheen as Mr. Wright. When she looked up at me, her eyes confirmed that this must be his daughter. Why hadn't this young girl remained at home with her mother?

I smiled warmly at the young girl. "Hello. My name is Esther, but everyone calls me Essie."

The young girl was reticent to reciprocate, but her father urged her to respond. She quietly said, "Hello. My name is Penelope, but everyone calls me Penny."

"How old are you, Penny?"

"Eleven," she replied. "But I'll be twelve in a few months, and Father says he will build me a playhouse out of trees from the forest."

"Oh, how nice! I hope I can visit your new playhouse, if it's all right with your mother and father."

With that intended nicety, Penny became sullen and turned away from me.

Mr. Wright tenderly patted his daughter on the back and addressed me with compassion. "My wife died last year. Smallpox. It was hard on us both."

I nodded and said, "I'm so sorry for your loss." It was not the time for sharing personal tragedy. I understood that it was not my place.

Mr. Wright helped me into the rear of the carriage, where I sat alone. He piloted the carriage with his young daughter by his side.

"How long is the journey to Harford County?" I asked.

"If we don't run into any trouble, we can be there by sundown."

"What kind of trouble might you expect?"

He paused, obviously not wanting to upset his young charge. "Indians, mostly. We could also encounter wildlife."

"Wildlife?"

"Yes, a coyote, or perhaps a bear." He patted the musket sitting upright between him and his daughter. "Not to worry. I'm a very capable shot."

"Who are these Indians you refer to?"

"They occupied these parts before European settlers arrived. They view us as squatters and will kill to preserve their land."

Penny turned squeamish at the suggestion, and judging from Mr. Wright's face, he knew he'd said too much. He added, "I've found that most the of the Indian tribes we encounter will be reasonable if we show mutual respect." For good measure, he added, "I've even successfully traded with the ones down by the river."

I let the subject rest. I had no experience with these Indian tribes and hoped we would not encounter any on our daylong journey.

We traveled in silence for quite some time, and then, as if to deliberately break the tedium, Mr. Wright proffered more information about his home.

"We live in the town of Cromwell. It's by the Bush River, near to Harford Town, the county seat."

"Do these Indians live by the river?"

"Not anymore. The tribes have migrated, mostly southward, into the Appalachian Mountains in the Virginia Colony and as far westward as the Oklahoma Territory. Still, a stray collection might be in the area."

Talk of Indians was unsettling. I badly wanted to change the subject. "Tell me about your home."

"Penny and I reside in a two-story home my family built when my grandfather arrived from England more than a century ago. King Charles granted him the land to farm, which he did until he died. My father took over and lacked the stomach for farming. He began a gristmill, which I took over once he passed on."

I considered this information and pondered the status of the land. Back in England, farms were expansive tracts with hordes of industrious men who labored from sunrise to dusk. I scratched my head in contemplation. "What became of the land once used for farming?"

"We built on a portion. The remainder is simply used for riding and hunting."

Penny had fallen asleep and was leaning on her father's side. Not much bothered him as he guided our carriage down the hardscrabble path.

Hours passed. The long carriage ride across difficult terrain was taking its toll. My body still ached from so many nights sleeping on unnatural surfaces in an upright position. I was malnourished and feared this would make me more susceptible to illness. I was lost in thought until a man in the road ahead, waving his arms, caught my attention and disturbed my rumination. I'd seen nothing like him before. His skin was as dark as the cauldron I once used to make stew for Thomas.

Mr. Wright stopped the carriage. "Sit back," he commanded of me. "Stay in the back." He then woke Penny and helped her sit by my side. "Watch her."

I became frightened. Mr. Wright was on high alert. "Was this one of the Indians you spoke of?"

"No," he replied brusquely. "Most likely a runaway slave."

"Slave?"

"Yes, I can explain later."

The dark-skinned man approached with his hands in the air. His clothes were dirty and in tatters. "Please, sir," the man beseeched. "I am trying to get as far north as possible."

"Where did you escape from?" Mr. Wright inquired.

"Farley's tobacco plantation in Cambridge, sir."

I noted the slave's difficulty with English and the sound of unfinished words. When he addressed Mr. Wright as *sir*, it sounded more like *suh*.

The slave pleaded with Mr. Wright. "I aim to go north, get me a job, and then bring my family up with me. I'm no danger, and I'd be mighty grateful for a ride."

Mr. Wright shook his head, as if he knew better, but was willing to help anyway. "What's your name?"

"Fred, sir. They call me Fred."

"I am Aquila Wright of Harford County. I am traveling with my daughter, Penny, and a servant. You will need to lie flat in the wagon and cover yourself with the tarp. I can take you as far as Joppa. From there, you may find passage on the river."

Fred smiled and said, "Thank you kindly, Mr. Wright."

A few minutes later, we were moving again. Penny remained with me, huddled close. I could tell that she was scared. So was I. The New World was aptly named for a reason.

I called to Mr. Wright. "Why can't Fred ride with us? Why must he hide under a tarp like a criminal?"

"The law, although it is wrong, considers Fred the property of Mr. Farley, the owner of the tobacco plantation in Cambridge. Militias will look for him. We will face serious consequences if they catch us harboring an escapee."

Now, my belly rumbled with anxiety. "I couldn't possibly go back to prison."

He demurred and finally replied, "I don't think you need to worry about it."

"Do you keep slaves as property at your mill?" I inquired, feeling somewhat emboldened.

He shook his head. "My father shunned the practice, and so do I. Everyone who works at my mill is free and receives a fair wage for an honest day's work."

I was relieved at this news. It reinforced my initial feeling upon meeting Mr. Wright. "Are there other indentured servants . . . like me?"

"No. In fact, you are the first one and probably the last."

"What made you seek an indentured servant?"

He sighed. "After my wife died, a friend of mine in the legislature urged me to pursue help to tend to Penny."

I considered his plight. A widower with varied business interests and what sounded like a role as a leader in colonial governance. I was keen to learn more about how things worked in the New World. My experience to date was like a story imagined from the reading of a Henry Fielding novel.

We rode in silence for quite some time. I looked back into the cart where Fred lay under an old tarp. The filthy cover probably secured payloads of dirt, logs for the fire, and other such items. Mr. Wright didn't even shake off the tarp's debris before covering Fred. The wagon was not long enough for Fred to lie extended. He bent his knees and curled up to remain unseen. I worried he might be uncomfortable. Lord knew I had an acute comprehension of the subject. I desperately wanted to inquire about Fred's well-being. Mr. Wright warned me emphatically not to. Even looking back into the cart might attract unnecessary attention.

"Cambridge is far away along the eastern shore. As a runaway, Fred understands the risks and knows the rules when accepting passage from well-meaning people."

The sun set and cooler air prevailed. I detected the unmistakable sound of the river residing on the forest's edge.

Mr. Wright stopped the carriage and secured the horse to an oak tree. He surveyed his surroundings and then lifted the tarp. "All right, Fred. We have arrived at the Gunpowder River. You must go. My advice is to travel the river south and seek a kind soul with a vessel who might take you to Spesutia Island. From there, you will need another vessel to sail north on the Chesapeake Bay—or better, a larger vessel to sail the coastline up to New York. Best of luck to you."

Mr. Wright handed Fred a half loaf of bread and two apples. Fred thanked Mr. Wright and nodded his goodbye to Penny and me. I delivered a smile of sympathy and hope for his safe passage and continued success.

Mr. Wright assumed his position in the carriage, and we were soon on our way.

"We have perhaps an hour of daylight. We will need all of it to arrive in Cromwell before dark," he proclaimed. "The bridge is up ahead. Once we cross the Nathaniel River, we will be close to home."

I gazed upon the river far below and marveled, as I always had, how one of God's creations provided a sense of calm. The rushing water parading gracefully over the jagged edges of the protruding rocks was breathtaking.

I sat back and found my eyelids becoming heavy. The anxiety of the past few days had taken its toll. I fell into a light sleep, still conscious of the bumps on the path and sound of the flowing estuary. The rickety noise of the old bridge was unmistakable. A similar bridge was part of our frequent journeys to visit relatives when I was a child. When the carriage stopped, I could see the outline of a fine home in the early evening dusk. A stable was off to the right of the house.

Mr. Wright helped Penny and me out of the carriage as my tired eyes strained to see the grounds.

I stretched my tired body and began walking toward the barn.

"Where are you going?" Mr. Wright asked.

Embarrassed, I replied, "I assumed I was to reside in the stable with the horses."

"Heavens, no. We have a room for you in the main house. It is off the kitchen and very private. Mrs. Greene will visit tomorrow and help you get settled."

"Mrs. Greene?"

"Her husband, Charles, is a friend, and she has been helping Penny and me since my wife's passing. The Greenes live nearby."

My heart lightened. A private room. An actual bed. And the Greenes! That was the name of the colonist with whom Hazel had been indentured.

When I bid them goodnight, I closed the bedroom door, lay back in the glorious feather bed, and allowed my head to rest on the overstuffed pillow. I pulled the quilt over my shoulder and fell into a sleep unlike any since before Thomas took ill.

## CHAPTER ELEVEN

## *Cromwell's Passage*
## the Maryland Colony

### 14 SEPTEMBER 1773

I soon learned that the estate of Mr. Aquila Wright, including its mill, was properly known as Cromwell's Passage. Mr. Wright's ancestor who settled this land at the behest of King Charles was his maternal grandfather, a Mr. Mordecai Cromwell. Mrs. Greene explained this to me as she showed me the wares of the house and listed my duties. I was to have responsibility for Penny, including getting her dressed and accompanying her to the schoolhouse each day. I was to assist the staff in preparing all meals, keeping the home tidy, mending the clothes, buying food, and if time permitted, tending to the stables. There would be no shortage of work, which meant a dearth of free time. I already missed my harp and longed for the serenity of reading a book. Mrs. Greene also told me that Mr. Wright expected me to accompany him and Penny to church each Sunday. The prospect of this did not thrill me. Thomas and I believed in God, but we somehow never found comfort in attending the Wickhamshire church.

"You will need to assemble a wardrobe," Mrs. Greene declared. "Mr. Wright has provided a purse for you to purchase a dress suitable for Sunday mornings. The rest is up to you. Can you sew?"

"Oh, yes, milady. I can make quilts. Clothing is not my strong suit, but I can get by. Is there money allocated to purchase material?"

"That won't be necessary. Mrs. Wright was a proficient dressmaker. We shall visit her drawing room today. There is an abundance of cloth, thread, and needles. She even has a reserve of imported silks and satins. Everything you might need." Then, after a long pause, "I can help if needed."

We walked up the grand staircase. Its handsome wood carved railings wound their way to the top floor in a wide, circular fashion, and as I ascended, I imagined I was a princess living in a fairy-tale castle. As I entered Mrs. Wright's drawing room, I could see that it had remained well preserved since her death. The room appeared as if Mrs. Wright had been sewing in it only a day earlier. A half-completed child's dress, intended for Penny, was draped across a velvet-covered bench. I understood why entering this room would be distressful for Penny and her father. I inspected the unfinished garment and pledged to complete it as my initial undertaking in this stately room.

"Look over there," Mrs. Greene declared. "That old travel chest."

"Yes, what of it?"

"Why, I'd forgotten all about it. I packed many of the missus's dresses in there. She wasn't much bigger than you. I am sure we can take them in to fit you just fine." Mrs. Greene was beaming at the prospect.

It made me anxious, and I was sure I wore my feelings on my sleeve.

"Aquila gave me free rein to get you settled, and especially with this room. I'm sure he would be delighted that these fine garments were being put to use."

I barely relaxed at the notion. Seeing another woman in his wife's clothes might elicit ill will between us. Cloth was abundant and scattered all around. I could fashion myself a few things to wear without disturbing the sanctity of Mrs. Wright's memory. First, I reminded myself, I would finish the dress for Penny.

An hour later, after I had a sense of the house, I accompanied Mrs. Greene to town. Learning the way to the market was crucial, she explained, as it housed the products and services necessary for fulfilling my responsibilities. The walk was pleasant, and early fall leaves were ripe with red, orange, and yellow hues. I longed to inquire about Hazel but didn't have the courage. If Mrs. Greene was showing me how to function in the New World, who was showing Hazel? I assumed her duties were like mine. We walked in silence for a bit, and I managed the courage to ask a question.

"Do you and Mr. Greene have children?"

It took her a moment to collect herself. I had hit a raw nerve.

"We had a son, John. The redcoats shot him while he was serving in the local militia. By the time they carted John back to Cromwell, Dr. Bradley couldn't save him."

"I'm so sorry for your loss." I presumed Mr. and Mrs. Greene were at least second-generation colonists. She spoke with nary an accent. Strangely, being British, I experienced guilt knowing that one of my countrymen had killed John. I wondered if Mrs. Greene resented me because of my heritage. She didn't seem like the type to engage in scorn without reason, but one never could tell at first blush.

When we arrived in town, the street was lined on both sides with businesses, and many people bustled about: a cobbler, a blacksmith, a produce store, and an emporium where one could purchase dry goods and other sundries. We visited all these establishments, with Mrs. Greene introducing me to the proprietors as Aquila's new servant. While it was a humbling sentiment, I reminded myself that my current situation far outweighed the London Debtor's Prison.

Our first stop was at the dressmaker. Mrs. Greene would collaborate with the seamstress to suitably outfit me for Sunday church. I concluded that such a garment would also be appropriate in the event I was to attend a wedding or funeral. Back in England, the wealthy ladies of London society wore sacque gowns for such occasions. They were loose-fitting, with pleats in the back and around the shoulders, and revealed a bit of one's petticoat. For my entrance into colonial Maryland, Mrs. Greene and I decided on a much more modest design with a full skirt enveloping the petticoat and enhanced by a white linen apron and bonnet.

I carried a long-handled basket from the kitchen of the Wright's home. Mrs. Greene and I finished in the market, having bought a chicken and some vegetables for stew. Mrs. Greene informed all the store proprietors that I was authorized to purchase whatever I needed and to place the charges on "Aquila's account." No one argued.

As we were preparing to leave, I stopped, and Mrs. Greene asked with a questioning tone, "Is something wrong?"

"It just occurred to me—we forgot to purchase the flour needed for baking."

She laughed and patted my shoulder, consoling my naivete. "Mr. Wright owns the largest mill in Cromwell. He supplies the town with flour. You needn't buy it. Whenever you require, you walk to the mill, and they will provide it to you free of charge."

I felt foolish.

Then she continued. "It is harvesting time now. You will probably see a steady stream of farmers bringing their corn and other grains to Cromwell's Passage for milling."

"Of course," I replied. It made perfect sense. We turned to walk back home. An approaching carriage interrupted our walk. The rider was an elderly man who was gaunt and wrinkled. His wispy white mustache had grown over his small round mouth and the goatee he sported formed a triangle below his chin. His string bowtie was askew. He appeared weary but greeted Mrs. Greene with a smile.

"Dr. Oliver Bradley, I'd like to introduce Aquila's new servant, Essie Lassiter. She's just recently arrived from England."

He hopped down from his carriage, removed his black top hat, and smiled, revealing a mouth full of crooked teeth. "It is my pleasure to make your acquaintance, Essie."

"The pleasure is mine, Dr. Bradley."

"Essie was a midwife in England."

Dr. Bradley's face brightened like a full moon. "Is that so? Our last midwife journeyed with her husband to the Oklahoma Territory two years ago. I hope I can call upon you from time to time."

His kind manner struck me. "Of course," I replied, "assuming Mr. Wright approves."

"Not to worry, I will make a proper inquiry of Aquila."

With that, he tipped his hat, boarded his carriage, and proceeded to town. The prospects of serving Mr. Wright and his daughter were pleasing, but if I were honest with myself, I did miss ministering to the needs of expectant mothers. I did so hope Mr. Wright would agree to my assisting Dr. Bradley.

# CHAPTER TWELVE

## Cromwell's Passage
## the Maryland Colony

### 15 SEPTEMBER 1773

I awoke ahead of the sunrise and ventured through the bedroom door to the spacious kitchen. Opening the cupboard, I removed a tin of milled oats, and prepared oatmeal and eggs sunny-side up using a cast-iron skillet hanging by the fire pit. Mrs. Greene told me that Mr. Wright enjoyed tea early in the morning, and so I brewed some and placed the teacups by each place setting, along with a pitcher of fresh water. Lastly, I found a partial loaf of bread and sliced it carefully. I made a mental note that I would need to bake more bread later that day.

As the smells of the kitchen announced a new day, Mr. Wright descended the grand staircase and entered the dining room. Dressed in tall boots, he was prepared for manual labor rather than the business of a large enterprise proprietor. He greeted me cheerfully and asked how I was getting along.

"Just fine, Mr. Wright. Mrs. Greene has been most helpful."

"Celia and Charles have been dear friends. I'm not sure what I would have done without them. After Rebecca . . . Mrs. Wright's unexpected passing, I was despondent. Melancholy overtook me. Were it not for the kindness of the Greenes, I'm not sure where we'd be."

I thought of his situation and considered the differences between our plights. Aquila Wright, with his wealth and circle of friends, sustained the loss of a spouse and grieved as one should. In time, he was able to recover through a nurturing community. After my husband died, having faithfully served the community for years, his debts were called in and I lost my home and everything in it—and to make matters worse, I was placed in a debtor's prison from which I was eventually sold into indentured servitude in a distant land. Time to mourn Thomas's passing was a luxury I could ill afford. My mind was resentful, and my heart was hollow.

Penny padded into the dining room in a white cotton nightgown and bare feet. Her dark brown hair desperately needed a brush and a ribbon. We would tend to that after the meal. It was Saturday, and school was not in session. Penny would spend the day with me. I would have to learn what this girl enjoyed and how to relate to her.

Mr. Wright sipped his tea and looked at his daughter. "I will help Mr. Trumbull, the foreman of the grist mill, today. We will be installing a new bed stone. The old one has a sizable breach, and grain is escaping into the void."

She observed him with a quizzical expression. "What's a bed stone, Father?"

"You've been in the mill. Remember how we drop grain from a large funnel into a hole in a top stone?"

"Yes, I remember."

"That is called the runner stone. The runner stone grinds the grain against a bottom stone, or the bed stone."

Penny became excited. "So, if the bed stone breaks, the grain can't be properly ground. Right, Father?"

He tenderly patted her hand. "That's right, my dear."

Learning how a grist mill operated fascinated me. I endeavored to meet Mr. Trumbull and see it for myself.

After Mr. Wright completed his meal, he removed a soiled work coat from a hook by the back door and headed out to start his day. I did not know when he might return or on what schedule he generally conducted his affairs. No one explained any of this to me. I would have to confer with other staff and learn as I proceeded.

"Penny, can I help you get dressed?"

She was still unsure about me. I was a stranger, nothing more. This young girl was on the cusp of womanhood and naturally needed her mother. My first impression was that Mrs. Greene, the only other female in her life, so far as I could tell, was not close to the girl. I needed to be mindful of my role. I was just a servant, not her friend, and definitely not her mother.

"I can dress myself," she replied.

"Fine. What would you like to do today?"

"Pick blackberries. Then, can we bake a pie?"

It lifted my mood. "Yes, that sounds splendid."

—⚬⚬—

I'd kneaded dough for the bread we would require while Penny retired to the outside patio with a book of poetry. By early afternoon, the smell of blackberry pie filled the house's lower level. Through the open window, I could see Penny sitting with proper posture, legs crossed, under a white parasol, turning the pages of her well-worn book.

I looked away to check on the pie when a bloodcurdling scream pierced the moment. My arm knocked into the rack holding the pie, and it slid from its place. Running to the door, I discovered a large black bear, its terrifying claws flexing in midair as the wild animal roared. Penny was only a stone's throw from the bear, and he had his sights on her. A gun rack hung by the door. I unhinged a musket from its grasp and calmly told Penny to get up and slowly move into the house. My father showed me how to load and fire a musket when I was a mere girl back in England. I had wanted no part of it and refused to shoot. But now, with our lives on the line, I quickly dropped gunpowder down the muzzle, inserted the lead ball, and used the ramrod to pack it snug.

This disturbance angered the enormous bear. It took a step toward the house, and although I'd never fired a musket before, I did my utmost to steady the weapon in the same manner as Father and did not hesitate to pull the trigger. As Penny made her way into the house, I slammed the door shut as the predatory beast fell backward to the ground. The thud nauseated me. Prior to this, I'd never killed another living thing.

I felt my insides rattling as I wrapped my arms around the petrified girl, unsure whether we were safe. The gun's blast wounded the bear, but I had no intention of venturing outside to confirm its survival. Penny and I huddled together on the kitchen floor, near to where the blackberry pie had splattered. In a matter of minutes, another gunshot startled both of us immensely.

The door swung open, and Mr. Wright stood tall, pistol in hand and a look of grave concern across his face. "Are you both all right?"

We both nodded, and he continued. "Tell me what happened."

After we recounted the story, he opened his arms and embraced his daughter. He looked at me and said, "You were very brave to shoot that bear. He could have killed you both."

Still shaken, I replied, "We didn't have bears in Wickhamshire. Can we expect more of them?"

Looking at the mess on the floor and detecting the scent of fresh baked goods, he replied, "It's not a common occurrence. Bears inhabit the forest on our estate. He was likely attracted by the smell of the pie." And then he looked at the floor, laughed, and said, "It looks like it would have been rather tasty."

Ashamed, I merely replied, "I will clean that up." Then I looked at Penny and said, "Perhaps we can try again tomorrow, after church?"

Tears were still in her eyes, and she trembled in her father's arms.

# CHAPTER THIRTEEN

*Cromwell*

the Maryland Colony

16 SEPTEMBER 1773

M y father built the Cromwell Church," explained Mr. Wright. "The beautiful river stones were brought by the cartload from Deer Creek. As a
youngster, I was part of a crew that worked tirelessly to build this shrine. My
father said it would pay homage to the churches Grandfather knew as a young
man in England."

"And so they succeeded," I replied. "It is reminiscent of the Victorian-style
churches common to the outskirts of London."

He nodded in appreciation. His expression revealed the pride he took in
helping to create a legacy structure in the town founded by his grandfather. The
front doors were whitewashed and rounded at the top, a sharp contrast to the
triangular roof with its black shingles and the majestic spire rising from the rear.
The steeple, constructed of river stones, held a window in its lower quadrant and
rose to a point of gray brick where an iron cross adorned the peak. An opening
was visible in the brick portion, where I could see a bell that resembled those
commonly found in the English countryside. The bell rang at the hour and filled
Cromwell with musical solitude reminiscent of the harp I once enjoyed.

The early morning sun was pouring down in complement to the fall weather.
The pastor stood at the top of the three wooden steps that led to the church

entrance. He instantly recognized Mr. Wright and zealously approached. He kneeled and looked Penny in the eye with a smile that warmed the child's expression.

"We have a new song to sing today," he gleefully declared.

Penny squealed with delight. "I love to sing. Is it a fast or slow song?"

"It's a hymn, but it has some . . . what's the expression?" The pastor paused for a moment and then resumed his train of thought. "Some pick-me-up at the end."

Penny smiled, and the pastor took Mr. Wright's hand and embraced him. "Aquila, it is good to see you. How are you on this fine morning?"

"I am well, Pastor Vinson. Allow me to introduce our new servant, Mrs. Esther Lassiter, recently arrived from Wickhamshire in England."

The pastor turned and, without warning, embraced me. His outpouring of love surprised me, for I was but a common servant. He pulled back and looked at me straight on. His blue eyes were comforting. He was a stranger, but I immediately felt I could tell him anything.

"Mrs. Lassiter. It is indeed a pleasure to make your acquaintance. I was raised in Aylesbury, a stone's throw from London." Then he laughed and said, "Well, maybe more like a long ride on a horse."

Aylesbury was familiar but not intimately. Thomas and I once passed through on a visit to his sister's house. The town exuded charm, and its residents were warm and welcoming.

"Pleased to meet you, Pastor Vinson. Please call me Essie."

He responded with a garrulous expression and said, "Essie it is."

We proceeded into the church. The affluence in the church overwhelmed me as I looked around. Having been polished to perfection, the pews gleamed as if they had never been sat upon. The pulpit shared the same characteristic. With reason, the Bibles and hymnals were worn. Many people attended and considered this church central to life in Cromwell. After all, Cromwell Church was the only place of worship in this growing town. People of differing faiths would have to travel a fair distance to attend another church. I spotted a row on the back right that held what my father would call "the ragged people." I looked down at Penny and said, "Stay with your father. I will be in the back, and we can meet up after the service."

"Nonsense," Mr. Wright answered. "You will sit with us. Penny would be more comfortable next to you."

I questioned this, as the child scarcely knew me. Still, it was not my place to proffer arguments, and I followed along. We sat down in the front row, which was always reserved for the Wright family as the descendants of the church's founder. I felt special. Seated in such a prominent position in this prestigious house of worship made me feel, for just an instant, that I was not here as a servant, a soul under duress, but a parishioner in good standing. I cherished that momentary thrill.

As a child, I had attended church with my family. Thomas and I were not religious. Thomas was agnostic, and as a dutiful wife, I succumbed to his way of thinking. After the horror of smallpox in Wickhamshire and the misfortune thrust upon me, my faith in God had waned, if not vanished altogether.

For the balance of the morning, Pastor Vinson and the Cromwell Church delivered a semblance of peace I thought lost forever. The highlight of the morning was seeing the glee in Penny as she sang the new hymn with the congregation. Like me, this child longed for a release of the grief from having lost someone close. I felt her pain, and I prayed that in time I might have some small impact on her life.

When the service ended, everyone stood while Pastor Vinson descended the pulpit and traversed the aisle to the church's front doors. The front rows exited first, and as I walked toward the rear of the church to leave, I glanced at the back row and saw her, my friend Hazel Giddings. Her sullen expression left me to wonder what happened to the high spirit that defined Hazel on the long journey from England. I smiled and waved, hoping we might get the chance to speak before heading back to Cromwell's Passage.

Hazel saw me and slowly waved to return my greeting. Her palm was red and raw. It held the countenance of a field hand.

CHAPTER FOURTEEN

## *The Greene Plantation*
## the Maryland Colony

### 19 SEPTEMBER 1773

Mr. Wright burst into the kitchen. A messenger had just left on horseback. "Celia has taken ill. Doc is with her now."

Alarmed and wanting to repay the kindness Mrs. Greene had shown me upon my arrival in Cromwell, I stated rather forcefully, "I wish to go there."

Mr. Wright appeared taken aback at my assertiveness. "Yes . . ." He stroked his rich brown hair. "I was preparing to ask you to do just that. We shall leave at once."

With Penny at the schoolhouse, it was just Mr. Wright and me riding in his carriage to the adjacent Greene Plantation. This would be my first trip there, and I hoped I would steal a few minutes to see how Hazel was getting along. I worried about her. The carriage ride took no time at all. Mr. Wright guided his horse at a furious pace, and we entered the long, pounded path leading past the fields toward the palatial home. I'd never seen so much of one crop before. It went on as far as the eye could see. Dozens of field hands worked the land to reap the harvest.

Spotting the bewildered look on my face, Mr. Wright said, "It's tobacco. This is the last of the fall harvest."

Shocked, I replied, "You mean there are more fields than what we can see?"

"Oh, yes. Charles has hundreds of acres. The field hands work the land from the farthest point in."

Field hands? I wanted to question the nature of their engagement but feared sounding belligerent. The preponderance of the workers were dark-skinned like Fred. They were slaves. The thought of these people being treated like property sickened me. As we made our way toward the house, I wondered where I would find Hazel. On the ocean voyage, she mentioned she enjoyed cooking. Perhaps they assigned her to the kitchen staff. A home like this would have a large variety of servants to cater to Mr. and Mrs. Greene's every need. The carriage came to a stop by the stable next to the house. Mr. Wright helped me down, and we narrowly missed hitting a woman in filthy rags pumping water into an old wooden pail. She looked up at me and quickly turned her head in shame.

"Hazel!"

In the three days since I saw her at church, her face had become haggard. Judging from the smell, I feared she hadn't bathed in weeks. She arched her back and walked past us without saying a word, her gait unsettled. Mr. Wright sensed the tension I felt, and he approached Hazel with care and relieved her of the heavy pail.

"Please . . ." he offered. "Let me take this where it needs to go. You visit with Essie."

His kindness overwhelmed me. Mr. Wright abhorred slavery. His compassion moved me as I embraced my friend.

"Let me look at you," I said. "You could do with a hot bath, a meal, and a few days' rest."

Hazel scratched an itch under her soiled garment. She replied calmly, "It's nice to see you." She attempted to smile, but it appeared as if she had no recollection of how to.

"I am a slave. My job is to pick tobacco and haul water to the others. They scarcely feed us, and our quarters are almost as bad as the London Debtor's Prison."

I tried to give her some hope. "With the harvest ending, surely they will give you easier chores?"

"I am told," she said as she caught her breath, "that winter chores are no less strenuous. They will assign me the task of mucking the stables and, once the weather improves, preparing the fields for planting."

I shook my head in despair. "But you are not a slave. You are an indentured servant, like me. One day, we will both be free and will start new lives."

Her eyes revealed the pain of misfortune and loss of hope. The high-spirited woman I met on my journey to the New World was gone, emotionally beaten into submission.

"I must return to work or risk facing the whip."

Aghast, I realized that Hazel's tendency to speak her mind had likely caused her to be disciplined. It explained the arched back and why she winced with every step. There were no words of comfort. I hugged her, but she recoiled from my embrace. The welts on her back protruded beyond her thin garment. In these moments, I was unsure of God's existence. I told myself I could only pray, hoping a higher being would respond on Hazel's behalf.

The Greenes' home was unlike the main house at Cromwell's Passage. They built a home that perched upon a dozen wide stairs and had a beautiful white picket fence surrounding a porch that meandered around the entire home. When we entered, I stood on a rug in the main hallway. It looked oriental and was plush beneath my feet. The grand staircase was circular and braced by wrought iron black railings decorated with forged roses in full bloom. Giant oil paintings of men hung on the walls. I presumed these were Charles Greene's ancestors. A manservant in an exquisitely tailored black suit greeted us.

"Mr. Aquila Wright and Mrs. Esther Lassiter to see Mr. and Mrs. Greene," declared Mr. Wright.

The man spoke in an English accent I couldn't quite place. "They are upstairs with Dr. Bradley. Please follow me."

The circular staircase made me lightheaded. There was an air about this house. It smelled of sickness, reminiscent of the last days in my Wickhamshire cottage. When we reached the top of the staircase, the servant led us into the bedroom where Mrs. Greene lay unconscious. Mr. Greene, looking distraught, rose and embraced his friend Mr. Wright.

Before I could take in the delicate nature of the scene, Doc Bradley looked up from the bedside and addressed me with some measure of relief. His wispy white mustache hung loosely, causing his lined face to appear more fatigued than usual. "Essie, I am glad you are here. Mrs. Greene has the fever. She will need constant attention for the next week, and there is no one here with any medical training. I must leave to tend to others. Can you stay?"

Stunned by the request, I wanted to immediately agree, but I deferred to Mr. Wright. Before I could reply, Mr. Greene took Mr. Wright's hand, locked eyes with him, and said, "Aquila, I would consider it a great personal favor if you were to agree."

Mr. Wright's look revealed his divided interests. On the one hand, Mr. Wright would drop everything for a friend in need. On the other, I assumed he was worried about who might care for Penny while I was away. Finally, after a long pause, he replied, "I would gladly loan Essie to you as long as Penny could accompany her."

Mr. Greene's face bore an expression of relief. "Of course, of course." Then he added, "The timing is poor, as you and I are due in Annapolis in two days' time."

Annapolis? I knew nothing of this. My assessment of Mr. Greene was already tentative at best. I respected his devotion to his wife but abhorred his ownership of slaves and especially his treatment of Hazel. And now he was planning to leave for God knows what? As was my downfall in the New World, I spoke up for my friend.

"May I suggest an added hand to help me? Penny will be of limited assistance, and Mrs. Greene should not be left alone."

Doc Bradley warmed to the idea. "Who have you in mind?"

"Mr. Greene's indentured servant, Hazel Giddings. She is not a midwife like me, but she ran a respectable home in England and would be very compassionate."

"Done," declared Mr. Greene. "Aquila, can you return with Penny by sundown? I will make sure Hazel gets cleaned up and assumes temporary quarters with the house servants."

"Very well," Mr. Wright replied.

Doc Bradley looked relieved.

Mr. Greene addressed Mr. Wright as we stood to leave. "As the newest representatives from Harford County's delegation at the Maryland legislative meeting, we can ill afford to be late."

Mr. Wright had failed to inform me of his appointment to the colony's governing body, but the news eased my tensions regarding Mr. Greene's departure while his wife lay gravely ill.

Although the next week would be hard, my troubled mind relaxed knowing Penny could accompany me and I had rescued Hazel from the misery of work as a field hand. Mostly, I hoped I could somehow nurse Mrs. Greene back to health.

# CHAPTER FIFTEEN

## The Greene Plantation
## the Maryland Colony

## 20 SEPTEMBER 1773

When we arrived at the Greene Plantation yesterday afternoon, the sweet smell of jasmine remained from the last of the season's tobacco crop. By sunset, Penny and I had settled in our rooms. The missus was still unconscious, and Doc Bradley was off to save other patients. Hazel enjoyed the pleasure of a warm bath and was grateful to be inside with the other house servants who addressed the daily goings on of the main house, one of the largest in the county and perhaps three times the size of Mr. Wright's enormous abode. Mr. Greene and his ancestors proved more cocksure than Mr. Wright and those who came before him. Although Mr. Wright was indeed a man of means, his demonstrable modesty was revealed in practice in his home and through empathy and kindness toward others.

The sun rose just before six o'clock in the morning. Mr. Wright appeared promptly at the top of the hour. He went inside to awaken Penny. This loving father wished to bid her farewell before his journey with Mr. Greene to Annapolis. Penny and I stood outside to see the men off. Before mounting his carriage, Mr. Greene gently placed his beefy hands on my shoulders, looked me straight in the eye, and said, "Take care of Celia. I place my faith and prayers in you."

I replied, "I will do everything I can."

Glancing over to Hazel and Penny, I smiled and added, "And I have plenty of able-bodied help." Without another word, the men departed, and I began issuing direction to Penny and Hazel. "I will go check on Mrs. Greene. Penny, go get ready for school, and Hazel, go to the kitchen and assist the cook with breakfast. Later today, I will show you how to prepare the diet Mrs. Greene will require during her convalescence."

Hazel looked at me and reverted to her sharp tongue from our time at sea. "You mean if she makes it that far."

Aghast at her apparent lack of commitment to the cause, I scolded her. "There shall be no such talk. We will concentrate on nothing else, and mark my words, we will get Mrs. Greene back to stead."

Hazel looked as if a drunken brute had slapped her. I didn't care. Repaying Mrs. Greene for her kindness upon my arrival is something I could never do. I would not waiver in my attempt to help in her hour of need.

I padded up the circular staircase and bent over Mrs. Greene. She was pale in complexion, and a light sweat appeared on her forehead. With a bowl of fresh water and a soft cloth, I gently cooled her face and then made a cold compress to rest on her forehead. Doc Bradley discussed his strategy for Mrs. Greene. He was a naturalist and shunned the old ways of treating a fever. Bloodletting, he said, was barbaric. Purging, however, was not, and this was the course he recommended, once she was conscious. Yesterday, Doc Bradley made a poultice from yarrow and toadflax. The paste from these local plants was applied to the patient's body to induce sleep and help pain to subside. Doc instructed that the healing remedy would last less than a day before it would need to be reapplied. Therefore, I expected Mrs. Greene to come to by midday.

After breakfast, I asked Hazel to walk Penny to the schoolhouse. I sat with Mrs. Greene for hours until she stirred and finally opened her eyes. Seeing me startled her, and it took her a long moment to process the scene.

"Essie?" she asked in a strained voice.

"Yes, Mrs. Greene. It is me. Your husband and Mr. Wright were called to Annapolis for government business. Doc Bradley asked me to care for you."

"How long have I been sleeping?"

"Little more than a day. Doc Bradley applied a plaster to your body to help you sleep and reduce pain."

"I feel depleted. My skin, it's so dry."

I dabbed her head with the cool cloth and replied, "It's from the plaster. When you feel up to it, I will cleanse the plaster from your body and change your nightdress. Perhaps tomorrow we will draw a warm bath."

She smiled faintly. "You are a godsend." And then she shook and pulled the blanket over her shoulders. "I am so cold."

Doc Bradley left the determination to me. Apply more plaster and let Mrs. Greene sleep, or transition to the medicine he left. I opted for the medicine. Moving to her dressing table, I took the brown glass bottle and removed the cork. Reaching for a small decanter, I mixed the powdered medicine with red wine.

"What is that?" Mrs. Greene asked.

"It is cinchona bark. I have mixed it with red wine to produce quinine. Doc says it will make you feel better."

"Quinine? Do I have malaria?"

"Doc couldn't say for sure. Your illness acts like malaria, and so this elixir should help."

I brought the small goblet to her lips and instructed her to sip slowly until she had consumed the entire amount. Inside of an hour, the chills subsided and her color returned. At Mrs. Greene's request, I helped her to sit up, and she expressed a desire to change her nightdress. Gradually, I removed the garment of her illness and tossed it on the floor. Bathed and dried to the best of my ability, Mrs. Greene was ready for a fresh gown from the tall dresser. With my aid, she got out of bed and into the high-back companion chair I'd sat in most of the morning. I poured her water from a pitcher and hurried to change the sheets. Then I helped her into bed and instructed her to rest.

"When will Charles and Aquila return?"

"Tomorrow evening."

"Who is caring for Penny while you are here?"

"She is staying in one of your guest rooms. When she returns from school, I will bring her in to visit."

"Will she walk alone from the schoolhouse?"

It was too much to take in. This fine lady was unwell yet more concerned about the welfare of a friend's child. "One of your servants, Hazel Giddings, will accompany her."

Mrs. Greene's confusion was evident. "Hazel Giddings? A servant of mine? I don't know that name."

I took her hand and responded. "Hazel and I journeyed to America together. She is indentured to you and Mr. Greene as I am to Mr. Wright. She's been working the fields since her arrival."

"But I have many fine house servants with whom I am familiar. Couldn't one of them assist instead?"

I squeezed her hand, looked into her tired eyes, and merely replied, "Trust me. You will see."

She nodded and her eyelids descended, showing she wished to rest. I stroked her hair, placed a bell on the nightstand, and said, "Ring this if you need me. I won't be far." Leaving Mrs. Greene to sleep, I picked up the laundry from the floor.

For the better part of the morning, Mrs. Greene slept. The house servants were loyal to her and assisted me wherever they could. One of them made a snide remark, however, regarding the need for Hazel. "I don't see why we need that field wench in the house when we have proper servants to assist Mrs. Lassiter." Having overheard this contempt, I responded with kindness, reminding the lady that Hazel was in the field under circumstances beyond her control and that she managed a proper home in England. The woman scoffed and walked away in a huff.

Fortunately, the house staff relieved me of the laundry burden and even the chore of keeping Mrs. Greene's room clean. I devoted my day to the tasks of medical care between visits from Doc Bradley, who appeared at the Greene Plantation in the late afternoon. I greeted him with a warm embrace and escorted him up the spiral staircase. Doc entered the bedchamber looking wearier than the prior day.

"Celia, it is good to see you awake," he said.

Mrs. Greene stirred, stretched, and replied through a hoarse tone, "Essie is taking good care of me." Mrs. Greene smiled at me, and I took her hand in mine while Doc examined her from the other side of the bed. I updated him on the decision to move away from another course of plaster in favor of cinchona, and he agreed.

"Let's stay with the cinchona for a few days with, of course, continued bed rest. Hopefully, we should have you up and about soon," he said.

With that, he disappeared down the staircase, and I was left to wonder, How did Doc Bradley make time to rest? His tasks seemed insurmountable given that he was the only doctor tending to sick people in a region that stretched from Cromwell north to Scott's Old Fields and the southern portion of Joppa. It was too much for one man to manage.

A short while later, I was sitting with Mrs. Greene and reading her a few of her favorite sonnets when Penny appeared with Hazel in tow. I introduced Hazel to Mrs. Greene, hoping she would be gracious. She did not disappoint me.

Mrs. Greene beamed at Penny and spoke directly to her. "You have grown just in the short time since I've seen you last. Come here and let me have a better look."

"I hope you are feeling better, Mrs. Greene. Essie is teaching me how to care for you."

"Essie is a shining star. I hope you two are getting along."

Penny hesitated. I was unsure of her reply to such an innocent inquiry.

"Aw, she's all right," she said, looking my way with a devilish grin. It was at that moment that I began successfully bonding with my young charge. My uncertainty up to that point was a source of anxiety, but now, I had something upon which to build.

Hazel volunteered to sit with Mrs. Greene and continue with the sonnets. I was grateful for the suggestion. It was important for Hazel to develop a relationship with Mrs. Greene. I left with Penny, and we walked down the corridor and around the bend of the great house to a series of guest rooms. Penny unloaded her schoolbooks on the bed, and we sat for a moment.

"Show me how to make the cinchona medicine," she said.

I smiled warmly and replied, "Perhaps tomorrow before school, you can watch me do it."

Penny beamed. "Father kept me from Mother's illness. Apart from brief daily visits, servants kept me away under their watchful eye." She began to cry softly. "I was always led to believe that Mother would recover."

"And this left you resentful?"

"Yes," she replied. "I was younger then and struggled to understand. You treat me like a grown-up. I appreciate that."

She came close and buried her head in my chest, seeking a compassionate embrace from a caretaker not much younger than her mother would have been. I felt deeply moved and held her close.

Unbeknownst to Penny, I would teach her more about medicine than she could imagine. Doc Bradley had advised that the Sons of Liberty, a growing colonial movement to oppose British rule, was forming new militias in Maryland. He was being asked to travel with them to tend to the ill and wounded. So far, he'd resisted these calls. There were not enough doctors in this region, and he was already at his breaking point. He warned that one day soon, he might have to speak to Mr. Wright about poaching me for my medical knowledge. I stroked Penny's rich walnut hair and held my worry inside.

# CHAPTER SIXTEEN

## The Greene Plantation
## the Maryland Colony

### 23 SEPTEMBER 1773

With help from Hazel and Penny, who was now an expert at applying cold compresses and mixing cinchona elixir, Mrs. Greene was on her feet. She was back to eating three meals a day and was regaining strength. Nightfall arrived and life settled down. Penny and Hazel retired to their quarters, and I sat with Mrs. Greene in the drawing room on the entry level of the home. A servant had built a fire, and we watched the logs burn as I spread a quilt over her lap. The house was serene, and for the first time in a long period, I relaxed. Mrs. Greene closed her eyes, and I took the opportunity to do the same. Soon, I would help her up the staircase, change into her nightdress, and settle her in bed. Doc Bradley thought Mrs. Greene could resume normal activities in a day or two. I agreed.

I was nodding off when the sound of an approaching carriage stirred my senses. It was too late for visitors, and the Greenes' butler was nowhere to be found. I looked around for anything I might use as a weapon. After being overtaken in Wickhamshire and the stray bear in Cromwell, I was less trustful than I once was. Grabbing a tall candlestick, I got up and crept to the door, being careful not to wake Mrs. Greene. I inched my way to the window and peeled back an edge of the drape. With one eye, I saw two men approaching the front door. All I could make out were silhouettes. They were laughing. As they drew near, they came into plain view, and I was relieved to see that Mr. Greene and Mr. Wright had returned from Annapolis.

I placed the candlestick on a table, opened the door, and the two men entered. Upon hearing her father's voice, Penny waltzed down the spiral staircase. Mr. Greene went directly to his recovering wife. I'd never seen a man so happy to reunite with his spouse.

Mr. Greene's rotund face might have split in two if his smile loomed any larger. "Celia, my love! You are looking amazingly well."

She addressed him with a loving but sleepy expression and, to my surprise, replied, "Thanks to Essie. She has barely left my side." Then she pointed to Penny and said, "And that one, she is a nurse in the making."

Mr. Greene addressed me directly. "I can't thank you enough, both of you."

"It was a privilege, sir. Your servant Hazel Giddings was also a tremendous help."

"Charles, she really was," offered Mrs. Greene. "A delightful woman. We had many conversations. And she can cook. I want to keep her in the house."

It had more of a commanding tone than a pleading one. Joy seemed to fill Mr. Greene, and at that moment, I thought he would have agreed to just about anything.

"Of course, of course, my love," he replied.

Mr. Wright embraced his daughter and then looked at me, placing one hand on my shoulder while extending me words of thanks.

"Essie, I am so proud of you. No small feat caring for the sick while also looking after an eleven-year-old."

"Almost twelve!" replied Penny. "I am practically a young woman, Father."

He picked Penny up and held her tight. "That you are, princess."

Mr. Wright put her down and said, "Let's all sit by the fire a brief spell. Charles and I have news from Annapolis."

Mrs. Greene perked up. "I hope neither of you have been asked to form a militia."

Mr. Greene patted her shoulder and said, "No, nothing like that. They asked me to lead a new Harford County delegation to represent our citizens' interests in Annapolis."

"A governor?" inquired Mrs. Greene.

"They refer to other county leaders as commissioners. I shall lead the Harford County delegation, to include Aquila and four other men."

"To what end?" asked Mrs. Greene.

"We will govern the county and ensure that there is law and order, and other basic needs required by our citizens." He paused and smiled at Mr. Wright. "On that front, Aquila has exciting news."

Mr. Wright blushed as he cautiously began speaking. "Well, it's a little surprising, given that I have no background in the matter at hand, but Governor Templeton requested I build a hospital in Harford County."

"That's extraordinary," stated Mrs. Greene. "But why you?"

"The governor acknowledged my ability to build the mill and expand it for the betterment of our county. He believes those skills are transferable to the creation of our first hospital."

"But where will you get the foundational knowledge?" she asked.

"I will spend time in Philadelphia to visit the hospital. It is there I will gain the knowledge and recruit a doctor to move to Cromwell to lead the effort."

I interjected. "What about Dr. Bradley? Shouldn't we give him due consideration?" I knew I shouldn't comment, but I felt compelled to speak up for a man who dedicated himself to the people of Harford County.

My interjection did not put Mr. Wright off. "Of course, Dr. Bradley is a fine man, but at seventy years of age, he may not live long enough to see the project through." Then he added, reflecting, "We will request Dr. Bradley to provide counsel as he is able."

"That's wonderful news for both of you. What did they discuss regarding British taxes and trade with England and its territories in the West Indies?" asked Mrs. Greene.

I found her knowledge of politics impressive. Many women in her position would not have concerned themselves with such matters. Mrs. Greene, however, was no ordinary woman. Knowing that the conversation was turning toward sensitive matters that might frighten Penny, I scurried her off to bed. When I came back, Mr. Greene was finishing his answer.

"These matters were raised by several delegations, but Governor Templeton is a Briton. No talk of rebellion could be held in his presence."

"There was another meeting, a clandestine one in the woods near the South River," said Mr. Wright. "A gentleman from Baltimore runs the local chapter of the Sons of Liberty. They asked us to join."

Mrs. Greene appeared cross. "Are these 'Sons of Liberty' engaged in violence? Must I worry every time you leave the house that you may not return?"

"There's no need to worry. The Sons are mostly a political group. They believe in no taxation without representation," Mr. Greene said reassuringly.

To calm the waters, Mr. Wright stated, "We only said we would consider the invitation."

Mrs. Greene sighed. "I can't tell either of you what to do. I can urge caution." She stood and extended her arm. "Essie, help me to bed."

# CHAPTER SEVENTEEN

## *Cromwell's Passage*
## the Maryland Colony

### 1 OCTOBER 1773

Dare I say, Isaiah Trumbull was a man of grizzled good looks. Mr. Wright's longtime mill foreman wasn't much older than his employer, but a life of hard work and a determined smile left his face with a certain allure. I lingered at the door to the main building. Mr. Trumbull had a line of local farmers with whom he was negotiating. I stood by and listened to the exchange as I took in the pleasant smell of fresh grain.

"Do you wish the wheat to be milled and sold or just milled?" Mr. Trumbull inquired of his customer.

"I have no means for commercial sale," the farmer replied. "All I ask is a fair price, and then you can export as you see fit."

"Very well," Mr. Trumbull proclaimed. "We shall pay you five shillings per bushel produced."

The poor farmer nodded in agreement. He lacked both bargaining power and the constitution to debate.

Mr. Trumbull left the farmer to unload his wagons and approached me forthwith. His dark eyes were embracing, although I just witnessed him as a man to be respected in all matters. I curtsied and introduced myself.

"Aquila said you would drop by. It is my pleasure to make your acquaintance. What do you require today? Cornmeal, flour, a bag of oats perhaps?"

I timidly stammered out, "Why, yes! I would appreciate all of that."

"It is done, then. I will have someone bring the sacks to the house. They can prove quite heavy."

I thanked him for his kindness. He appeared to have a busy day, and I didn't wish to encroach on his time or good nature, but my curiosity overwhelmed my better instincts to leave.

"Mr. Trumbull, if I may. You offered that poor farmer five shillings per barrel. How much do you earn from the resale?"

"You have a head for business, do you?" he said somewhat sarcastically. I feared I'd offended him. Why would a woman of my station care about such matters? Mr. Trumbull, a formidable and strong man, placed his arm around my shoulders, which I deemed untoward. I bristled at his touch, but he seemed to relish the contact. His dark eyes looked down at me, not in a lustful manner but more like a boy with a schoolhouse crush. Then his voice softened as he explained the history of the mill.

"We mill the crops and then export the bushels of finished product to the West Indies, and sometimes merchant vessels take them to the northern colonies. Our price is one pound and sixpence, a fine profit."

While I was rotting in the London Debtor's Prison, I had plenty of time to ruminate on the value of money and how to avoid future debt if I were ever placed back into a normal societal role. "That's a handsome return," I remarked.

"Yes, but to be fair. The farmer was free to pay a fee for the milling and sell the bushels himself to the highest bidder."

I considered that for a moment. "Mr. Wright is quite wealthy, then, wouldn't you say?"

Mr. Trumbull furrowed his brow. "You could say that. When his father died, the mill was only one building. Today we have four. Cromwell's Passage produces and exports more grain than any mill in the Maryland Colony. Mr. Wright conceived of the plan to expand the mill. I oversaw construction and operations while he traveled extensively to the West Indies and other places to establish buyers, transportation, and trade."

"Trade?" I inquired.

"Yes, Aquila sometimes accepts rum and other commodities as payment for grain. Then, he resells the rum across the colonies through general stores."

"Did Penny accompany him on these trips?" I worried that Mr. Wright's daughter was being asked to forgo a normal childhood in deference to her father's business.

"No, he did all that travel in the early days, after his father passed away. Penny was just a wee one and would stay home with Rebecca. After her unfortunate demise, Aquila appointed several buyer's agents to keep the business growing."

Contemplating building a business and exploiting diligent farmers was captivating. I didn't know whether to respect the former or empathize with the latter. I did, however, admire how modestly Mr. Wright lived, given his abundance of wealth. Unlike Mr. Greene, who boasted a much larger home, imported rugs, and treasures for all to see, Mr. Wright was a man grounded in principle.

A strong breeze blew through the grounds, kicking up the dust outside the main building. It was my reminder that I had lingered too long. I wished Mr. Trumbull a good day and began the walk to the house. Dark clouds rumbled above, and before I made my way to the main road, a heavy rain drop slapped me on the cheek and ran quickly down my face. Later, in my room, writing this passage, it occurred to me that the drop of rain and the approaching storm were an awakening of sorts. I pondered on Trumbull's apparent infatuation with me and how it made me feel. I suppose I should have taken it as a compliment. Instead, I realized that without Thomas and the few remaining relations in England, no one on this earth genuinely cared about my existence.

## CHAPTER EIGHTEEN

# *Cromwell Church*
# the Maryland Colony

## 3 OCTOBER 1773

I was warming to the idea of attending church each Sunday. While my faith had not strengthened, my enjoyment of the people and their activities brought a sense of belonging. My feelings of beleaguerment were not a task for the church, at least in my eyes. At the very least, however, the church helped me to rediscover a piece of the happiness missing from my heart.

Pastor Vinson bestowed an honor upon me for weekly services. I was the new church harpist, an unfilled position since the role's prior occupant migrated north to Boston. I perched delicately by the beautiful instrument. To play the harp is to be one with the device. I needed time to acclimate to the nuances of the pedals and the texture of the strings. My first service required me only to play something pleasing as people entered and exited the church. That was easy. The music returned to my mind effortlessly as I played Handel from memory. Many of the parishioners noted the music and softly applauded. One townsfolk told me afterward that my music was a pleasant departure from the silence to which they had become accustomed.

I completed the piece, and I observed Penny beaming in my direction as the parishioners were seated. The music touched her, and I was pleased. I sat upright and listened as Pastor Vinson spoke to the congregation.

"Good morning, and let us express our thanks to our new harpist, Essie Lassiter." He turned, looked over his shoulder and addressed me directly. "Essie, what a beautiful job!"

Then Pastor Vinson looked back at the congregation. "Essie works in a domestic capacity for Mr. Aquila Wright, our town's benefactor and the grandson of its founder, Mordecai Cromwell. Aquila, we thank you for lending us Essie each Sunday morning. You are both blessings of the Lord."

I almost blushed at this sentiment. But Pastor Vinson possessed an undeniable quality. I have a strong sense of people, and I knew from the instant we met he was as genuine as they come. I listened as he continued.

"After our service concludes this morning, Aquila Wright has asked that you stay for a few announcements. I trust it will not take long, and I have reminded Aquila that today is the Lord's day, and he should not conduct any town business."

With that, Pastor Vinson proceeded with his sermon. His message was about kindness and working together as a community. "We are stronger together," he said. The oration moved me. It emphasized that if one member of the community was in need, then the entire community was in need. The possibility of another widow in the New World experiencing what happened to me in Wickhamshire was beyond imagination. Since arriving here, I had found myself homesick on more than one occasion. That day, for the first time, Pastor Vinson, a fellow Briton, made the thought of returning to England repugnant.

When the service concluded, Pastor Vinson reminded everyone to remain, and Mr. Wright was invited to address the congregation. He ascended gracefully, dressed in his Sunday best. The ruffled shirt and fine blue coat accentuated his thick, rolling waves of chestnut hair. The sun shone on him through a side window, and I thought him more handsome than usual.

"Governor Templeton has tasked me to create the colony's first hospital. Hospitals have appeared in Philadelphia, New York, and Boston. I have accepted this assignment and will travel to Philadelphia to meet with their hospital's founders. Once I have gained sufficient knowledge, I will work with Cromwell leaders to find an appropriate tract of land upon which to build and develop a plan to find a doctor to operate the facility."

I knew Doc Bradley was uncomfortable with this topic. He held hands with his wife. After so many years of marriage, I suppose she could sense his anxiety. No doubt he knew the plan well and they had discussed it in detail.

One parishioner called out, "Why isn't Doc Bradley handling this?"

Mr. Wright nodded in Doc's direction, and the elderly medical man rose.

"I have been consulted and will offer Aquila the necessary advice. My current practice has me covering every town in the county north of the Bush River. If I stop to build a hospital, then I will be of little use to any of you."

The same parishioner called out again, "Doc, will you run the hospital once it's built?"

Doc rose again. "No, friends. I am a country doctor. I know little about hospital procedures. Besides, at seventy years of age, Edith is encouraging me to slow down."

This appeased the curious parishioner.

"With all due respect to Pastor Vinson and the sabbath day, I shall conclude by saying that I will disclose more information when I return from my trip to Philadelphia to visit with their hospital's founders, Dr. Thomas Bond and Dr. Benjamin Franklin."

"Not so fast, Aquila."

A man stood from the front row on the aisle opposite Mr. Wright's pew. He was tall, with flax-colored hair pulled back with a black ribbon near the collar. His gold pocket watch glimmered on his torso.

"Yes, Mr. Amos Haverford. Do you have a question?" asked Mr. Wright.

Haverford's face held a long, raised scar along the right cheek and he wore a monocle from behind which he glared at Mr. Wright with a scowl.

"I believe this hospital project might overwhelm you what with the grist mill and all. And I understand that you and Mr. Greene have been asked to serve as county representatives for the colony. Maybe others would be better suited to manage this project."

Mr. Wright's disdain for Mr. Haverford was not in doubt. "Like whom, Amos? You? I cannot imagine anyone more overwhelmed than thee. You already own the bank and the general store, not to mention being a prominent dealer in the moonshine trade." Mr. Wright paused to let the admonishment sink in.

"I will delegate the business of my mill to our family's longtime foreman, Isaiah Trumbull," Mr. Wright proclaimed to the churchgoers. "This will afford me adequate time to pursue the hospital project."

Mr. Haverford was less than pleased. "Well, just because your granddaddy founded Cromwell doesn't give your family the right to rule its province forever. We are not a monarchy. This is the New World! I demand that we elect a mayor and a town council."

Many in the crowd applauded this insolence and began pumping fists in the air, chanting, "Haver-ford, Haver-ford."

Pastor Vinson stepped in. He glanced my way with the unmistakable signal to play. The crowd was becoming unruly. I played Mozart as Pastor Vinson raised his voice and declared, "Friends, I remind you that this is the Lord's day. These matters are to be settled in the town hall. Our service is now concluded. Please file out in an orderly manner."

I continued to play while the crowd settled, and I waited for Pastor Vinson to leave first so he could thank people for attending and wish them a good day. As my fingers skillfully danced across the strings, Amos Haverford spoke to another man in the pew behind him. I couldn't hear what they were saying, but they were angry and up to no good—of this, I was certain.

On the walk home, Penny held my hand, and much to my surprise, Mr. Wright asked me to accompany him to Philadelphia.

"I have asked Charles and Celia to allow Hazel to stay with Penny. Your medical knowledge will prove to be of value."

I felt flabbergasted. Me? A value in the commencement of a hospital? Why, the thought was preposterous. I gathered my courage, hiding my ever-present self-doubt. "Where shall we stay in Philadelphia?"

"We will be guests in the home of Dr. Benjamin Franklin, a prominent statesman, and the hospital's cofounder."

# CHAPTER NINETEEN

## *The Home of Benjamin Franklin*
## the Pennsylvania Colony

### 10 OCTOBER 1773

Two days of travel, including one night at a stately inn deep inside the Brandywine Valley, finally reached an end. Knowing that it would be improper for a man and woman who were not married to travel so far alone, Mr. Wright employed his largest carriage, pulled by two of his finest horses and operated by an ancient servant with a lined face named Clement. Clement said little but had served the Wright family for generations. Inside the carriage, there were two benches, and the interior was outfitted with soft, crushed Vienna velvet lining. The burgundy fabric was so soft, I pressed my hands down and flexed my fingers in the plush material to quell my frayed nerves. Mr. Wright sat opposite me and observed with concern.

We arrived just after dawn on the morning of 10 October. A distinguished gentleman and lady padded out of the door on Second Street in Philadelphia to greet us. My first glimpse of Benjamin Franklin brought a feeling of reverence. On our journey, Mr. Wright delighted me with stories of Dr. Franklin's accomplishments, the hospital not being the only one. Although he wasn't a medical doctor, Benjamin Franklin was bestowed honorary doctorates from the Universities of St. Andrews and Oxford for his scientific accomplishments. The many achievements were remarkable, and I only hoped that this great man would be benevolent in spirit so we could learn all that was possible.

Clement helped me out of the carriage, and as I stepped down onto the cobblestone street, I stood tall next to Mr. Wright feeling honored to be where I was.

Benjamin Franklin approached with a warm smile. His long, rotund face portended kindness. "Welcome to Philadelphia, Mrs. Lassiter. Mr. Wright has told me of your medical training." He took my hand and kissed it.

Now, I felt embarrassed. I glanced at Mr. Wright with a look that begged for help. I was not a woman of any standing, and I hadn't earned the respect of this great man.

I softly said, "Thank you, Dr. Franklin. I am a midwife and was the spouse to the doctor of a quaint village in England. I am here to learn."

"And so you shall," he replied. "First, let me introduce you to my wife, Deborah. We have prepared breakfast for you, and then we will meet Dr. Bond for a tour of the hospital."

Deborah, or Miss Reed, as she was called, had a similar build to Dr. Franklin, her common-law husband. They were both on what my mother would have called "the plump side." Her plain features blended in with her simple saxe blue dress and its single ruffle. Deborah Reed bore a striking resemblance to Benjamin Franklin, almost as if they could be siblings. I admonished myself for the shameful thought.

We entered the stately home, and a butler immediately greeted us, asking whether we needed to freshen up before seating us in the dining room. Ten minutes later, we were at a table artfully carved by hand from the trees of a nearby forest. The linen-covered table was ornamented with the finest lace and a silver teapot that glistened, while the smell of fresh-cooked bacon, poached eggs, and smoked whitefish filled my nostrils.

Miss Reed offered warm cornbread and apricot jam. A servant poured tea, and I thought this might be the finest meal I'd ever seen. Mr. Wright thanked our hosts, and we began discussing the day ahead.

Dr. Franklin enjoyed storytelling. He conveyed his warm manner in each word he spoke, in contrast to his female companion, who had a stoic, cynical persona.

"Nearly a quarter century ago, Thomas, Dr. Bond, that is, longtime friend that he is, approached me about starting a hospital here in Philadelphia. He and his brother, Phineas, also a doctor, saw a great need, and we opened modestly to much delight in 1752."

"And you have no background in medicine?" asked Mr. Wright.

"Heavens, no. I consider myself a printer and an inventor mostly, although truth be told, the business of politics occupies more of my time than I would like."

"Could you tell us of your inventions?" I tentatively asked.

In the manner of his smile, one would have thought I'd given him the key to a long-lost treasure chest. I saw that Benjamin Franklin wanted the world to know of his ingenuity.

"I was a curious lad growing up in Boston. I was born the tenth of seventeen children. My father was a man who made candles and soap from the most meager materials. When I was twelve, my older brother, James, apprenticed me as a printer. I had no formal education, but I learned to read easily and was naturally curious. Learning to write proficiently made me a standout, first as a journalist for my brother's publication, *The New-England Courant*, and then as a statesman in important matters on behalf of the colonies."

He paused, sipped his tea from a bone-colored cup with a pinky finger extended outward, and then continued. "But to answer your question, Essie, if I may call you Essie . . ."

I smiled and said, "Of course."

"As a boy, I invented fins so people could swim as easily as fish. Later in life, I brought forth the idea for a lightning rod to be mounted on buildings to prevent fire from errant bolts." He furrowed a brow as if trying to recall the events of his own life and said, "And then there was the new wood stove for warming homes, the twenty-four-hour, three-wheel clock, the glass armonica, and—well, I should stop. Deborah doesn't like me to boast."

Now, fascination overwhelmed me. My interest in the harp stressed my thirst to learn more about this glass armonica. I asked him to elaborate.

"It's a simple musical instrument made from spinning glass. Before you return to Maryland, I will show you."

"That would be lovely," I graciously replied.

"Dr. Franklin need not boast," claimed Mr. Wright. "His accomplishments go far beyond what he says. As a philosopher, he proposed the first police force and volunteer fire department. More importantly, he founded the Academy of Philadelphia as an institution of higher learning."

Mr. Wright took a bite of whitefish, swallowed, and then added, "And let us not forget to mention the prominent roles in Pennsylvania's governance, including service as the postmaster and the organizer of militias to guard against feared invasions from France and Spain."

"Politics are a delicate matter. My extensive time in London and Paris has caused me to be a world diplomat of sorts, a role I have relished, but I fear that some question my American allegiance."

"Nonsense, sir. You are a true patriot," Mr. Wright proclaimed. "In fact, the Sons of Liberty approached me, and I was hoping to gain your counsel on the matter."

Dr. Franklin's mood demurred. His tone became stoic when he stated, "Let's concentrate on the hospital, shall we? Deborah doesn't care for political conversation at the dining table nor, for that matter, talk of my years away in Europe."

—W—

The hospital occupied an entire city block from the corner of Spruce and Pine to the intersection of 8th and 9th Streets. The cobblestone structure boasted three stories, with windows complemented by black shutters and rooftops dotted with chimneys to support the need to heat the buildings. As we stood on the street, the view was magnificent. I could only imagine how many men, materials, and years it took to build. Dr. Franklin broke my errant thought and rattled me back to the moment at hand.

"You know, Essie, this hospital began in 1752 in a house on High Street. A lady named Elizabeth Gardner, a Quaker widow, received the position of the matron."

"Really? That's remarkable," I replied. I found it astonishing and refreshing that people in Colonial America would give such responsibility to a woman.

In the lobby, the high ceilings and cylindrical columns whispered the history that occurred in these hallowed halls. The unavoidable scent of antiseptic filled the room. A man greeted us in a black topcoat. His face appeared as if someone had chiseled it in stone. His eyes were serious and his lips devoid of any glee.

"Aquila, Essie, permit me to introduce my friend and cofounder, Dr. Thomas Bond. Dr. Bond will conduct the tour of the hospital."

Before anyone could say another word, Dr. Bond shook hands with Mr. Wright and regarded me with nothing more than a casual grunt. I thought I might share with Dr. Bond that my husband was also a doctor named Thomas, but after meeting him, I concluded that he likely wouldn't care.

"Pardon the smell. Benjamin and I are firm believers in reducing the spread of germs. Ours was the first hospital in the colonies, and as such, we are obliged to put forth new medical breakthroughs as often as possible."

Mr. Wright simply nodded. We walked through the entire complex encompassing patient rooms, surgical theaters, the apothecary, and specialty rooms. In the latter, I spied devices the likes of which I'd never seen in my days of assisting Thomas in Wickhamshire. Glancing at a flexible tube of some length, I asked Dr. Bond what it was.

"That is but one of the many things my friend Benjamin invented. It's a flexible catheter. It easily catches the patient's urine more comfortably and deposits it into a chamber pot for analysis."

I shook my head in amazement. The tour whizzed by, and I was taken by the advances in medical care. I wish my Thomas were alive to see this.

Mr. Wright was a bit overwhelmed. He asked Dr. Bond whether he could spend some time with the person in charge of the hospital's administration.

"Well, at present, my niece Antonia oversees those tasks. We will stop by her office and say hello, but you will meet her more formally at tonight's dinner in your honor."

I was oblivious to any dinner but swiftly discovered that Dr. Franklin and Deborah Reed were hosting said dinner and the guests included Dr. Thomas Bond, his brother, Dr. Phineas Bond, and the esteemed governor of Pennsylvania, John Penn.

Our tour concluded with Mr. Wright being taken by Dr. Bond to see his niece about administration and me being whisked away to learn from the head nurse. When the day was over, I was exhausted. It was a good tired. I gained much knowledge and looked forward to learning even more.

—⁓—

Antonia Bond was ravishing. Her fiery red hair and azure eyes gave her a sultry appearance, and, if I may say so, she wore it well, in addition to the black gown cut much too low. She revealed the swell of her generous bosom in a manner unbefitting to a lady. From the looks of her, I would guess her about my age. I wondered why she wasn't married or betrothed. She made haste for Mr. Wright, interlocked her arm in his, and asked him to escort her to the austere dining room where she ignored the place cards and sat herself next to him. The situation appalled me. There was a definitive story about this woman, and I was bound and determined to discover its meaning.

Miss Reed was none too pleased at the disrespect shown to her as the hostess. Mr. Franklin gave her a love pat as if to say, *I understand your angst, but let the moment pass.* We enjoyed a fine squab, with a mix of fresh vegetables raised from Miss Reed's own garden.

Governor Penn inquired of Mr. Wright whether he had accomplished everything in the short trip to Philadelphia.

"Mostly, I would be grateful for more time to learn the administrative side of the hospital and speak to the architect."

Antonia jumped in. "I will have time tomorrow and can show you everything and then introduce you to the architect, a man named Barkley."

"Fantastic," he replied. "Essie and I will meet you promptly at the opening of business."

She grinned at me cunningly and then squeezed Mr. Wright's arm. "Essie? Why, might I suggest that you let me arrange for your servant to spend the day with the finest seamstress in Philadelphia. I am sure you want to treat her to a new dress."

Mr. Wright blushed. In short order, Antonia had wrapped him around her little finger and was enjoying the manipulation. "Splendid," he replied. "If there is time, perhaps you would do me the honor of accompanying me on a carriage ride. My coachman would, of course, serve as a chaperone."

Antonia beamed. Mr. Wright was smitten, and she was basking in the glory. As the dinner wrapped up, the men retired to Dr. Franklin's library for brandy and cigars. The butler walked Antonia to the door, and before I ascended the stairwell to my guest room, she shot me a look to kill.

# CHAPTER TWENTY

## *The*

## Journey Home

### 12 OCTOBER 1773

The dressmaker, a portly figure, proved rather perfunctory in performing her duties. Of course, except for the small shop in Cromwell, I had nothing by which to judge. Every other garment I'd ever owned came from my mother, was a secondhand relic, or was a creation of my limited ability. The Cromwell dressmaker I visited upon my arrival was far less regal in her approach. Nevertheless, I chose something practical. The deep wine fabric of the long-sleeve dress contained fashionable ruffles from the hand to the mid-forearm, a high neck with a flat collar, and a delicate display of subtle dual-rowed brass grommets running from the waist to the bosom. The dress had a long length, making it warm for the upcoming winter months and suitable for most social occasions in Cromwell. I was grateful to Mr. Wright for his generosity and expressed this to him as we entered the long path through the winding hills of the Brandywine Valley.

"It is my pleasure," he replied. "It is I who am grateful to you. Your help with Penny, our home, and caring for Celia when she took ill. Well, it goes without saying that you are truly a blessing."

My heart warmed at such a kind sentiment. I didn't know what to say, so I just smiled and changed the subject. "Will we stay at the same inn in Delaware, or shall we journey all the way home?"

"We will spend tonight at the inn and continue in the morning. The horses require rest and water and . . ." He laughed. "I suspect old Clement does as well."

"Did this trip accomplish all your objectives?" I asked.

He beamed and said, "Heavens, yes."

"Will you need to return to Philadelphia?"

"Perhaps. We made good use of our time. I am sure I will have many more questions for Dr. Franklin and Dr. Bond. Writing letters back and forth takes so much time. I aim to open the Cromwell Hospital in some modest form by spring. Antonia will be of much help."

"Antonia?" I asked, shocked at the insinuation that she would remain involved in our lives. I was hoping I'd seen the last of the manipulative, opportunistic witch. As the thought screeched through my head, I immediately felt guilty for thinking such ill thoughts. Perhaps, underneath her exterior, there was a decent person.

"Antonia lost her betrothed on a militia run several years back. Her father, Phineas, later agreed to a union between his daughter and a wealthy industrialist, but he was an older man—fifties, I think—and Antonia talked her father out of the arrangement."

This information did not surprise me in the least. Her powers of persuasion extended to her father as well. I was sure Antonia was confident in her ability to get what she wanted with whomever she desired. Once again, errant thoughts made their presence known. I berated myself inwardly and listened to Mr. Wright opine on the future.

"We will build a fine hospital. We will start in a manner much like they did in Philadelphia . . . with a simple structure, a manageable number of beds, and a small staff tending to urgent medical needs." Then he ran his hand through his thick brown hair and spoke again. "I have met with Mr. Barkley, the architect, who believes that they can condense the time from design to completion of construction to one year if the coming winter is not too harsh."

"Will you run the new hospital?"

"No, as we said in church last Sunday, I will find a doctor to move to Cromwell. In the meantime, I will oversee the plans, the construction, the recruitment of staff, and the organization of the venture."

I sighed. "It sounds overwhelming."

He broke out in a crooked grin, the likes of which I'd yet to see. "Antonia is coming to Cromwell to help. Her role at the Philadelphia hospital was temporary, and she has relevant experience."

My stomach soured at the notion of seeing Antonia regularly. "But where will she stay?" I asked, praying it would not be at Cromwell's Passage. The thought of having to care for Antonia Bond's needs made me melancholy.

"I have sent a messenger to the proprietor of the Cromwell Inn. Antonia will reside there for as long as it takes. The community fund to establish the hospital will pay for her lodging."

I was relieved that she would not be at the house. Penny would hate her. There was something about a woman like Antonia, who always tried too hard. These types were obvious to me, but so many others tend to suffer fools, and upon this fact, Antonia was reliant. As sure as I was sitting there, I knew Antonia was not coming to Cromwell to help establish a hospital. Her true aim was to marry Mr. Wright and assume a place of societal prominence. Were this to occur, my remaining years of indentured servitude would indeed become a living hell.

# CHAPTER TWENTY-ONE

## *Cromwell's Passage*

## the Maryland Colony

## 15 NOVEMBER 1773

A month had passed since the journey to Philadelphia. Antonia arrived the previous week and was spending considerable time with Mr. Wright in town as they searched for temporary quarters with which to open the hospital. I was thankful she had scarcely appeared at Cromwell's Passage. Her presence in town was already causing a stir, and rumors of a courtship between Mr. Wright and the eligible Miss Bond sprang to life.

My life had returned to normal, whatever that was. The emotional rescue of the daily household routine was a welcome respite for my nervous stomach. I admit I was a worrier. The ruminations of my mind often deprived me of sleep, and my body felt as if I hadn't slept in a fortnight. I sat on an old wooden rocker in Mrs. Wright's former sewing room and taught Penny the art of stitching a wound on an old straw doll. My eyes were heavy. The bright afternoon sun broke through the bay window, causing sleepiness. I drifted off into an involuntary slumber until Penny's vigor jarred me awake. Her enthusiasm knew no bounds.

"Miss Essie, is this correct?"

Penny held up the ragged toy and showed off the crude stitching on the doll's arm. I smiled at her attempt to sew a wound. The bright orange thread zigged and zagged across the arm's surface. If this was a person, I fear they might scar beyond that which was necessary. I gently corrected her.

"Did you clean the wound before stitching?" I asked.

She presented me with a small piece of old cheesecloth. "Yes! I soaked this cloth in boiling water and cleaned the wound." Holding up one of her mother's larger sewing needles, she grinned and proclaimed, "And then I sutured the wound like you showed me."

Before I could respond, Clement peeked into the room and nodded for me to join him in the corridor. His face revealed enormous distress. I joined him in the hallway and softly closed the door behind me so Penny wouldn't overhear our conversation.

"I can tell from the look on your face. What's wrong?" I inquired.

The old man's face bore the burden of angst, and I braced myself as he spoke.

"A messenger just came by. Aquila was injured. He was traveling alone up north in Harford Town to get supplies for the new hospital when the Nathaniel River bridge gave out beneath him. Some locals rescued him. They are bringing him here and will arrive any time."

I fought back the tears and instantly considered Penny, the bright youngster who had already lost her mother. How would she manage this news?

"How badly was he hurt?"

Clement shrugged. "I don't know for certain. All the courier knew was that Aquila fell into the river, hit a rock, and a splintered bridge board impaled him."

"Impaled?" I exclaimed, unwittingly alerting Penny to the crisis.

I was utterly unprepared for the conversation that ensued. I needed to collect my emotions and remain strong to insulate Penny from distress.

Penny appeared in the now open doorway. "What does *impaled* mean?" she asked curiously.

Clement stepped back. "I have sent for Doc Bradley. I trust you will make any necessary preparations." And with that, he retreated down the grand staircase.

I turned to Penny, kneeled, and looked her in the eye. "Your father has been in an accident."

Her gleeful expression of a few moments ago vanished like the late-day sun.

"Is Father . . ." She sobbed, and I took her in my arms and answered the question that was foremost in her mind.

"No, your father is alive, but seriously hurt." I explained the accident as Clement had to me, in more gentle terms, of course. Penny trembled. I held her close and patted the back of her head. I didn't want to let go. At that moment, my only thought was protecting this child at all costs. After a few minutes, she settled down.

"I will need your help. Men from Harford Town are bringing your father here. He may not be awake, and there may be a lot of bleeding. You must be brave. I will be by your side every step of the way."

She nodded, and with the small piece of cheesecloth, I dabbed the tears from her forlorn eyes.

—ɷ—

A few hours later, the *clip-clop* of approaching horses drilled through the day's peace. My stomach fluttered. Alarm ran through my mind like a shotgun in the dead of night. What would I face? When would Doc Bradley arrive? Thomas encountered many odd maladies in his Wickhamshire practice, but I couldn't recall a single impalement. I'd no experience treating such a trauma. While my faith in God was still waning, I kneeled at my bedside and hurriedly said a prayer for Mr. Wright's recovery and for Doc Bradley to arrive with haste.

Taking a deep breath, I walked to the front door and prepared myself for the worst. The commotion outside was Clement arriving with Hazel and Mrs. Greene. I forgot I asked Clement to retrieve Hazel with Mrs. Greene's consent. I should have surmised that Mrs. Greene would also come. She was a kindhearted soul. Hazel would be helpful in shielding Penny from her father's injuries.

Mrs. Greene stepped out of the carriage with the aid of Clement's hand and promptly embraced me. "Has he arrived?" she inquired.

I shook my head and thanked her for coming.

"Charles is away on a business venture. I have sent word for him to return. Hazel can stay here for as long as you like."

"Bless you, Mrs. Greene. You are a dear friend to Mr. Wright, and I so appreciate your kindness." I surprised myself with the religious overtone. Perhaps I was rediscovering my long-lost faith in God.

"Of course," she replied. And then she smiled warmly. "I am *your* friend too."

I clung to her and held on for longer than I should have. I drew strength from Mrs. Greene's iron clad will.

"Do you know anything about Aquila's condition?" she asked.

Frustrated, I shook my head and told her what little I knew: Clement went to retrieve Doc Bradley and bring him to Cromwell's Passage. "We can prepare his bed chamber and begin gathering supplies that Doc Bradley will probably need."

We toiled for the next hour, gathering everything we could think of. Hazel and Penny walked to town and procured surplus laudanum, cloths, and bandages to treat the wound. We assumed Doc Bradley would have only enough to treat the wound but not to change the dressing. Mrs. Greene brought materials to mix the plaster we had used on her in case we needed it. We were straining to think of everything. We lacked proper information with which to prepare.

Finally, we were as ready as we could be. Clement had not yet arrived with Doc Bradley, and the four of us took up residence on the front porch of Mr. Wright's stately manor. Penny and Hazel sat on the top porch step while Mrs. Greene and I occupied two oversized rocking chairs. Conversation was stilted as we anxiously awaited Mr. Wright's arrival. I glanced at the sky and felt a slight chill from an approaching storm. The gray clouds billowed across the remnants of the peaceful blue sky. I couldn't help but feel those dark clouds were a sign of what was to come. I shivered momentarily, crossing my arms over my chest to shake off the cold. I drew a deep breath, again praying for strength and wisdom to help guide Mr. Wright to health and shield young Penny from the fear of losing another parent.

Finally! An approaching carriage. Two riders traveled alongside the main carriage. I couldn't yet see Mr. Wright. He was inside the covered wagon. The horses came to a stop in front of the house, and I ran to the wagon's rear. I couldn't help myself. I shrieked at the sight. Mr. Wright was unconscious, almost gray in complexion. He resembled more a rotting corpse than a man with a severe injury.

The men from Harford Town introduced themselves and expressed their sympathies. They spoke of Mr. Wright as if he had already passed. I signaled to Hazel to whisk Penny into the house, which she did. The man who was in charge addressed us.

"The bridge gave way early this morning. A passerby saw the collapse and watched Mr. Wright's horse and carriage fall into the Nathaniel River. Several of us retrieved him and placed him in the wagon. Fortunately, people in Harford Town know Mr. Wright very well. We sure hope he'll make a full recovery."

Mrs. Greene thanked the men, and the three kind souls gently moved Mr. Wright from the wagon into the house. I was surprised when Mrs. Greene ordered the men to place him on the large dining room table in lieu of his bed.

She patted my arm. "Doc Bradley will have an easier time here."

Looking at Mr. Wright's stomach and the protruding splintered board, I understood her reasoning.

"I will go boil water. We need to clean the wound," Mrs. Greene stated authoritatively.

Looking at Mr. Wright, I feared the worst. I felt for a pulse. It was present, but extremely weak. His forehead was cold and clammy.

"Let's remove the board. Be prepared for a lot of bleeding. We will pack the wound and pray it holds until Clement arrives with Doc Bradley." I tried to sound self-assured, but I knew better.

Mrs. Greene came into the dining room with the boiling water and a pile of cloth from Hazel and Penny's trip to the apothecary. I gently removed the board and was relieved that it came free with relative ease. I worried that deep penetration might have caused irreparable harm to an organ. A pool of blood gurgled up and filled the cavity in Mr. Wright's belly. We packed the wound with boiled cloths and prayed Doc Bradley would arrive soon.

Not knowing what else to do, I sat in the dining room, holding Mr. Wright's hand and repacking the wound every fifteen minutes. Time inched forward. Mrs. Greene and I were there to support each other in this time of tragedy even though neither of us found words to suit the occasion.

I was so preoccupied that I was oblivious to the sound of the approaching carriage until I saw Clement enter the dining room, hat in hand, without Doc Bradley.

He looked at us as if he were attending a funeral and was comforting the bereaved. "I regret to inform you that Doc Bradley passed away yesterday evening. Yellow fever."

My spirits sank. No other doctor resided within the region, and the nearest hospital, located in Philadelphia, required a two-day journey from Cromwell's Passage.

# CHAPTER TWENTY-TWO

## Cromwell's Passage

## the Maryland Colony

## 16 NOVEMBER 1773

Three male servants and Pastor Vinson delicately carried Mr. Wright to his chambers. Mrs. Greene directed Clement to begin the journey to Philadelphia. "Go. Make haste," she decried. "And do not return without a doctor!" She retired to a guest room while I tended to Mr. Wright's bedside. Sleep was not possible. Mr. Wright's life was touch and go. It was Hazel who finally coaxed me to take a break.

"The youngster is asleep. I can watch Mr. Wright, dress the wound as needed, and still get Penny off to school. Now go on! Get some sleep while you can. I'll wake you if anything changes."

I agreed with reluctance. Mr. Wright remained unconscious. We prayed with Pastor Vinson that the bleeding would not grow worse. I told Mrs. Greene that if a doctor didn't arrive soon, I would need to suture the wound and pray it did not become infected. Mrs. Greene agreed. I couldn't, however, suture until I was sure the preponderance of bleeding had ceased.

"I will continue to pray for Aquila," said Pastor Vinson. "The Cromwell community will come together and help with whatever you need." I hugged this kind man and walked him to the front door.

The hours passed slowly. Hazel was good to her word. She minded Mr. Wright for three uneventful hours before seeing Penny off to school. Thereafter, I checked the wound and elected to begin the sutures. Mr. Wright was still devoid of color. I was not a betting woman, but if I were, I would not have given him odds of recovery. It took thirty minutes to suture the wound and apply fresh dressing. I placed a warm cloth on his head and covered him with a second quilt. The additional quilt was heavy and contained a landscape of Cromwell's Passage, at least as I imagined it. I had made only one quilt since working on Lord Hall's family crest in the London Debtor's Prison. I was pleased with the outcome and had planned to surprise Mr. Wright on his birthday. Now, not knowing if he would see the next year, I placed it in early use.

I made him as comfortable as I could and sat in the high-back chair by his bed. An angry rapping on the front door disturbed the momentary peace. The cadence of the knocking reminded me of the awful day of Thomas's death and the intrusion from that horrible man, Elias Carmichael. I'll never forget his lack of empathy nor his tasteless behavior.

Mr. Wright's valet answered the door. A loud voice declared that Amos Haverford had arrived with his entourage.

I walked to the top of the stairwell and gazed down upon the foyer. "What is the meaning of this?" I asked. "A gravely ill man is trying to rest."

"That is exactly why we are here," Haverford replied. "With Aquila on death's door, I have persuaded Governor Templeton to turn the hospital construction over to me."

Before I could reply, Mr. Wright's trusted foreman from the mill, Isaiah Trumbull, burst in the foyer. He was sweating intensely and struggling to catch his breath.

"Miss Essie, I tried to stop these charlatans from coming to the main house. They wouldn't listen."

Haverford jumped in. "It is you who will be listening to me. With Aquila out of commission, I intend to purchase the mill, this estate, and even that pretty indentured servant at the top of the stairs."

I was mortified. Before I could say a word, Mrs. Greene appeared from behind me.

"Amos, you may have persuaded Governor Templeton to let you build a hospital, but I'll be damned if you'll own one shred of the mill or Cromwell's Passage."

Haverford snarled at Mrs. Greene. "I can't imagine what you could do to stop me."

Mrs. Greene held up her hand. "When Charles returns, he will affirm the bad news for you. When Rebecca died, Aquila appointed Charles and me Penny's legal guardians in the event of his demise. Further, it is Charles who will oversee Aquila's business interests and this land, not the likes of you. Now get out!"

Mr. Haverford and his men retreated but not before making an angry declaration. "I'll come back with a judge's order to sell the mill and the estate." The door closed.

I turned to Mrs. Greene and embraced her heartily. "I don't know what I would have done if you weren't here."

She patted my back as a caring mother would. "He's nothing more than a bully. Charles will set him straight."

# CHAPTER TWENTY-THREE

## *Cromwell*

## the Maryland Colony

### 17 NOVEMBER 1773

On the afternoon of the third day after the bridge collapsed, Clement had not yet returned with a doctor. Mr. Wright remained the same—no worse, no better. The sutures were holding, and the wound appeared clean. Hazel and Mrs. Greene tended to Mr. Wright while I went into town for provisions. Mrs. Greene suggested I have Mr. Wright's valet escort me, but I chose to walk. I needed little in town and desired the fresh air. A brisk fall stroll would improve my demeanor.

The sky was clear, and colorful leaves had fallen. There was something pleasing about kicking the gold and orange maple leaves from the path with each step into town. About halfway there, my mind was on the deplorable Amos Haverford. I hoped Mr. Greene would produce the documents needed to restrain him. He struck me as an evil man filled with hate and greed. I believed him to envy Mr. Wright. From the time I laid eyes on him in church, it was obvious to me.

At that moment, my right foot knocked into something beneath the leaves. It moved and took me by surprise. I feared I accidentally bumped into a wounded critter beneath the leaves, but it was not the case. A large black snake lifted its head from the pile. Its tongue ambled out while the steely eyes stared me down. I jumped back, and my foot slipped on the moist leaves. I landed on the sodden path, making my backside wet as the snake grew closer. Paralyzed with fear, I could only retreat on my rear end, my feet pushing me backward through the leaves. Retreating off the path, I found my back against a tall maple which served as a prop for me to stand and run. I deviated from the path, unaware of the snake's precise whereabouts.

When I felt safe, I returned to the leaf-covered path and brushed the debris and mud from my dress. I was sure I was unfit to enter any of Cromwell's shops. I pondered turning back, but since I was closer to town, I went to the church. Pastor Vinson kept a collection of used clothing where I could find something dry to change into.

What a sight I must have been for Pastor Vinson as I entered his revered place of worship. "My goodness! What happened? Are you all right?"

Embarrassed, I explained myself and inquired about the used clothing collection. Pastor Vinson pointed me to a storage closet in the back of the church. Rummaging through the box of retired clothing, I found a simple gray dress, the likes of which Mrs. Allen gave me on my first day in Annapolis. It lacked a good fit and attractiveness, but it was clean and dry. I swiftly changed and bundled my soiled garment into the basket I'd brought to fill with provisions. Entering the main sanctuary, I found Pastor Vinson waiting in the front-row pew where I sat with Mr. Wright and Penny on Sunday mornings.

"How is Aquila?"

"The same," I replied. "Which I take as an estimation of his status. My late husband always said the body possessed remarkable powers to heal under the right circumstances."

Pastor Vinson smiled warmly. His right eyebrow arched. "Your late husband was a wise man. I think the Lord has a direct hand in these matters, and I shall continue to pray for Aquila."

Pastor Vinson offered tea and more conversation, but I felt the strong need to return to Cromwell's Passage with food and medical supplies. As I rose to leave, the church doors flew open as if a gust of wind barreled into them. Antonia Bond fainted in the doorway. Her dress was dirty and torn, and her face showed bruises. Two black eyes and a puffy lower lip were all we needed to see to know someone had beaten her to a pulp.

Pastor Vinson and I rushed over. The two of us carried Antonia to the meeting room and placed her on the old chaise lounge.

She regained a partial awareness of her surroundings.

"Child, what happened to you? Who did this?" inquired Pastor Vinson.

Antonia mumbled incoherently. Her mouth was bleeding, and her two front teeth were missing.

"Do you have any clean cloth and cool water?" I asked the pastor.

He nodded and left us alone. I took her hand and ran my other through her red hair. Her eyes revealed the horror of the attack, and she forced some guttural syllables.

"Have . . ."

"Have what? Do you want something?"

She vigorously shook her head. "Have . . . eh . . . fold."

At first, I wasn't sure what she was trying to convey, but then it struck me as sure as Amos Haverford's bare fists had landed upon my own flesh.

"Don't try to speak," I counseled. "We can talk when you feel up to it."

Pastor Vinson returned, and I used the cool cloth to clean her wounds and ease the sting. Taking a piece of cloth, I mixed it with salt and placed it in Antonia's mouth to halt the bleeding and promote healing. I told Pastor Vinson what I heard, and he shook his head in disgust.

"The town council just appointed a new sheriff, a Mr. Zeke McCarron. I'll send for him."

Upon this news, the fear in Antonia's eyes grew wild. She yanked the cloth from her bloody mouth and began an anguished protest. "No, no, no," she proclaimed as tears streamed down her swollen cheeks.

Trying to calm Antonia, Pastor Vinson inquired, "What are you afraid of? The sheriff will seek justice on your behalf."

Antonia remained vigilant in her protestations. Although her words were muffled, Antonia's meaning was clear. "McCarron works for Haverford. They took turns raping me."

Cromwell's new lawman was corrupt, likely on the payroll of one of the town's wealthiest men, a man who was aiming for more. More power, more money. My sense was that Amos Haverford would spare no expense to run over the town of Cromwell and anyone who got in his way.

# CHAPTER TWENTY-FOUR

## *Cromwell's Passage*
## the Maryland Colony

### 17 NOVEMBER 1773

Dr. Phineas Bond arrived well past supper. He was a man who appeared much older than his age. His gray wig hung regally past the collar of the white ruffled shirt and dark overcoat. He looked drawn, almost haggard, as if deprived of sleep.

"We journeyed directly here," he offered without being asked. Carrying a black cowhide medical bag, he asked to be taken to Mr. Wright's chamber. Penny was already asleep, and Mrs. Greene had gone home to await her husband's return. Dr. Bond followed me up the stairs. I wondered if I should wake Hazel for additional assistance.

Mr. Wright remained unconscious as Dr. Bond set his bag down and immediately went to work. He asked me to tell him the story of the bridge accident, and I relayed the details as told to me.

"I shall examine the wound," he stated. Then, after a few moments. "I was expecting to see a wound full of pus. Someone did well by Mr. Wright."

I blushed and told him of my experience in Wickhamshire as a midwife and medical assistant to Thomas.

"It is common with these sorts of wounds that the patient falls into a coma. It's the body's way of healing. Had you not prevented the wound from infection, he would have spiked a high fever and likely died in the first day or so."

"So you think he will recover?"

"Yes, thanks to you. You saved his life."

I didn't know how to reply. I simply regarded Dr. Bond's praise with humility.

"I shall give you an antiseptic balm to promote healing. He is not running a fever and should be awake any time now. Clean and dress the wound daily and have him stay in bed for two or three weeks."

I nodded and asked him if he needed anything, food or drink, before retiring for the evening.

"No, thank you. I am exhausted. If you would show me to my room, I shall rest, check on the patient in the morning, and then go visit my daughter."

"Your daughter? She lives here in Cromwell?"

"Why, yes. Aquila invited her here to assist in the opening of the new hospital."

The blood must have drained from my face. I felt silly at having forgotten the connection. Antonia's last name was Bond. Of course they were related! And Dr. Bond did not know his daughter had sustained a savage attack. I bit my bottom lip and dragged my foot on the floor. I always employed a delay mechanism when I needed to deliver troubling news.

"Dr. Bond. I don't know how to tell you this. I didn't recall that Antonia was your daughter. She was beaten and . . . raped this morning. I tended to her at the church in town. She is resting in her room at the inn. I am to check on her tomorrow, as our only doctor passed on a few days ago."

The man's cheeks became crimson, his anger apparent. "Who is responsible for this atrocity?"

"Antonia said it was a man named Amos Haverford and the new sheriff, Zeke McCarron."

"Take me to her, NOW!" Dr. Bond would not listen to reason.

"Let me find Clement, Mr. Wright's coachman. He can take you."

"Nonsense," he bellowed. "I have a horse and carriage outside. You will accompany me and show me the way."

"Of course," I replied obediently. I went and got Hazel, leaving her instructions on the care of Mr. Wright and getting Penny off to school in the morning in the event I had not yet returned.

The short ride in the hour past midnight plodded. Dr. Bond's coachman was unfamiliar with the route, and despite two carriage lamps, I feared we would veer off into the woods. When we arrived at the inn, the town was eerily quiet. In my brief time in Cromwell, it was the first time I'd been in town after dark. A bright yellow moon broke through a sea of puffy clouds, giving the night a ghost story feel. Dr. Bond wasted not a moment dismounting from the carriage, and he helped me to the ground.

"Which room is Antonia in?" Dr. Bond barked.

I didn't take offense. He was of a singular mind to address his daughter's plight. Any upstanding parent would have done the same.

We knocked on the door until finally a mousy man answered, no doubt wondering what was the nature of this late night disturbance. Before I could say a word, Dr. Bond snapped at the innkeeper.

"I am Dr. Phineas Bond of Philadelphia. My daughter is here. I demand to see her at once."

Fear petrified the meek innkeeper.

"Yes, yes. Of course, Dr. Bond. Let me see which room she is in."

"I know the way," I offered and led Dr. Bond through the corridor and down to the right.

Dr. Bond rapped on the pine door calling his daughter's name until she appeared at the door, her red hair askew and her patrician face a puddled mess of black and blue.

Through sleep-ridden eyes, she appeared confused. "Papa, what—"

"Antonia, your father came to treat Mr. Wright. When he heard of your misfortune, he insisted we come to see you."

Dr. Bond embraced his daughter. The love that a father has for a daughter is immeasurable. Dr. Bond's hug was like a rainbow appearing after a summer storm.

"Let me examine you, and then you will tell me who did this and why."

Antonia lay still on the small feather bed. I assisted Dr. Bond. After completing the physical exam, he spoke to me directly, expressing his concern about his badly beaten daughter and hoping that her attackers had not violated her.

I placed my hand on his shoulder to express my sympathy for his daughter's plight. I could not find the words to adequately pay my respects to the situation. We approached the bed where Antonia lay half-awake, and her father addressed her again.

"My dearest, I know you wish to sleep. Tell me if you can, who did this?"

Antonia, through the haze of trauma and the need to sleep, whispered, "Haverford . . . and the sheriff."

Looking at me, Dr. Bond asked, "Do you know these men?"

I nodded. "I suspect that neither of them will be difficult to find. From what I have come to learn, they fancy themselves invincible, especially with Mr. Wright out of commission. He unofficially governs Cromwell as the sole descendant of the town's founder."

"What do you suppose was their motive?"

Before I could answer, Antonia confirmed my suspicion. "They said that Aquila Wright is not a king and doesn't have a say in all matters of Cromwell." She paused, and a tear trickled down her swollen cheek. "And the sheriff said he'd not stand by and watch a woman do a man's work."

And there it was. The resolute affirmation that women were to be bound forever to an apron and a broom, nothing more. I was appalled but not surprised. I witnessed the same, if not worse, in Wickhamshire.

"Antonia, rest now. I will take you home at first light." Then he spoke to me in a tone that I knew meant business. "When Aquila awakes, let him know what happened and that I, along with my brother, and Benjamin Franklin, will form a militia to capture these corrupt men. Let it be known that Cromwell will continue to fall prey to charlatans until you have duly elected town officials, a mayor, a judge, and a real sheriff."

I nodded and prayed that Mr. Wright was soon back on his feet.

"Make no mistake about it. We will bring these men to justice."

# CHAPTER TWENTY-FIVE

## Cromwell's Passage

## the Maryland Colony

## 20 NOVEMBER 1773

When I was Penny's age, I often rearranged the modest furnishings in my room. Somehow, a new configuration provided a fresh outlook on the burdens holding me captive. I hadn't thought about that in years. In the time since Thomas died, I had found myself angry, melancholy, and without hope, all plenty of reason to justify rearranging the furniture. Strangely, now as an adult, the changes were not happening to the items in a bedroom but rather to my life. Unlike the inanimate objects with which I was free to create placement, life events were conspiring to dictate the circumstances governing my narrow band of choice.

I hadn't considered my status in the world for some time. Thomas passed just over six months previously. So much had happened. Now I cared for Mr. Wright and his daughter and was a churchgoer. My life had changed before my very eyes, yet I considered that Mr. Wright could claim a similar sentiment. Circumstances beyond his control altered his life. I witnessed firsthand the gleam in his eye when he met Antonia in Philadelphia. Although I am sad about what transpired with her, Antonia would have made a fine wife for Mr. Wright. Now, I suspected she would never return to Cromwell. What would Mr. Wright do, I wondered? He was a devilishly handsome man with a kind manner. I enjoyed how he doted over

Penny. In my dream world, I sometimes imagined that I might be his wife and become a second mother to Penny. We could build a life together in the manner Thomas and I dreamed of in Wickhamshire. And every time these fantasies danced across my mind, I was fraught with the guilt of a woman in mourning.

While I did not own the house in which I lived—or my freedom, for that matter—I had taken to appeasing the guilt by rearranging the furniture in my mind for each room of Mr. Wright's stately abode. Upon commencement of that exercise, my dream returned, and the guilt with it. If I were Mrs. Wright, I could remake this home in the way I desired. I pinched myself as penance for the inappropriate thoughts and walked to town. I promised Penny I would make a proper English beef stew for dinner.

As I entered the general store owned by Amos Haverford, his clerk, a friendly older woman, offered to help me find what I needed. I located the ingredients or comparable substitutes for my mother's recipe and proceeded to the counter to settle the bill. The general store also served as the drop-off point for the daily post, and the clerk presented me with a letter from Philadelphia addressed to Mr. Wright. I tucked it inside my basket and stopped by the church to visit with Pastor Vinson.

"I hope you are here to practice the new music for our Thanksgiving service."

I felt foolish. I hadn't remembered that he asked me weeks ago to perform a new piece.

"I have time to run through it quickly," I replied.

I sat with the harp and the sheet music Pastor Vinson provided. The melody was enchanting, and the music effortlessly emanated from my hand and the strings. I wondered what an accompaniment from Benjamin Franklin's glass armonica might sound like. When I completed the song, Pastor Vinson was pleased.

"Essie, you are a gifted musician." He beamed, but as usual, I felt inadequate. Perhaps by Cromwell standards, I was considered gifted. In England, I was just a face in the crowded field of players more talented than I.

Not satisfied, I promised to practice more. "I'll be ready for the service," I said, as if he required my assurance.

I aimed to get back to the house in time to greet Penny and begin the stew. By the time I made my way up the long, winding path at Cromwell's Passage, Hazel was running toward me with a look of glee rarely exhibited.

"The master . . . Essie . . . the master . . . he's awake!" She was bouncing with joy, her arms flailing about like a child on her birthday.

I handed her the provisions, grabbed the Philadelphia post, and raced up the stairs, bursting into the entryway of his chamber.

Mr. Wright sat upright. The color had returned to his cheeks, and those brown eyes sparkled at his own rebirth. I couldn't help but beam. My heart sang. Pastor Vinson promised me that prayers do come true.

"Hazel tells me I've been asleep for five days."

"Yes, milord. Can I get you anything? Water, some bread, perhaps?"

"Water, if you please."

I placed the letter on his nightstand and handed him a glass of water. He sipped gently. "How much do you remember of the accident?" I inquired.

He furrowed his brow and scratched his head. "I recall all of it, and I'm sure my favorite horse could not have survived the fall into the Nathaniel River."

I shook my head. "No, I'm afraid not. We lost both horses, the wagon, and all the provisions you carried. But you! You are here and are looking well."

I didn't yet know if he was aware of Antonia's attack and sudden departure. Or for that matter, Haverford's brazen attempt to assume the leadership of the hospital and the town itself.

He sensed the angst on my face and prodded me gently. "I can see you are troubled. What is bothering you? Is it Penny?"

The last thing I wanted to do was upset him so soon after emerging from a weeklong sleep. "No, no. Penny is fine. She's been very worried about you, but she has been so good about everything. Mrs. Greene has been a tremendous help."

"Then what, Essie? You can tell me anything."

Mr. Wright had a greater capacity for compassion and empathy than anyone I'd ever known. Here he was emerging from a near-death experience, and his first thought was about what might be troubling me.

I was unsure how to respond. If I chose to be forthright with the truth, it might cause Mr. Wright an unfortunate setback. If I concealed what I knew, he would easily see through me, and it would shatter my credibility. As was my habit, I fidgeted. My right leg moved forward and backward, and I played with a lock of hair draped across my forehead. I could see he was eager for a reply. Before I could utter a coherent phrase, a noise erupted from the foyer, and heavy-footed steps were marching up the staircase. Fear gripped me. Was Haverford here with his henchmen to do us harm? I was now shaking, and sweat broke out across my nose and cheeks.

A moment later, Mr. Wright smiled, and I felt foolish. Mr. Greene had returned and was simply visiting his old friend, surprised to finally see him awake and alert.

"Charles! You look like you are on a mission."

"Aquila, I am glad to see you recovering. I have been away. I have the most extraordinary news on multiple fronts."

"Do tell," Mr. Wright eagerly replied.

Mr. Greene hesitated. He focused on me, and Mr. Wright quickly ascertained that Mr. Greene wished to speak in private. Taking the hint, I respectfully excused myself, closing the door to Mr. Wright's chamber almost all the way.

I must confess my curiosity regarding Mr. Greene's extraordinary news overwhelmed my better judgment. I positioned myself close enough to the opening in the doorway where I could hear their conversation.

"I told Celia that I was on a business trip. She would frown on the real reason for my absence. I have been in Baltimore meeting with the Sons of Liberty. The colonial patriots have become fed up with British rule, including their taxes, laws, and governance."

Mr. Greene paused. I could hear him pacing back and forth on the creaky floorboard at the foot of the bed. Then he continued.

"Aquila, there is going to be a revolution. Our path to independence is a dangerous road. We will need to be steadfast but covert in our efforts. You and I will help to usher in a new nation."

"That's remarkable!" Mr. Wright was tiring. I could hear the strain in his voice. The water pitcher chugged as he refilled the glass. A breeze entered the chamber from the open window and raced through the crack in the door where I stood. A new tenor to their conversation emerged with the wind.

Mr. Greene's voice turned down an octave or two. "I am raising a small militia to settle the score with Haverford."

Mr. Greene was about to reveal the upsetting news that Mr. Wright was still not ready to hear. All I could do was wait and brace myself for the reaction lest I give away my position by the door as an eavesdropper.

"Haverford? What has that scoundrel done now?" Mr. Wright asked nonchalantly.

Then, Mr. Greene realized he unwittingly stepped into a pile of manure.

"Oh, uh . . . well, I . . . you don't know?"

Mr. Wright smiled and replied, "I've been asleep. Out with it, my man."

Mr. Greene sounded uncomfortable and unsure of how to proceed. Through the narrow opening, I could see it in his manner. He was fidgety, like me. Finally, he stammered out a reply.

"Haverford and his handpicked sheriff, Zeke McCarron, paid a visit to Antonia."

Mr. Wright immediately grasped the magnitude of the proclamation. "How badly was she hurt?"

Mr. Greene shook his head, pulling a handkerchief from his breast pocket and wiping his brow. "It was bad. She was beaten and raped. Her father came to tend to you and then took her back to Philadelphia."

The heat rose in Mr. Wright's face. With crimson cheeks, he sat upright in the bed and angrily replied, "Do we know the reason for this atrocity?"

From outside the room, I scoffed at the question. From what I'd seen of Mr. Haverford, he didn't need a reason. He was just a mean-spirited man intent on causing angst wherever he went. My mother would have said he'd been kissed by the devil himself.

"Celia tells me that in view of your accident, Haverford has made himself the de facto town leader. He appointed McCarron and attempted to take over the hospital project. It was Celia's opinion that Haverford wanted to send the message that a woman would not be able or welcome to administer a hospital."

Mr. Wright swung his legs over the edge of the bed and straightened his night-shirt. He grabbed the bandage over his near-death wound and, through a wince, declared, "I need to dress and hunt him down."

"You are in no condition. As I mentioned, I am forming a small militia. Me, Isaiah Trumbull, and a handful of others. We are assembling this evening to formulate a plan."

As Mr. Wright took in this devastating news, he turned to the nightstand for a sip of water and noticed the letter I had left.

"What's that?" Mr. Greene inquired.

"It's a letter from Dr. Bond in Philadelphia." Mr. Wright broke the seal and began reading. "Antonia lost her two front teeth, and her eyesight is now in question. The attack traumatized her, and she will not be returning to Cromwell." He continued reading. "It looks like your plan is getting help. Dr. Bond and his brother worked with Benjamin Franklin and Governor Penn to form a militia. They are coming for Haverford and McCarron and after justice is served, they intend on working with Governor Templeton to establish the hospital and proper governance in Cromwell." Mr. Wright continued to read and then sighed. "Dr. Bond says I should be grateful for Essie. Were it not for her forethought in the aftermath of Doc Bradley's passing, my wound would have never healed properly, causing a certain death."

"Celia would concur with Dr. Bond's sentiment that Essie saved your life, Aquila."

"I am grateful, although I was unaware of Doc Bradley's passing. I am sorry to hear such sad news."

"Celia informed me that he died around the time you were brought back to Cromwell's Passage. It was yellow fever."

I listened attentively and regarded what I heard as bad news on all fronts. The credit afforded to me by Dr. Bond for saving Mr. Wright's life was flattering. I suppose my work with Thomas in Wickhamshire made my judgment feasible. While I appreciated the praise, I was more concerned with the plan to avenge Antonia. Any local militia formed by Mr. Greene might find an uphill battle in bringing two dangerous men to justice. Governor Penn, Dr. Franklin, and the Bond brothers working together would be a stronger effort. I tiptoed down the steps toward the kitchen. I did not want to be caught lurking.

As I made my way toward the staircase, I heard Mr. Greene console his best friend. "I know you had feelings for Antonia and viewed her as a potential spouse. Fear not. Often opportunity arises from the depths of despair."

I concurred with Mr. Greene's sentiment and harbored a secret hope that I could be Mr. Wright's opportunity.

# CHAPTER TWENTY-SIX

## Cromwell's Passage
## the Maryland Colony

THANKSGIVING DAY, 25 NOVEMBER 1773

I was not familiar with the traditions of this American Thanksgiving holiday. Penny did her best to educate me. Early that morning, the cook slaughtered, plucked, and bathed three prime geese from Cromwell's Passage before seasoning them with a variety of spices, which aroused my senses as the birds roasted. Another servant worked on a fig pudding while they peeled, chopped, and boiled vegetables. Mr. Wright extended an invitation for me to sit at the table with him, Penny and the Greenes. The gesture was well-received but awkward. Despite my dream of a future with Mr. Wright, I recognized my role as an indentured servant and felt more at ease with the staff rather than the family.

The meal preparation would take hours, and I sat with Penny on the porch. The November morning was delightfully mild. We rocked on side-by-side chairs and took in the pleasant smells of the kitchen wafting from the windows onto the porch. Colorful maple leaves had fallen and covered the path that would return Mr. Wright to his home in time for the Thanksgiving celebration.

"I am worried about Father," Penny confided.

I valued this trust in me. I had made slow and steady progress, building her affections. I reached for her hand and embraced it affectionately. "May I ask why?"

She looked up at me with the last vestiges of a little girl's puppy dog eyes and replied, "Dr. Bond said Father should rest for two to three weeks upon awakening, but off he went to Annapolis just days after. Suppose he takes ill while away?"

I couldn't fault Penny for the way she felt. I shared her concern but understood that Mr. Wright was not a passive man who let life come to him. He was the sort who took charge and pursued objectives as he saw them.

"Mr. Greene is with your father. So is Clement. At least your father is not on horseback. Sitting in the comfort of his carriage will be much safer." I tried to sound reassuring, but as we both knew firsthand, the carriage ride from Annapolis was long, bumpy, and sometimes treacherous. There was a strong possibility that the carriage would not travel unimpeded. I remembered the fear of rogue Indians and desperate runaway slaves who might not be as gracious as Fred. Mr. Greene's presence on this journey was a godsend. While I didn't approve of his position on slavery, he, unlike his friend Mr. Wright, would not help a runaway. This I saw as a safer choice for a man impaled and still physically inept. I revealed none of these worries to Penny. I just patted her arm and reassured her that her father would be home soon to enjoy a festive meal.

Since I could not play a meaningful role in the preparation of the holiday feast, Penny and I walked to town and visited with Pastor Vinson. Penny asked if I could teach her how to play the harp. With the pastor's consent, I showed her proper seating and hand position and taught her how to strum and create basic chords. The glee on her face reminded me of my own when my mother did the same for me when I was a few years Penny's junior. I let her practice while I spoke to the pastor.

"Are you eager for your first Thanksgiving celebration?"

"I am, although I confess I feel rather inadequate in the preparation."

He placed an arm around my shoulder in a fatherly gesture and said, "It's all right to let others take the lead sometimes."

He was right, but it was not in my nature to be served.

"Pastor Vinson, may I confide in you?"

"Of course. Anything you say remains between us and us only."

While he offered a sense of reassurance, I felt timid in an instant. I hadn't planned to come to church today and pour out my innermost feelings. I made a sudden decision and immediately regretted speaking. Tears streamed down my face as I looked down at my feet. I hated myself for submitting to weakness. If the past few months taught me anything, it was to put on a brave face.

"What is it, Essie?"

I looked up, dabbed my cheek with the bottom of my apron, and whispered so Penny would not overhear. "I feel my place in this world is in between."

He appeared bewildered at my statement. "In between?" he asked. "Help me understand."

"Not long ago, I was a happy wife to a man with whom I was deeply in love. We built a fine life in Wickhamshire, and the community valued us as members." I paused, dabbed the apron to my eyes again, and continued. "Now, I am an indentured servant in a foreign land with an uncertain future and a feeling of despair."

"Are you melancholy?" he inquired.

I considered his question. "No," I replied. "I am happy when I am with Penny, and helping Mr. Wright back to health reminded me of my days back home. It is just that . . ."

"What, child?"

I peered into his eyes, seeking reassurance of the sincerity I perceived. Finally, I said it out loud for the first time. "I think I have feelings for Mr. Wright."

Pastor Vinson was surprised but quickly regained his composure. "Do you mean romantic feelings?"

I nodded and again began to cry. "Is that wrong?"

"The Lord teaches us to love everyone. How could it be wrong?"

I hadn't considered this in religious connotation, but my reemergence into the church gave me comfort on the issue.

Penny finished playing the harp and skipped down the steps of the altar toward the back pew where we sat.

I wiped the last vestige of tears from my face and said to Pastor Vinson, "Thank you for the pleasant conversation. I trust this remains between us?"

"Certainly," he replied. "You have nothing to worry about."

We wished Pastor Vinson a happy Thanksgiving and shuffled through the fallen leaves on the road back to Cromwell's Passage.

—⁂—

I delighted in the father-daughter reunion. Penny leapt into the arms of her father, whose recovering body was not ready for such an exuberant embrace. To Mr. Wright's credit, he did not let his pain deter his daughter's glee.

"Did you bring me anything from Annapolis, Father?"

Reaching for a satchel, Mr. Wright removed a small bag tied at the top with a thin piece of twine. "Here you are, my dear. Save these for after supper."

"Chocolate squares!" Penny was ecstatic. "Just one now, Father. Please."

"All right, my sweet. Just one."

Penny scurried off and left Mr. Wright and me alone on the front porch. He directed me to the companion rockers. "Essie, sit. Can we have a conversation?"

I sat. I started fidgeting, as I was a bundle of nerves. "Have I done something wrong, milord?"

"Heavens, no. To the contrary. I wish to thank you."

"Thank me, sir? What for?"

"For starters, for saving my life. Dr. Bond wrote to me of your heroics. He said I would have died were it not for you. Celia tells me how collected and deliberate you were in the face of a crisis after the accident, and the other servants told me how much they respect and defer to you. You are a genuine leader."

"You are too kind."

"And then there is my daughter. As you know, she does not easily give her affections. But I see how she admires you, and I am grateful. It is difficult for a girl approaching womanhood to grow up without a mother."

My heart began fluttering. Where was this leading? Was Mr. Wright proposing a different relationship? I drew in a breath to calm myself, not knowing how or whether to reply.

"Essie, I am granting you your freedom. You are no longer indentured to me and are free to leave if you wish."

Leave? I was flabbergasted. Of course, my freedom was my utmost wish, but with no means of supporting myself and no place to live, what would become of me? Should I go back to England or perhaps travel amongst the other colonies? Sometimes getting what you want is not as appealing when it sits in the palm of your hand. I felt crushed. Defeated. Lost. I was certain it showed on my pale expression.

"Thank you, milord," I said stoically.

"But I hope you will give consideration to my plan."

"Plan? What plan?"

He reached into the inner pocket of his azure coat and removed a rolled piece of parchment secured by a blue ribbon. "This is a writ from Governor Templeton granting me full authority over all matters of the hospital's construction and operation. It will remove threats from derelicts like Haverford."

"That is wonderful news, sir."

"I don't think you understand," he proclaimed. "I want to name you the administrator of the new hospital. Your medical knowledge and leadership skills are evident. You have proven yourself capable. You will receive the same salary as Antonia, and if you prefer, you can live in the cottage on the east side of the property without paying rent. Rebecca's father lived there in his final years. It has a bedroom, kitchen, living area, and its own garden. Anyway, the arrangement will help you save some money so you are never beholden again to debt, yours or anyone else's."

I was overwhelmed. My mind flooded with errant thoughts. What about Penny? Who would care for her? And Antonia? My God, how could I attempt such a feat as starting a hospital and remain safe? What if they don't apprehend Haverford and McCarron? I became dizzy from the torrent of ruminations.

Mr. Wright was determined and ignored my flight of disarray. "I will prepare documents certifying your freedom with no further monetary or service obligations. I shall have your things moved into the cottage. Charles and Celia have a niece in Virginia who will become a nanny to Penny, and we can begin working together on the hospital next week."

The fear in my eyes must have given me away. Before I could respond, he took my hand and stated boldly, "I will keep you safe and sound, surely as if you were my wife."

Although it was meant only as a metaphor, my heart still raced.

With no proper choice before me, I said, "I am grateful and gladly accept your kind and generous offer."

—ᘰ—

The Thanksgiving meal was divine. The goose was tender and succulent and the fig pudding a sweet delight on which to conclude the feast. As we sat and drank tea, Mr. Wright announced my freedom, new residence, and responsibility to start the Cromwell hospital. Mr. and Mrs. Greene offered their congratulations. Penny looked wounded.

I swiftly wrapped my arms around her, proclaiming, "We shall remain the best of friends. I still have much to teach you."

She laid her head on my shoulder. "Do you mean it?"

"Of course. When your new nanny arrives from Virginia, the three of us will forge an unbreakable bond."

For the first time, Penny kissed my cheek, and my lower extremities went almost numb with joy. I'd never realized how much the love of a child could soften my indomitable will to achieve life's other objectives. At that moment, nothing else mattered.

Mr. Greene turned the conversation toward his plans. "The Sons of Liberty beckon. We must heed the call to lead the Harford County contingent. I propose we resign our commissions as county representatives in Governor Templeton's legislature. Why pander to the British any longer?"

"Charles, I urge cautious deliberation on the matter. Would it not be wise to remain in both groups—secretly, that is?"

Mr. Greene furrowed his brow. "I suppose you are right, Aquila. We can better aid the patriots if we know what the British are thinking."

"Precisely," Mr. Wright replied.

And with that, a loud rap on the front door concluded a most pleasant Thanksgiving dinner. A band of six men entered the foyer and called for Mr. Wright, who, along with Mr. Greene, went to see what the unexpected visitors wanted.

From the dining room entrance, I could see the leader was a tall, burly man with a bushy red beard and a scowl. He wasn't someone with whom I'd like to tangle in a conflict. I feared he was here to wreak havoc. Again, my initial fear betrayed common sense.

"Evening, Mr. Wright. We are sorry to disturb your holiday meal, but we are the militia sent by Governor Penn to apprehend Messrs. Haverford and McCarron.

Since they attacked a Philadelphia citizen, they are to be extradited and tried in Pennsylvania."

"I see," Mr. Wright replied. He offered each a plate of food left over from the evening meal.

As they sat and talked, I accompanied Penny to her room for a private moment.

She looked at me with those warm brown eyes. Her hair glistened like her father's. This girl would one day be a stunning young woman. I hoped I could be here to see her grow.

"Did you mean what you said earlier?" she inquired.

I squeezed her with all my might, kissed the top of her head, and said affectionately, "Nothing is more important to me."

After I accompanied Penny to her chamber, I retired to my room. On this day of giving thanks for our blessings, I'd gained my freedom, a prominent role in Cromwell's society, a home of my own, the love of a child, and, most important, hope for the future.

# CHAPTER TWENTY-SEVEN

## Cromwell's Passage
## the Maryland Colony

## 5 DECEMBER 1773

The new nanny's arrival was delayed, so I sat with Penny in the sewing room and quizzed her on English literature. We were making fine progress when Benjamin Franklin arrived from Philadelphia. A young surgeon who bore a striking resemblance to my Thomas accompanied him. It was undeniably strange!

Dr. Timothy Clarke was tall, at least six feet, and while thin, he had a muscular frame accompanied by thick sandy blond hair, blue eyes, and a face that betrayed his probable age. At first blush, one could assume he was younger than I. To be a surgeon, it couldn't be so.

After the servant who answered the door invited the two visitors to wait in the parlor, I told Penny to keep reading and made my way downstairs to greet the renowned man I'd met in Philadelphia. Truth be told, I also wanted to meet his new charge.

Benjamin Franklin was thrilled to see me and attempted to introduce Dr. Clarke. "Timothy, allow me to introduce Mrs. Essie Lassiter. She is . . . Well, I know you have been released from servitude, and a new nanny is coming, so I . . ."

I offered my assistance. I curtsied to Dr. Clarke and stated proudly, "I understand we are to work together in establishing the Cromwell hospital. I am your administrator."

Benjamin Franklin was relieved, although he hadn't yet moved past his sense of awkwardness. "Of course she is. How silly of me," he said in an obvious attempt to save face.

"It shall be my pleasure to collaborate with you, Mrs. Lassiter," stated Dr. Clarke in a rich baritone.

"Please call me Essie. All my friends do."

"I understand your husband was a doctor and you were a midwife back in England."

"Yes, that's correct. My husband died from smallpox."

"Dr. Franklin briefed me on your history. I am sorry for your loss."

"Where is Aquila?" inquired Franklin. "We have much to discuss."

"He is at the mill but should return any time. May I offer you gentlemen some hot tea?"

"That would be lovely," replied Dr. Clarke.

I showed them to the dining room and made my way to the kitchen. I wasn't expecting Benjmain Franklin—just the new doctor. Franklin helped found the Philadelphia hospital twenty-two years ago, and I knew his counsel would be invaluable.

Before the water boiled, Mr. Wright arrived and greeted his guests. I took an additional cup from the shelf and brought three servings of black tea with milk into the dining room.

The four of us sat at one end of the table, with Mr. Wright occupying the head.

"Did the militia arrive yet?" inquired Dr. Franklin.

"Yes," Mr. Wright said. "They have been here since Thanksgiving. I am afraid they have had no luck apprehending Messrs. Haverford and McCarron."

"They vanished?" asked Dr. Franklin.

"At least for now. Haverford has too many business interests in these parts. He can't keep away for long. He is probably thinking he can lie low for a spell and everything will blow over."

Dr. Franklin shook his head. "Well, that brings up the matter of Essie's safety in assuming Antonia's role. How will we keep her safe?"

Dr. Clarke was the first to respond. "I propose that Essie never works alone. I shall remain in her presence while all work takes place, and if I must make a house call, she shall accompany me."

"Aquila, does that meet with your approval?" Dr. Franklin asked.

Mr. Wright blanched. "I was going to have at least two men watch the front door of the temporary hospital quarters while Essie is inside."

"You may do so, if you like," offered Dr. Clarke. "But take solace in the fact that I was the prize fighting champion of Pennsylvania three years running, and I'm not ashamed to say I'm pretty handy with a musket."

Looking at me, Mr. Wright said, "Essie, what would make you feel most comfortable?"

I appreciated that he considered my opinion. "I suggest we try Dr. Clarke's plan and add guards if that proves too little."

"Done!" declared Dr. Franklin. "Now, let's discuss hospital plans. The first order of business is finding a temporary location while we construct the permanent building."

"I have a place in mind," replied Mr. Wright. "It's an old boardinghouse on the west end of town. Since the inn opened some years ago, it hasn't been in use. It will be sufficient for the short term. I have already made the arrangements to purchase the building with our hospital funds."

"Excellent," stated Dr. Franklin. "I suggest we tour the boardinghouse tomorrow. Then, we may evaluate needed equipment, supplies, and medicines."

"Dr. Clarke," I said. "You may be aware that Dr. Bradley, the only doctor for Cromwell and the surrounding towns, recently passed away. These people have no one else. How will we assist them?"

"We shall not leave them in a lurch. While we cannot make rounds like your Dr. Bradley, we will designate one or two days a week to see those in need. Once we build the hospital, we can entice more doctors to come to the area, thus making the job easier."

"Benjamin, the letter I received from Phineas said that he wanted to establish proper elected authority in Cromwell," said Mr. Wright.

Dr. Franklin presented an amiable smile as if he intended on speaking to this very topic. And perhaps he did. "Yes, I have had much influence in these matters, in Philadelphia and across the colonies. For now, I suggest you hold a simple election process for a mayor, a sheriff, and a judge. I can draw up the documents and oversee the printing of the announcement, the ballots, and the voting to take place at your town hall on a designated day and time. Officeholders will need to be reelected each year."

"That seems like a stalwart plan," replied Mr. Wright.

"It is indeed." Dr. Franklin clapped his hands together and grinned. "Few people know this, but we will soon form a Continental Congress. It will meet in Philadelphia, and delegates from all colonies will attend. I am certain that the Maryland Provincial Convention will appoint you."

This beckoned the conversation Mr. Wright had attempted at Dr. Franklin's dinner table in Philadelphia. He inquired about the Sons of Liberty. As I recalled, Dr. Franklin was not eager to conduct such talk then. Now, the tide had turned.

"That's welcome news," replied Mr. Wright. "Charles was lamenting the depressed price of tobacco. The British are still attempting to tax everything they can. We fought off the Stamp Act and the Townshend Act, but the tax on imported tea from England remains. The people have had enough."

Again, Dr. Franklin grinned like he knew something the rest of us did not. "I still have friends in Boston. The British have a surprise coming soon regarding their unreasonable tax on tea."

"They deserve whatever they get," added Dr. Clarke.

"I agree with you, Dr. Clarke," I said, surprising myself for adding a political opinion.

"We will work closely. Shall we dispense with the formalities? Call me Timothy."

I blushed but agreed. Quickly, in a sudden panic, I looked over at Mr. Wright. I had overstepped my bounds. "Milord, is it appropriate to do so?"

Mr. Wright took my hand and gently embraced it. "Essie, you are a free woman. You no longer need my approval for so simple a gesture from a gentleman. That decision is yours to make. In fact, I shall rather enjoy it if you would call me Aquila."

"And while we are at it, you may call me Benjamin," added Dr. Franklin.

Pride flushed through me. I skipped in glee on the path back to my little cottage. While I remain frightened of the return of Haverford and McCarron, I couldn't wait to commence work on the Cromwell hospital. Timothy was not one to scoff at a woman's brain or skill at achieving an arduous task. I'd only just met him, but I had a sense of the man. I believed I would learn much under his tutelage.

As I turned the knob on the cottage door, I stepped inside. I didn't feel like rearranging my furniture. Things finally fell into place. . . except I couldn't help but wonder whether Aquila was jealous of Timothy.

# CHAPTER TWENTY-EIGHT

## *The Road Back to Cromwell*

## the Maryland Colony

### 17 DECEMBER 1773

Benjamin's words regarding a surprise for the British in Boston turned out to be true. News spread through the colonies of how patriots took 340 cases of imported British tea and dumped them into the Boston Harbor. The revolt was on against taxes and the general economic depression caused by British rule. Talk of revolution was everywhere. In towns much larger than Cromwell, people ostracized British sympathizers. Mr. Greene reported as much from his frequent trips to Baltimore. Rumor had it that the Maryland Provincial Convention would soon require all men between ages fifteen and sixty to train for war against the British. Aquila told me he would leave to fight if called. Timothy and Mr. Greene as well.

Aquila explained to me how the French and Indian War depleted England's financial resources and placed pressure on King George III to raise revenue by further taxing the colonies. Colonial leaders argued that extreme taxation was crippling the economic potential of the colonies to aid England's plight. But beyond the economic factors, the patriots of this land sought independence for other reasons. Freedom was a central tenet—freedom to choose one's religion and not be bound by the Church of England. They spoke of a democratic governance that shunned monarchies and recognized all men as being equal. I was just beginning to comprehend these complex issues as America prepared for war against the country I once called home, a country that had cast me aside like unwanted rubbish. When it arose, I was determined to support the revolution in whatever way I could.

All these thoughts burdened my mind as Aquila, Timothy, and I worked to prepare the old boardinghouse for use. Benjamin had been away in Baltimore. He attended meetings that none of us dared to question the nature of. The boardinghouse was in a general state of disrepair. Time and neglect had had their way. Our first order of business was removing debris. Rooms overflowed with dusty, broken furniture, crates of irreclaimable old clothing, peeling paint, and cobwebs in every corner. It would take weeks to get the dilapidated building in order. Then we could begin bringing in new beds, fixtures, and supplies. Aquila asked Isaiah and three men from the mill to complete the job as quickly as they could.

While they worked, we spent time with an architect recommended by Benjamin who had designed the current Philadelphia hospital. I'd seen that magnificent structure occupying an entire city block. Cromwell would require nothing as elaborate. A modest building that housed twenty-five patients was a start. With the architect ready to begin his work, my immediate task was accompanying Timothy on rounds throughout Cromwell and the surrounding areas. Since I was the hospital administrator and the head nurse, in fact the only nurse, and Timothy a doctor, it was not considered inappropriate for a single man and woman to travel together. We journeyed as far south as Joppa and as far north as Scott's Old Fields, just east of the Nathaniel River. As we treated people, we spoke of the hospital plans. It surprised me that so many Harford County residents were thinking about war. The sentiment was so strong that I wondered if a twenty-five-bed hospital would be enough. I said as much to Timothy on our journey from Scott's Old Fields.

"I cannot say you are wrong. The site Aquila chose has plenty of room for expansion when the need arises," Timothy said. He paused in contemplation, as if he already realized the fallacy in his statement. "Of course, if we are in the throes of war, it would be nearly impossible to begin a construction project."

I smiled in agreement. Experience taught me that allowing a man to believe he knows best is always preferable. "Perhaps we should prevail upon Aquila to expand before the architect delves too deeply in his work."

"I see why Aquila and Benjamin think so highly of you. You are always think-ing ahead."

"And with a larger hospital comes the need for greater quantities of doctors, nurses, and equipment," I said. This made perfect sense to me. What did not was how the excess would be paid for.

He pulled the reins gently, bringing the carriage to a stop. "The horses need to rest. We can sit under the big shade tree just over there," he said as he pointed to an ancient oak tree twenty paces to our left.

"So what of the money needed to expand the hospital plan?" I inquired.

"Governor Templeton allocated adequate funds for the current project. I am sure he would be open to increasing the budget. And, if I dare say, we may enjoy assis-tance from a few wealthy benefactors, namely Aquila and his friend Charles Greene."

I hadn't considered this. Managing the monetary needs of the hospital was something I would need to learn and master. "Benjamin proposed a tax on Maryland colonists. He suggests that those men of wealth who live the closest pay the most and poorer folks pay less and less, depending upon their distance from Cromwell."

Timothy raised an eyebrow. "It makes sense. I must, however, question the citizens' appetite for yet another tax. I am sure Governor Templeton would not object. The British appointees have a penchant for taxes."

I thought about the revolution and considered whether Governor Templeton might be worried about a colonial revolt. Would he pay for an expanded hospital that might aid the enemy? Perhaps he was indifferent and regarded the matter as just another tax to be levied upon the subservient colonists.

A chill December wind rushed in. A cloud of dust and fallen leaves envel-oped us without warning, and before I knew it, Timothy shielded me in the folds of his long overcoat. I hadn't been so close to a man since Thomas died. I hadn't imagined Timothy romantically, but his gesture to shield me from nature's harsh force was both selfless and appreciated. I pressed my cheek into his shoulder and was ashamed to admit that I welcomed the warmth and comfort of a man's body. When the wind subsided, I looked up into his eyes and, for a moment, felt lost in those inviting deep blue pools. Our eyes locked, and I thought he might kiss me. I'm not sure I would have resisted had he tried, but chivalry took hold, and we rose from the ground and returned to the carriage.

"Are you all right?" he asked. "I didn't mean to pull you so close. It was just my instinct to protect you."

I think I may have blushed, although the frigid December air could have been the culprit. "It is all right," I replied as I brushed dirt and debris from my coat. "Thank you for shielding me."

As we resumed our travels back to Cromwell, I could tell Timothy was deep in thought. I was feeling giddy, like a schoolgirl, at the notion that he, too, might dwell on our moment under the tree. My silliness ended when he finally disclosed the nature of his silence.

"If there is to be war, we need to recruit and train nurses now. Beyond Philadelphia, they have established hospitals in New York and Massachusetts. I may be able to get doctors from those institutions. I also believe that the Bond brothers know of credible surgeons in France and Holland who may oppose England by coming here to work in our new hospital."

"May I suggest someone to assume my title as head nurse?"

"Certainly. That would be wonderful. Is she local?"

"Yes, and while she is not a nurse by training, she has aided me since my arrival in America and has strong aptitude."

"And she would sacrifice her responsibilities to her husband and home to work at the hospital?"

I hesitated.

Timothy discerned a deeper narrative and awaited my voluntary disclosure of the truth.

"I speak of my friend Hazel Giddings. She has no family here, nor does she maintain a household. She is an indentured servant to Mr. Greene." I waited for his thunderous dismissal of my foolhardy proposal. My stomach fluttered. I was sorry I had let the words escape my mouth.

But Timothy's reaction stunned me. "Would Mr. Greene be amenable to relieving Hazel of her debt of servitude?"

I was unsure how Mr. Greene felt but stated Mrs. Greene would enthusiastically agree. Hazel had been instrumental in Mrs. Greene's and Aquila's recoveries from illness.

"Essie, I will make you this pledge. When we return to Cromwell, I will speak with Aquila, and together, we will approach Mr. Greene. If he won't outright grant Hazel her freedom, then I will personally retire her debt."

"That's astoundingly generous. Thank you for agreeing to bring Hazel on. She can share the cottage with me and be of such help."

He gazed at me with kindness and proclaimed, "The choice of nurses will always be yours. You are the administrator. I am merely here to lead the medical practice and support your every need."

"Thank you, Timothy. It will take me time to become accustomed to having authority over such matters."

A sense of peace washed over me. The cool December wind picked up once more. I closed my eyes to shield them from flying debris, and when I opened them, the horses had stopped and the wind died down. And who did I see standing in our path? None other than the fugitives Haverford and McCarron.

I informed Timothy who the strangers were as they remained out of earshot.

"Essie, take the carriage and ride to the clearing just over yonder," Timothy instructed, pointing to an opening just past a small bluff. He hopped down and retrieved a musket and a leather satchel filled with ammunition and gunpowder from the wagon. He quickly attended to the loading of the weapon and advanced toward the fugitives.

"Be careful," I said and then did as he asked. I was still close enough to see and hear every word that was spoken.

Holding the musket in plain sight, Timothy peered into the steely eyes of Amos Haverford and declared, "I am Dr. Clarke, the new doctor for these parts. You men are fugitives. I know your stories. In ordinary circumstances, I must escort you to the legal authorities, but I am ill-equipped to do so. I suggest you move on."

Haverford snarled, "Legal authorities?" He nodded toward his companion. "This here is the sheriff of Cromwell, Mr. Zeke McCarron."

Timothy was undismayed. "We are not in Cromwell, and both of you are wanted men. The father of the woman you attacked has organized a militia that's here from Philadelphia. You should know Governor Penn sponsors the effort. Keep moving while you can."

McCarron spoke first. "What supplies do you have in that wagon?"

"I assure you it's empty. The wagon is for transporting the ill and injured. That might be you if you don't move on."

Timothy was so direct. His strength comforted me even though I feared for my life, knowing full well what these animals did to Antonia.

McCarron did not easily intimidate. "We have muskets too. I could shoot you and have my way with the young lady over there."

Timothy fired his musket, skillfully wounding the right shoulder of Zeke McCarron. "That is a warning shot, I assure you. The next one goes right between your eyes. Now move on!"

And they did. Haverford shouted a threat. "This isn't over," he proffered as McCarron held his shoulder, writhing in pain while attempting to still ride.

I waited beyond the bluff for Timothy to walk over. He mounted the carriage and maintained the musket in position between us. "Are you all right?" he asked.

I nodded, but truth be told, I was terrified. His gallantry touched me. I should have been the one asking him that exact question.

"We should have no more trouble from those two. Mr. McCarron may bleed to death before they can harm anyone else."

I hesitated and spoke. "As a doctor, do you not have an obligation to heal the ill and injured?"

His stern look belied the words that followed. "These men are criminals and were intending to harm us. I suspect they are British sympathizers. And this is war, which supersedes my moral obligation as a healer."

I couldn't challenge his logic. "What will become of them?"

"When we get back to Cromwell, I shall send word to the militia. With McCarron's shoulder in the state it's in, they won't get far."

I softly murmured a prayer, hoping he was right. It astounded me how, in times of strife, I returned to the faith abandoned in early adulthood. Was it the influence of Pastor Vinson? I wondered—or perhaps my finding that prayer in the worst of recent times brought me to a better place.

# CHAPTER TWENTY-NINE

## Cromwell's Passage

## the Maryland Colony

### 25 DECEMBER 1773

Snow descended softly for the second day in a row. The rolling hills outside the cottage window appeared like a blanket made of soft cotton. Despite its beauty, walking up to the main house would become more challenging. Hazel and I would lean on each other. She had moved in a few days earlier and was ever so grateful for my influence in securing her freedom and new position as head nurse. I promised to teach her all I knew about medicine and even midwifery. Mr. and Mrs. Greene joyfully released Hazel, freeing Timothy of the financial burden he so generously offered on our journey from Scott's Old Fields.

I had worked late into the evenings, completing two quilts as Christmas gifts for Aquila and Penny. Aquila's featured the Cromwell family crest brought to the New World by Aquila's grandfather, Mordecai Cromwell. The quilt resembled the pattern I used for Lord Hall's family crest when I was in the London Debtor's Prison. Penny's quilt featured the forest and the woodland birds and animals she so adored. For Mrs. Greene, I made a fine white linen tablecloth laced with a green-edged pattern common to the part of England where I grew up. And for Mr. Greene, Timothy, and Benjamin, I stitched monogrammed handkerchiefs. Hazel and I packed up these items in a basket to prevent the snow from infiltration during our walk to the main house. As she headed to the door, I said, "Wait. Before we go, I also have a Christmas gift for you."

Blood drained from her face as she drew near and wholeheartedly embraced me. "My dear Essie. Since the day I met you on the godforsaken boat, you have saved me time and again. You rescued me from the brute sailors, from indentured servitude, and even from myself. You needn't give me anything else. It is I who owe thee, and I fear I have no present to give."

Her embrace and friendship were the only gifts that mattered to me, and I told her as much. I handed her my gift, a candle I had made, scented with rose petals pressed into the pages of a book before the cold season approached. Hazel took the candle and sniffed its subtle aroma. She threw her arms around me again, and a tear fell from her eye.

I was so glad Hazel was with me. I dreamed of the day, in the distant future, when we were both married and our children would play together by the river as we ate biscuits on a blanket with our husbands. Then the door to the cottage opened, and the brusque winter air called me back into the present.

Bundled up as we were and walking against the winter wind, the ten-minute walk took much longer. When we arrived at the main house, the butler took our coats and escorted us to the great room where the fire was roaring and Christmas morning bacon, crumpets, and tea were being enjoyed by all. Aquila hugged me, and Penny tugged at my waist, waiting her turn. Hazel walked to the kitchen, fulfilling her instinctive need to help the staff.

"We were just about to pass around gifts," Aquila said.

I took a seat near the fire and allowed the chill to leave my bones. From the basket trudged up the hill, I gave out my gifts to an appreciative lot. Penny wrapped herself in her new quilt and spun around like a gleeful top. Aquila was moved by the quilt with his family's crest. Benjamin interrupted Penny's dance by offering a gift of his own.

"Penny, I understand you have taken to the harp."

"Yes, Dr. Franklin."

"When my daughter, Sally, was even younger than you, she enjoyed music as well. I gave her one of these."

Benjamin indicated a spot behind the chair in which he sat. There it was! A new glass armonica. Benjamin had ingeniously assembled glass bowls of different sizes on a long rectangular device and skillfully created harmonious musical tones using a flywheel and wet fingers. Borrowing a bit of water from the pitcher on the dining table, he showed Penny how to make simple sounds. Her happiness gave me joy. I thought the gift exchange had been successful and was content to remain by the warmth of the fire and partake of some food.

"Essie," Aquila stated. "I have one more gift to give." He handed me a small blue box with a hinged lid and fine silver wire decorating the surface.

"What is this?" I asked. "You have already done so much for me. A gift is quite unnecessary."

He smiled and simply replied, "Open it."

I lifted the lid and what did I see but the most elegant pendant on a gold chain. The oval shape held a surface laden with ivory and a simple raised butterfly, all backed by gold. I was overwhelmed.

"It was my mother's. Rebecca wore it for years, but now, I'd like you to have it."

"It's beautiful," I said. "But it's too much. Penny should have this, perhaps when she is older."

Penny chimed in. "Father and I discussed it. We both want you to have the pendant."

I impulsively blurted out, "Thank you both. I love how much you have made me feel part of your family." And before I knew it, Aquila was behind me. I lifted my hair so he could fasten the pendant around my neck. Penny handed me a mirror, and the grandeur of the piece struck me. I had never owned a real pendant or any jewelry of significance. This would be a gift I would treasure for all time.

After exchanging all the gifts and consuming the morning meal, we sat by the fire and conversed for hours as the snow continued to blanket the world outside. I huddled with Penny and Hazel by the hearth. A servant brought us warm apple cider. The hint of cinnamon it contained was a pleasing aroma. Timothy and Benjamin occupied two stuffed chairs on the opposite side of the room while Aquila sat with the Greenes on the long couch facing the fire.

"I understand the fugitives are still at large," stated Aquila.

"McCarron's injury is severe. Without medical treatment, he likely will bleed to death, if he hasn't already," Timothy proclaimed.

He still showed a callous view of shooting another man, even if the scoundrel's actions warranted it. I was so torn.

"Haverford has many business interests in Cromwell. I have difficulty believing he would abandon all he's built," said Mr. Greene.

"What choice does he have? He committed a serious crime and, when caught and tried in Philadelphia, will most certainly never return," Aquila replied.

"What becomes of his business interests?" inquired Mrs. Greene.

I admired her so. She had a mind for business and could stand toe to toe with any man.

"The new Cromwell government will place the property and businesses up for sale. In no time, Haverford will be little more than a sour memory," her husband stated.

"Is the militia still searching for the fugitives?" I asked.

"Oh, yes," Benjamin replied. "Phineas sent me a letter yesterday. He reports the militia has grown to two battalions of ten men each, with one stationed in the northern part of Harford County and the other in the south. Phineas has a close relationship with Governor Penn and will not let the matter rest until justice prevails."

"I thought it was you that persuaded Governor Penn to organize the militia," stated Aquila.

"Heavens, no," Benjamin replied. "It's fair to say my relationship with the Penns is strained at best. They view me as something of a troublemaker."

"A curious term indeed," Timothy said. "Troublemaker?"

"Well, yes. Pennsylvania, unlike Maryland, is a proprietor state. The King granted the Penn family the land, and they feel they have domain to rule with an iron fist. They defy the Assembly and wish all lands to be taxed except their own. I do not ascribe to that view—or, for that matter, the notion of a proprietor state. I view all the colonies as one America."

Benjamin was a learned man. When he spoke, his words captured the attention and imagination of everyone around. It's no surprise that he received acclaim in both America and Europe. I felt smarter just being in his presence and held him in the highest regard.

I sat and listened to the banter in silence for an hour or more.

Then Timothy announced that he'd found another doctor to join the new hospital. "His name is Henrik Van Der Beek. He is highly credentialed and arrives from Holland in two months' time."

"I understand the Dutch have made considerable progress in the medical field. A wise choice, Timothy." Benjamin's praise obviously pleased Timothy, who was still feeling his way through the unlit path of the task at hand.

"As you know, I have spent considerable time in England. A colleague of mine, a fellow printer, in fact, took ill, and it was a doctor from Amsterdam who correctly assessed the problem as an abscess. He employed a new procedure to drain the wound for proper healing. It was quite remarkable," Benjamin stated.

Timothy continued, "Dr. Van Der Beek and his wife, Fleur, will arrive in time for us to complete the plans for the permanent hospital. I have functioned as the intermediary for his purchase of Doc Bradley's home. I understand Doc's widow moved in with her daughter in Joppa."

"That was good of you," Aquila remarked. "Have you found a place of your own?"

"In time. I am planning to build a small home within walking distance of the hospital site. Until then, I shall maintain my residence at the inn."

"Nonsense, we have plenty of room here," Aquila offered.

"As do we," said Mrs. Greene. "We would be honored to have you as our guest for as long as you need," Mrs. Greene said.

Timothy smiled. "I shall gratefully consider your generosity."

Several hours remained until the evening meal, and the inclement weather prevented anyone from venturing outside. Mr. Greene asked for a private talk with Aquila and Timothy, and they reverted to the study. Mrs. Greene took Hazel to oversee preparations for Christmas dinner, and Penny ran to her chambers to lay her new quilt atop her bed and practice on the glass armonica. Suddenly, I found myself alone by the hearth with Benjamin, who, as he was in his later years, looked as if he required a nap.

"Shall I leave you be?" I asked.

"No, no. I always enjoy spirited conversation with a beautiful young woman."

Benjamin owned a reputation as something of a philanderer. I viewed him as harmless. He was an old man who was flirtatious.

"Tell me," he said. "Do you not see this hospital as an impediment to your role as future wife and mother? Do you not wish to make a home and raise a family?"

I hesitated before replying. I wasn't sure if he meant to express concern on my behalf or if he was just another man with a narrow view of women and their aptitude for things beyond homemaking. As my mother always taught me to do, I chose the high road. "Is it not possible that I can achieve all of these things?"

He almost laughed at me when he said, "Possible? Yes. Probable, no."

Now I was certain that Benjamin Franklin held an old-world view of women, and I was determined to mete out common ground.

"When we first met in Philadelphia, did you not tell me of a woman who ran your first hospital? She took care of all nonmedical matters so the Bond brothers could build the larger enterprise."

"Your memory is intact. That lady—How shall we put it?—was of a certain age. She was widowed and had surpassed the childbearing years."

"I see. So, in your opinion, a woman of childbearing age should prioritize husband and babies?"

He smiled warmly, clearly meaning no malice. "Of course." And with that, the crackling of the fire and its warmth aided Benjamin in a sleep-laden stupor.

I let the matter rest. In my view, the priority was evident. Aquila needed my help to bring Maryland's first hospital to fruition. War was on the horizon, and time was of the essence. Like America, I was seeking my independence from Britain. Not only from the land I once called home but from the men who ruled it and, by design, me. Despite the shortsighted views of Benjamin Franklin, the hospital project meant everything to me. This was my moment to seize. My opportunity to prove myself and, for that matter, the worth of a woman in the new American society. I want to—no, I need to—learn to stand tall. Should love follow, whether it be with Aquila, Timothy, or someone still unforetold, I would not shun it, although I knew in my heart the hospital was a personal beacon. I had followed my path to break free from forces that could confine me to a world I didn't choose. But Benjamin's comments aside, if I were honest, love itself was still my strongest need.

# CHAPTER THIRTY

## Cromwell's Passage
## the Maryland Colony

## 10 JANUARY 1774

The new year fell upon us with more snow, more cold, and it seemed, a standstill to life. The weather prevented any real progress in preparing to open the hospital. With the design of a larger, permanent building complete, Aquila hoped to begin construction as soon as the weather broke. Benjamin was waiting out the weather for his return to Philadelphia. Timothy had accepted Aquila's offer of room and board, and Hazel and I hunkered down in our little cottage. The snow was simply too deep to walk to the main house. I began work on sewing linens for the hospital beds, and Hazel was stuffing pillows with feathers from the coop.

"Any word on the fugitives?" Hazel asked with her nose twitching from the tickle of an errant feather.

"No. They were last seen by me and Timothy, and the militias to the north and south have discovered nary a trace."

"That McCarron fellow could not have survived on the run in this weather without a doctor. And you said that Dr. Clarke is the only one in these parts."

"Aquila thinks they had help. Haverford is wealthy, smart, and resourceful. They likely headed west toward the Ohio Territory. Haverford could find help there."

"Blimey," Hazel declared in her sharp Cockney accent. "Ohio? How they come up with these names bewilders me."

"It's an Indian name. Penny learned in school that the word *Ohio* is Iroquois for *a beautiful river.*"

"Who knew?" Hazel stated deferentially. "Why don't the militias turn west?"

"Governor Penn is hesitant. He is looking for more land west of Pennsylvania and doesn't wish to upset the prime minister."

Hazel sneezed as tiny feathers danced around her face. "The bloody English have their hooks in everybody's business."

Like me, Hazel had no love left for England. Our motherland took away everything we owned, everyone we loved, and our last shred of dignity.

"So what of the fugitives? They head west and wait it out? Must we worry every time we go to work that they will show up and do to us what they did to poor Antonia?"

I couldn't blame Hazel for being scared. Truth be told, so was I.

"Benjamin has distributed wanted posters through the entire postal system. Phineas Bond has put forth a handsome reward. I am sure that someone will see the notice and turn them in." I tried to sound reassuring, but my voice cracked, betraying the confidence I hoped to convey. I threw two more logs on the fire and noticed that our stack of firewood was dwindling.

Isaiah occupied another cottage on Cromwell's Passage. He came by every few days and delivered more wood for us. He also brought food from the main house. Our cottage was on the way to the mill, and despite the inclement weather, he felt a strong obligation to make sure it was operating.

"When this bloody snow is gone and spring finally graces our land, I am going to start a vegetable garden," Hazel proclaimed. "Young Penny said she will help."

"That sounds lovely. What will you plant?"

Hazel's eyes twinkled in reply. Gardening was a passion she had longed for since her departure to the London Debtor's Prison. "I miss fresh tomatoes and cucumbers."

"Might I suggest some others?"

"Of course, anything you desire."

"I wish to grow a variety of medicinal plants to keep our hospital costs low and supply strong. I'll make a list. But to start, I think sage, mint, licorice, horsetail, yarrow, hyssop, and perhaps a few others."

"Consider it done," Hazel replied. "An extraordinary idea! Where will we procure the seeds?"

"The general store in town should have most, if not all, of them. I've come to learn that the Indians have vast experience using plants like these for medical purposes. They barter at the general store for blankets and other goods."

Hazel turned her head and sneezed again as she stitched the last of the hospital pillows.

I smiled and gazed out our window. The pine trees' branches were laden with snow and sagged. I understood the weight of their burden.

We had a plan for food and medicines. Even though the weather was prohibitive, we made progress where we could to aid the opening of Maryland's first hospital. Timothy asked me to prepare for the arrival of Dr. Van Der Beek. Our temporary hospital would use a first-floor room as a shared office for myself and the two doctors. Aquila and I received the authority to manage the colonial fund for renovation to the boardinghouse and construction of the hospital. I would need to hire a carpenter skilled in the way of desks. We would need two rolltops, one for each doctor. I would work on an old serving table donated by the Greenes. The carpenter would also need to construct cabinets to hold medicines and supplies. There were numerous tasks to complete, and time had a tendency to slip away. I tired of winter and was eager for the warmth and freedom that spring promised.

# CHAPTER THIRTY-ONE

# *Cromwell*

# the Maryland Colony

## 5 MARCH 1774

Sunshine and warmth delighted my spirit as I sat in the office of the temporary hospital. A gentle breeze came through the open window, and I detected a pleasing but unfamiliar scent. It was some sort of cologne. It contained a citrus mixed with oleander and perhaps a bit of tobacco. Two voices beckoned outside the window, and upon hearing the Dutch accent conversing with Timothy, I knew that Dr. Van Der Beek had arrived.

They entered the hospital and made introductions. Dr. Van Der Beek took my hand and softly kissed it. To me, this was a trait of the cultured European man. He was polite and charming with an old-world manner. Judging from the gray in his vandyke beard and the crow's feet surrounding his eyes, he was older than Timothy. I would guess him around fifty.

"Henrik is already teaching me about medical practices in Holland. Our hospital will be the envy of the colonies," proclaimed an exuberant Timothy.

"That's wonderful," I replied. "You'll let me know what additional supplies you may need, Dr. Van Der Beek. Hazel Giddings, our head nurse, and I are here to help in any way possible."

"Please call me Henrik. Timothy is in charge. I shall merely make suggestions and let him decide. Now, if you please, may I see our temporary hospital? I am particularly interested in the operating area."

"Where is Hazel, anyway?" Timothy inquired.

"She is at the cottage with Penny. They are clearing land for our new garden. We will be growing herbs to make medicines."

"Delightful news," stated Henrik. "I shall look forward to meeting Hazel and Aquila's daughter, Penny."

"Do you have children, Henrik?" I asked.

His mood turned somber, and he paused for an interminable period. I regretted the question, for I unintentionally upset him. Finally, he stammered out, "Fleur and I welcomed three beautiful boys into the world. Each one died before the age of five. After that, we didn't have the strength to try again."

"Did you identify the cause?" Timothy inquired.

"It is difficult to say. Unfortunately, it is an all-too-common occurrence throughout the civilized world."

Timothy draped an arm over his new colleague's shoulder and offered what I thought was an admirable gesture. "When time permits, you and I shall collaborate on the cause. Maybe we can save the children of the world with a proper serum."

Henrik loosened up. "I'd like that." And off they went to tour the temporary quarters of the still unnamed hospital.

I followed the doctors to the operating theater. I wished to inventory the supplies received to date. Each day, I went to the general store, where parcels arrived from overseas. Some instruments required were difficult to procure. I opened the drawers of the recently completed medical cabinet. The fresh smell of varnish was pleasing. I counted one set of amputation knives, some with curved blades and some that were straight, forceps for removing bullets and musket balls, tweezers for pulling teeth, and a drill made for creating holes in the skull, a most extreme occurrence with which I had no experience. Thomas was not a surgeon, and my Wickhamshire days were dotted with a combination of natural therapies and medicines coupled with rest. The surgical instruments took all forms of shape and size. I was becoming familiar with their names but had little stomach for understanding the intended uses.

The front door opened, and a man's voice called out.

"Yes, hello," I called out. "I'll be there momentarily."

I approached the front door and found an older man in a dark tricorn hat with wispy gray sideburns and long flabby jowls. His posture and expression conveyed contempt.

"Good day, Madam. I am Arthur Bartholomew, the mayor of Cromwell. I should like to meet the gentleman in charge of this establishment."

"How do you do, sir. I am Essie Lassiter, the administrator of the Cromwell hospital."

He guffawed. "Surely you jest. A woman in charge of my town's hospital? I think not! Now, tell me who is in charge?" he demanded angrily.

"I am responsible for the operation of this hospital. We have two surgeons, Drs. Clarke and Van Der Beek, and our benefactor is Mr. Aquila Wright, a descendent of Mordecai Cromwell, the town's founder."

"I know who Aquila Wright is," he bellowed. "Where is he?"

"I don't know. But I can assure you that Governor Templeton has given him full authority to open this hospital and oversee all manner of issues."

"I shall take up my concerns with Mr. Wright, and then we shall return you to your proper place in whatever man's home you belong to tend to a woman's chores."

Before I could call out to Timothy for assistance, Mayor Bartholomew turned and left, slamming the door, and leaving a cloud of dust in his wake.

I tried to apprise the doctors about the abrupt visit from the new mayor, but they blew past me on the way to meet people in town. I fretted about for hours, pursuing my chores with my mind elsewhere. When Pastor Vinson entered with a jolly demeanor, he disturbed my frantic state.

"And how are things coming? It's beginning to look less like a boardinghouse and more like a hospital."

I nodded.

He knew in an instant something was wrong. "Out with it," he commanded in his fatherly way.

"I had the unfortunate occasion to meet our new mayor, a dreadful man."

Pastor Vinson turned somber. "Yes, he ran unopposed at last night's town meeting."

"Unopposed? No one wanted the job?"

"Aquila was nominated and received strong support, but he declared he would not serve if elected."

"I'd no idea." Not that I could blame Aquila. With the hospital project, the mill, raising a daughter, and the prospect of having to go to war, how could he also serve as mayor? But Arthur Bartholomew?

"Bartholomew is a tanner. He and his wife live quietly on the northern side of town. No one really knows him. We had no idea he'd throw his hat in the ring."

"What shall I do when he aligns the new town council against me? Will Hazel and I be tossed out on our ear? Destitute?"

He offered a comforting embrace and his handkerchief to dry my eyes. "Aquila will support you. Your appointment as the hospital administrator is solely up to him, and let us not forget, Aquila has the backing of Governor Templeton."

"Why must men view women with such disdain? Do we not have the ability to read, learn, and think for ourselves, just like any man would? What are they afraid of?"

"My best guess is that men like Bartholomew fear not what women might accomplish but rather that women will cast them in a poor light."

I stopped to consider his words. Perhaps Pastor Vinson was right. Without being deferential all the time, how was a woman to make her mark on the world— or this small town, for that matter? I sought no personal acclaim. I only wished to serve and be respected for my efforts and my judgments.

—◊◊—

The day finally concluded. I lay in my bed, weary to the bone, and reflected on the evening. I hadn't seen Aquila all day. Timothy and Henrik had vanished, leaving me alone in my despair. Hazel and I had received an invitation to dinner at the main house. The guests also included the Greenes and the Van der Beeks. The conversation was brisk, although I must confess I was only half there. I could not rid myself of the horrible encounter with Arthur Bartholomew. He reminded me of that wretched Elias Carmichael, the man who callously came to my door the day Thomas died and demanded payment of outstanding debts. There was no reasoning with Carmichael, and Bartholomew gave me the same prickly feeling.

"I received a letter from Benjamin today. He inquired of our progress with the hospital and wanted to let me know he is journeying to France on a diplomatic mission with his grandson, Temple," Aquila stated.

"France is charming," replied Henrik. "Fleur and I have visited on several occasions."

"Do you speak French?" asked Penny.

"Oui mademoiselle, *le français est une jolie langue*," answered Fleur.

Penny giggled. "I have no idea what you just said."

Henrik emitted a smile. "She said, 'Yes, young lady, French is a beautiful language.'"

"I hope to learn one day," Penny answered.

"And how is the hospital coming along?" inquired Mr. Greene.

"Splendidly," said Aquila. "Essie, Timothy, and Henrik are ready to open the temporary building, and construction on the permanent hospital begins next week."

"From what I hear, everyone is pleased with the efforts," Mr. Greene answered.

"Almost everyone," I blurted out, as I tended to do.

"Ah, yes, Pastor Vinson told me you met Bartholomew, the new mayor," offered Timothy.

"Did that not go well?" asked Aquila.

"He said he will seek an audience with you to find a proper administrator and return me to the home of whatever man I might belong to."

"I'm aghast! He has no such power. I have complete domain over the hospital. If he persists, we will need to pay him a visit and tan *his* hide."

Mr. Greene laughed at Aquila's comment. His wife elbowed him. I imagine the smirk on his face foretold his mind, conjuring up the very image Aquila described.

Aquila looked at me. "You needn't worry."

I only wished I could rely on his assurance. By nature, I was indeed a worrier. Throughout my life, I had struggled to let go of that suffocating appendage to my mind's logical ability.

# CHAPTER THIRTY-TWO

# Cromwell's Passage
# the Maryland Colony

## 12 APRIL 1774

I completed my day at the hospital, stopped in at the church to greet Pastor Vinson, and began my walk to the cottage. It had been a hectic day. Word of the newly named Maryland Hospital spread rapidly, and our old boardinghouse was now half full. The town debated names for months, including the Cromwell Hospital, the Harford Hospital, and even the Templeton Hospital after the governor who commissioned it, but in the end, Aquila chose the name that most obviously fit.

Timothy and Henrik treated many maladies, ranging from fever to gangrene. I had trained Hazel, and in turn, she'd hired two more nurses and trained them. To keep things moving in an orderly manner, I worked both as an administrator and a nurse. I was pleased with the progress so far. We experienced shortages of bandages, crutches, and medicines, but we were getting by, and no patient was worse for the wear. Aquila and the two doctors found our hospital's modest start satisfying. We met one evening each week to discuss pressing issues and ways we might improve. Aquila spent most of his time tending to the business of the mill and overseeing the construction of the new hospital. We were all busy, but the work was gratifying and that, in my estimation, made the long days worthwhile. Oh, lest I forget, today the Greenes' niece, Prudence, finally arrived from Virginia to become Penny's new nanny.

I padded down the hard-packed path leading to the cottage. When I spied Penny in the garden feeding a baby black bear, a feeling of horror washed over me. She was there to plant seeds we'd purchased at the general store.

"Penny, do not move an inch," I said as softly as I could while still being heard. I did not want to alarm her or the bear. The horrid memory of shooting a large black bear soon after my arrival in Cromwell was fresh in my mind.

"It's all right. She's just a cub. Look, I'm feeding her biscuits. She likes me."

Every sensation in my body screamed. There was no availability of a weapon, unlike on the previous occasion. I was no authority on black bears, but I was sure that a mother would lurk with the instinct to protect her young from perceived danger.

"Penny, you are not safe. I need you to leave the biscuits on the ground. Let the cub have them all. Then, you get up slowly and back away from the garden. Go into the cottage and close the door."

"But this bear is friendly," she replied. Ignoring my instruction, Penny sat with her new friend and continued to feed the cub one biscuit at a time.

Before I could react, the mother bear appeared from beyond a tall oak and roared like rolling thunder. On her hind legs, she bared her teeth and charged toward Penny.

I inched toward the garden, taking one baby step at a time, while trying to stomach my fear. Without forethought, I yelled, "Penny, run! Run to the cottage. Now!"

This time, she listened. As she rose from the ground, leaving the biscuits, the mother bear swept her arm across the garden until her long, sharp claws penetrated Penny's left cheek. Penny let go of that same bloodcurdling scream from our first black bear encounter. She fell backward into the freshly hoed soil, bringing her hands to the torn flesh on her youthful face. The mother bear scooped up her cub and receded into the forest as I ran to Penny's aid.

Kneeling at Penny's side, I used my apron to quell the bleeding. Then, I helped her to walk to the cottage where I laid her down in my bed and attempted to clean and dress the deep wounds.

Penny trembled. Her voice quivered as she struggled to express herself.

"Don't talk," I said as I worked furiously to ease her suffering. The bleeding was severe, and despite my limited medical knowledge, I struggled to contain the flow. I packed the wounds with fresh cloth and told Penny to hold it against her face while I ran to the cabinet in the other room. I brought a small bottle of laudanum and instructed Penny to drink the entire contents to help with the pain. It would also help her sleep once the pain subsided.

"Hello," Hazel called as she came through the cottage door. "What's that mess in the garden?" When she walked into my bedroom and saw Penny, she inquired, "Oh my Lord, what happened?"

"Attacked by an angry bear," I hastily replied. "Quick, run to the mill. As fast as you can. Get Isaiah and tell him to bring a carriage. We must get Penny to the hospital."

Hazel blew a kiss to her young gardening compatriot and ran out the door.

It felt like hours before Hazel returned with Isaiah. He carried Penny out the door and carefully laid her in the carriage for the short ride to town.

I climbed in and called to Hazel, "Quickly, go to the main house and find Aquila. Tell him to meet us at the hospital."

# CHAPTER THIRTY-THREE

## *Cromwell*

## the Maryland Colony

### 13 APRIL 1774

Aquila was in a near rage when he walked out of the hospital room where Penny was being treated by Timothy and Henrik. I'd never seen him truly angry. He confronted me. My back was against the corridor wall, and a cold sweat broke out across my face. His normally placid eyes breathed fire, and for the first time, I feared the man I dreamed of marrying.

"My daughter was nearly killed on your watch and not one . . ."—he huffed and puffed as his voice got louder—"but five, *five* scars on her cheek. These will never go away. You've extinguished any chance of a future marriage."

Before I could reply, Aquila held up his hand, commanding me to stop.

Mr. Greene implored Aquila to join him for a brief respite at the tavern.

"No," he replied. "I shall not leave Penny's side."

Not knowing what else to do, I approached Timothy, who had just left the treatment room where Penny lay.

"What is the prognosis?" I inquired.

He shook his head and, with a handkerchief, swabbed his brow. "Well, she will live, but her face—I'm afraid the scars will never heal."

Nausea overwhelmed me, and I thought I might faint. I loved Penny. The thought that I couldn't save her from the bear attack was devastating. Even though

Penny was not "on my watch," at the time of the attack, as Aquila stated, it didn't make me feel any better about her future prospects.

"Essie, are you still with me?" Timothy asked.

"I'm sorry. My thoughts drifted."

"Yes, I said that the young lady is lucky she didn't lose an eye."

How horrifying a thought that was. As if I could feel any worse.

Just then, Henrik emerged from Penny's bedside. "She is resting comfortably. I don't see any infection, but we will continue to treat and redress the wounds every few hours until healing begins. I do not want to stitch the wounds quite yet."

"For goodness' sake," replied Timothy. "Why not?"

"I have applied minimal stitching to promote healing. The next phase of treatment will be determined once the risk of infection has passed."

"What do you see as the next phase of treatment?" I asked.

Henrik grinned. "I shall need to confer with her father. In Europe, surgeons have experienced success with a procedure called skin grafting to eliminate scarring."

"Skin grafting? What on earth is that?" I wondered aloud.

"I've read about the procedure," Timothy stated. "An Italian doctor or maybe a British fellow, I can't recall."

"Both, actually. They tested the procedure in Italy using sheep," Henrik replied. "And then it was conducted on humans in London."

"Would someone please enlighten me as to the nature of this procedure?" I implored.

"It is straightforward. Once the flesh has healed on its own, the surgeon will cut away the scarred tissue and replace it with a patch taken from another part of the body. For facial tissue, a surgeon may graft from the abdomen or the thigh. Once the graft heals, the original wound will be nearly impossible to see."

"Magnificent," declared Timothy. "Have you performed such a procedure?"

"I have not. Therefore, we must confer with Aquila. The questions before us are whether he will allow the procedure, and then, would he prefer a surgeon with more experience? We could do it here but would need sufficient time to research and practice."

"Practice," I said. "How would this be accomplished?"

"All surgeons learn on cadavers, sometimes with animals. It's all standard procedure," Henrik replied.

And with that information, I was glad my medical work did not include surgery. Training alone would have sickened me. The skin graft was encouraging news, and I hoped it would quell Aquila's anger. The two doctors left to tend to other patients, and I went to check on Penny, who was asleep. Hazel was by her side, singing an English lullaby.

I whispered to Hazel about Henrik's skin graft proposal.

"It sounds almost too good to be true," she remarked.

We sat in silence, intent on keeping Penny in our thoughts and prayers.

Pastor Vinson walked in and offered comfort. "I know it is not only the youngster who is suffering," he observed.

Aquila and a spritely young woman with long blond hair wrapped up in a laced-lined bonnet joined the three of us. Her brown eyes sat atop an aquiline nose, sprinkled with freckles. Before we could make introductions, the young lady gasped at the sight of Penny's face.

Aquila placed an arm around her shoulders. "It is normal to express alarm. But I shall caution you not to do so in Penny's presence. I wish her to view herself as she always has, not as some freak."

He paused, took a deep breath, and said, "Prudence, meet Pastor Vinson. He is the clergyman at our church here in town. Pastor, this is Prudence Greene, the niece of Charles and Celia, and Penny's new nanny."

"I look forward to getting to know you, Prudence. Please visit our church anytime. You always have a friend in me." And he smiled in that cherished manner of a grandfather.

Then, as an afterthought, in a cold, flat voice, Aquila looked my way and said, "And this is Essie and Hazel. They work here at the hospital."

That was it. No acknowledgement of my former role as Penny's unofficial nanny, and absolutely no reference to our friendship. I suppose I understood Aquila's disposition, but I'd be lying if I didn't say that I was devastated.

Looking toward Prudence, I extended my arms to warmly embrace her. I understood the importance of feeling welcomed upon arriving in a strange place.

"Please call upon me for anything. Penny and I are very close, and I'd like to help you however I can."

"That won't be necessary," Aquila interrupted. "Essie has her hands full here at the hospital."

I was stunned. The situation grew worse when Aquila pulled my arm and "asked" to see me in the next room.

"Let me make myself crystal clear, Mrs. Lassiter. You will not have any contact with my daughter while she is in this hospital. You must not go to her bed. Once she is released, you must act as if you do not know one another."

"But Aquila, I . . . I tried to save her."

"You shall address me as Mr. Wright, and I do not believe you."

My spirits sank like a rock in the river. With my head down, I wandered outside. The sky, laden with dark clouds, released heavy raindrops, hiding the tears falling from my eyes.

# CHAPTER THIRTY-FOUR

## *Cromwell*

## the Maryland Colony

### 29 APRIL 1774

I'd little choice but to throw myself into the work of the hospital. Aquila's anger toward me had yet to subside, and Penny, I was told by Hazel, wondered why I abandoned her in a most desperate time. Hazel stopped short of telling Penny that her father had ordered me to stay away. I hoped Hazel and Pastor Vinson would vindicate my honor with my former charge. I was in the shared office when Henrik came in for a cup of tea.

"You are one who wears her emotions on her sleeve," he remarked.

"Is it that obvious?"

He chuckled in a filial manner and said, "Yes, I am afraid so. I am a good listener, and I have time between patients." He sat down beside me, inhaled the steam from his tea, and sipped at a leisurely pace.

"I wish I could be with Penny. I know Prudence is here to look after her, but I can't escape the guilt of abandoning her, even if it wasn't my choice."

"You have every right to feel conflicted. Perhaps once they return, the ill will may have subsided."

"Return from where?"

"I have arranged for Aquila, Penny, and Prudence to travel to England for a skin graft. They will be gone for several months."

I had no idea. My mother used to say that time heals all wounds. I hope she was right.

"When do they depart?"

"Tomorrow."

"Who will look after the hospital's affairs, the construction, the mill, and Cromwell's Passage?"

"As I understand it, Mr. and Mrs. Greene will oversee Cromwell's Passage, Mr. Trumbull will manage the mill's affairs, while myself and Timothy will be responsible for the hospital as a committee. The construction project will also be the responsibility of Mr. Trumbull."

"What of my role in the hospital's daily needs?"

Henrik sighed. "I was hoping Aquila would speak to you directly, but apparently, he has not. So I will tell you. Your future here, I am sorry to say, is quite uncertain. Aquila has directed that Timothy and I hold all authority over hospital matters and that you are to oversee administrative duties and assist with nursing when needed."

"To what end? Am I to be cast out like a leper?"

Henrik shrugged his shoulders. "I would hope not. This hospital would not be open were it not for your extraordinary efforts. Aquila said he would decide when he returns from England."

I let that proclamation sink in. Aquila's misguided feelings angered me, and frankly, I was weary of another man dictating my future. I was a free woman. I had experience as a medic, a midwife, and now as a hospital administrator. Perhaps I would leave before Aquila returned. Maybe I would travel south to Virginia or North Carolina. Surely they needed help starting their own hospitals. Would they accept a woman? Likely not. To stay or to go? The conflict raged in me like rising bubbles in a boiling cauldron.

Henrik placed his teacup on his desk and leaped up from the chair. "Did you hear that?"

"No, what?"

"The horses, many are approaching. Something is wrong."

Henrik's hearing and anticipation of danger was uncanny. His intuition did not betray him. Something was clearly amiss. We were about to experience our most challenging day since the hospital commenced.

The door burst open. Men who had been shot were carried into the room on stretchers. Pandemonium reigned. Many of these men needed immediate surgery. We had one operating area and two surgeons, and the hospital could not manage the influx.

Timothy ran in and took charge. "Essie, Hazel, go to each man and assess their status. If they are dead, place a sheet over them. Henrik and I will each tend to those who need surgery. Have a bed brought to the operating room, and we shall double up. Place the rest of the patients wherever you can but leave the hospital doorway free in case more patients arrive."

We sprang into action. A dozen men sustained injuries. In the mayhem, we determined that eight of them already passed away or would soon. Determining the latter was terrifying, but it was our only hope to save those who had a chance. The first two moved to the operating room sustained bullets to the chest. Based on the amount of blood loss, Timothy assessed they had a chance at survival. The others took shots to limbs and would live with amputation still a possibility. Hazel and I tended to these two men, packing the wounds and administering laudanum for the pain. When things settled, I asked a woman in tears what happened.

"It was two men. One had a musket, and the other bore a pistol. They came into the bank, demanded money, and told all the customers to give up their belongings. My husband works at the bank. He did as they asked, and they shot him anyway."

She sobbed, and I held her close. Timothy emerged from the operating room, ready for the next patient at the same time that Mayor Bartholomew entered the hospital.

"What's all this commotion?" he demanded. Then, looking at me with contempt, he said, "If a man were in charge of this place, I very much doubt I'd be witnessing this travesty." Spittle accompanied his words of disdain.

I elected to ignore his ignorance and explained what the aggrieved woman had just told me.

Looking at the sobbing woman, Bartholomew asked, "Did you see the men who did this?"

She nodded, and through a strained voice, she replied, "The man in charge, he had a musket. He was a tall blond-haired man with the eyes of a wolf and a scar on his left cheek. His right eye had a red ring around it."

"A red ring?" asked the bewildered mayor.

"Yes, you know. A mark left from a monocle."

"And who did you say was with him?"

"An even taller man with blond hair and blue eyes. He had only one arm and was a deadeye with that pistol."

Bartholomew sighed.

"Any idea who they are?" inquired Timothy.

"Based on the descriptions, I'd say we are being revisited by Messrs. Haverford and McCarron."

"Yes, McCarron would have had to lose the arm to survive. I aimed precisely to cause maximum damage."

"I am serving as mayor and sheriff until I get a new lawman appointed. A group of men will ride out to apprehend the fugitives. They cannot have gotten far."

"Doesn't Haverford own the bank? Why would he rob his own establishment?" I asked.

Bartholomew scoffed, as if the mere thought of speaking to a woman about something other than a domestic matter was repugnant. "As mayor, I convened a town council meeting to seize all assets of Mr. Haverford and to formally dismiss Mr. McCarron as sheriff." He huffed again and added, "Aquila Wright voted in favor of both measures. I am surprised he didn't relay this to you."

I didn't want to give this brute the satisfaction of knowing that my relationship with Aquila was in tatters. He turned and left.

Timothy went to operate on the next victim, and Henrik emerged to speak to the wife of the man he had just operated on.

"I am sorry," he said as gently as one could. "Your husband lost too much blood from his injuries. Saving him was a long shot from the start. You have my deepest sympathies."

The poor woman broke down again. Knowing full well what it was like to lose one's husband, I stayed with her for as long as I could. Henrik left to tend to the next patient, and I thought the horror of the day was finally behind us.

As I held the widow, I looked around our little hospital. Dead bodies, bloody linens, and stained floors were all the eye could see. Once we removed the bodies and stabilized the patients, the entire crew of nurses would need a day or more to restore the hospital to pristine condition. The widow's sister arrived to accompany the poor woman home. I stood and sighed. My bones were weary. It'd been a day that tested my resolve. Our staff had nary a break all day, and I hoped that moment was finally upon us. When the last surgery was completed, I would take tea and crumpets to the doctors and nurses. The group needed a brief respite from the trauma of what we'd experienced. None of the nurses had been so for long. This was their first experience dealing with a mass tragedy. I felt for each of them. In truth, I felt for myself. This was also new to me, but given the experiences of my life since Thomas died, I'd gained a measure of reserved strength I never knew I possessed. Now, however, at this late point in a much too long day, I could feel the depletion.

Before I could move to prepare the tea and crumpets, the finest carriage I ever saw rolled up to our front door. Two coachmen rushed to the door and helped a pregnant woman to the ground. She teetered on the brink of collapse and was barely conscious. From the other side of the carriage, a man emerged who commanded the scene. I assessed he was a man of great importance based on the exquisite carriage, the fine liveried dual coachmen, and the beautiful dress on the pregnant woman.

"I am Governor Templeton," he proclaimed. "As you can see, my wife, Olivia, is pregnant and in distress."

I quickly introduced myself and directed the coachmen to bring Mrs. Templeton into the main drawing room. "Lay her on the chaise lounge," I directed.

"This place is deplorable," the governor barked. "This is what I have commissioned? It is unclean and unworthy. Move my wife to a proper room for treatment immediately!"

I was terrified. This man's mere presence in a more placid time would have intimidated me. I had to stop myself from visibly trembling.

"Milord, I offer my humble apologies. Earlier today, someone robbed the bank, and we had a dozen wounded. The last victim just finished surgery, and we still need to clean up. The hospital is presently at capacity."

"Well, then move someone else to this drawing room and give my Olivia the care she requires." His voice thundered through the small room as fear pricked my crimson cheeks.

"Perhaps, Governor, in the interest of time, you would allow me to examine Olivia here."

"Fine, fine," he grumbled. "Just get on with it."

"If I may, it might be a good idea to ask your men to excuse themselves."

And with a wave of his hand, the room was just me, the governor and Olivia Templeton.

"Where are the doctors?" Governor Templeton asked.

"Still in surgery. I am sure one or both will join us as soon as they are able. In England, I worked as a midwife. I have delivered more babies than I can count. Everything will be just fine."

I tried to reassure the governor, but Olivia Templeton being unconscious alarmed me.

"How far along is your wife?" I asked.

"Eight months and change. We were on our way to Philadelphia for a meeting of governors. We figured Olivia could give birth at the Philadelphia hospital under the watchful eye of Dr. Thomas Bond."

"I see."

"You must see to it this baby arrives without any problems. We have lost four children at birth, and Olivia is of an age where it is ill-advised to try again."

I used smelling salts to awaken Mrs. Templeton. She slowly came to.

"Mrs. Templeton, hello. My name is Essie. I am a midwife, and you are at the Maryland Hospital. May I examine you?"

She nodded slowly. Her husband kneeled beside her head and held her hand as I removed her garments.

"You are not in labor. Often, the body prepares for the birthing process by offering preliminary discomfort."

Mrs. Templeton smiled. I could tell she was a good soul from that smile alone. "Thank you, Essie."

"When can we continue our journey?" asked the governor.

"It is not advisable to move her. Philadelphia is a good two days' journey. Mrs. Templeton might go into labor anytime."

"I see. We are due there tomorrow. I shall send a courier to inform the other colonial governors of my delay."

Timothy emerged from the operating room with his shirt stained with patient's blood and his hair disheveled. Unaware of our guests, he walked in chatting about the surgery as he wrung his hands in a wet towel.

"We saved the man, but unfortunately, we had to amputate a leg. One of our nurses fainted, and it was—" And then he realized it was not just him and me in the drawing room.

"My apologies," he said. "I'd shake hands, but I am a frightful mess. I am Dr. Timothy Clarke, the head of medical matters for this facility. And you are, sir?"

Before the governor could respond, I chimed in. "This is Governor Templeton and his wife, Olivia. Mrs. Templeton will stay here until she gives birth."

"Pleased to meet you, Governor, Mrs. Templeton. We shall take excellent care of you and your baby. First, we shall get you to a proper room. We have one private area on the third floor. I believe the patient there now is well enough to go home. We shall move Mrs. Templeton in a short while."

"I should hope so," the governor replied. He was not a man to be managed. "Where is the finest lodging in town?"

"We have only one inn, but I am sure Mr. and Mrs. Greene or Mr. Wright would be glad to have you and your men stay with them. The accommodations would be far nicer," I offered. Then, I regretted once again putting my foot in my mouth. Had Aquila and I not been in a state of disrepair, I might have felt more comfortable making the offer of lodging, and I was ashamed of offering the Greenes' plantation when I'd no right to do so.

"I assume the inn is nearby. It will suffice. I wish to be as close to Olivia as possible."

"Of course, milord. I understand. Please allow me to make the necessary arrangements on your behalf."

When the day finally concluded, I sat by candlelight at the cottage dinner table with Hazel. "It was you who fainted in the operating room?" I asked sympathetically.

"There's a stark difference between emptying a chamber pot and seeing someone's leg come off."

I told her about my encounters with Bartholomew and the governor.

"You know what your problem is? You bend to the will of these men like a willow in the wind. If it were me in your shoes, I'd have left them with a piece of my mind."

I laughed. "I remember how well that served you on the boat to America."

She pointed a finger in the air as if to make her point. "Yes, but without the expression of truth, we would not have become friends, would we?"

Hazel was right. Perhaps there was a lesson to be learned in not always taking the safest path.

# CHAPTER THIRTY-FIVE

## *Cromwell*

## the Maryland Colony

### 30 APRIL 1774

I entered the hospital just after sunrise, eager to see Mrs. Templeton. The night nurse reported no issues. Timothy was off making house calls in the country and would be gone all day. Henrik had not yet arrived. He would be here soon with Fleur, who had no medical training but wanted to help however she could.

Mrs. Templeton looked pale. Her hair was undone. She was not running a fever, although she felt clammy. If anything, I would have said her flesh felt cold. She was barely conscious but lucid enough to ask for water. I happily obliged and told her to rest. I wanted to begin the cleanup from yesterday's events.

Henrik had worked late into the evening. Mayor Bartholomew sent a few men to help transport the deceased to the undertaker. Today, we would remove soiled linens and begin a top-to-bottom scrubbing of the hospital. I would lead the effort with help from Fleur and whatever nurses were off duty. We had another long day in front of us.

Governor Templeton walked in about an hour later. Pleased at the cleanup effort, he brushed past me on the way upstairs to the private patient room. I was laboring on my knees with a scrub brush when the governor yelled for me.

"My wife is in distress. Come quickly."

I dropped the brush and ran as fast as I could up the stairs. Along the way, I passed a nurse and instructed her to run to Dr. Van Der Beek's house and urgently ask him to come to the hospital. When I arrived upstairs, Mrs. Templeton was writhing in pain. She was sweating profusely and let out a bloodcurdling scream, one that was not familiar to the childbirth process.

I knew something was wrong before I began the examination. To maintain my composure, I needed to stay calm. I was a midwife. Presumably, I'd seen it all. I had experience. I could do this.

"All right, Mrs. Templeton, you are in labor. A small issue is present. Your baby is in the breech position."

"What on earth does that mean?" asked Governor Templeton.

"The baby is turned around. Its feet are in line to be out first."

"Is that dangerous?" asked Mrs. Templeton.

I drew a deep breath before answering. "It can be. Discovering this weeks ago could have enabled doctors to attempt a maneuver to reverse the baby's position in the womb."

"And now?" the governor barked.

"It's too late. We must do the best we can with the situation at hand."

Right then, Henrik ran in, and I updated him promptly. He nodded his understanding.

Looking at Mrs. Templeton, I said, "Now, Mrs. Templeton, we are going to take this as slowly and deliberately as we can. Once the feet and legs are out, the buttocks will pass through the vaginal canal, and our last concern will be the head. I will tell you when to push."

She screamed again. Hazel entered the room and dried her brow with a wet cloth.

"Why is the head a concern?" the governor wanted to know.

"In a normal birth," Henrik explained, "the head comes out first and experiences minimal pressure on the skull. In this situation, the opposite is true."

Governor Templeton placed his hand over his eyes as if he could hide his outward agony. After losing four other children at birth, I could only imagine the pain he and his wife must be experiencing. I knew Henrik could empathize with the Templetons' plight.

"If the head passes through the canal quickly, there should be no issues," I added.

The feet and legs emerged a quarter hour afterward. The next worry was that the baby's arms would not be at its sides, causing another potential trouble spot. But the buttocks slid through, and I saw both arms. Now, we just needed to get the head through quickly.

"Mrs. Templeton, we are almost there," I said. "Let's try one more push, and we will get the head through."

Mrs. Templeton pushed and, with her effort, let out another of those blood-curdling shrieks. When the head came through, her body slumped in the heap of sweat-laden bed linens. There was no crying from the newborn.

I knew instantly, and Henrik looked at me in a way to indicate that he knew as well.

"There is no crying from the baby," declared the governor.

I held the baby and rose from my position to present the Templetons with their son. The umbilical cord had wrapped around his neck. A stillborn. My heart ached for these two people.

The governor broke down, falling to his knees and taking hold of his wife's hand.

Mrs. Templeton didn't speak. She expressed no sorrow over the death of her son. Her face was devoid of color.

"Olivia?" cried the governor. "I'm not sure she's breathing. Her hands are as cold as ice."

Henrik took Mrs. Templeton's pulse. He looked at me, shaking his head, and then toward the governor. "I'm sorry, sir. Your wife is gone."

One would have expected tearful sorrow from a man who lost his wife and yet another child at birth. That is not the reaction we witnessed.

The governor rose from his wife's side and, with vitriol the likes of which I'd rarely seen, berated us.

"The astounding level of incompetence at this hospital is remarkable. Why is a woman yielding authority in an institution I have commissioned and funded? When Aquila returns from England, I shall discuss whether this hospital is to remain open and which doctors will work here. Now, all of you, get out of my sight. I wish to be alone with Olivia."

Another devastatingly bad day. I'd neither the mind nor body to continue cleaning yesterday's mess, and so I left the hospital, my tail between my legs, and trudged toward home. I thought about stopping at the church. Pastor Vinson was always such a comfort. I opted to continue along my way. I couldn't bear the thought of Pastor Vinson trying to tell me the Templetons' tragedy was not my fault and I did all I could. He would tell me what a good person I was and that God believed in me and truly loved me. At that moment, nothing was farther from the truth. How could God love me? I brought death and tragedy to all whom I loved. I was unworthy and knew it to the depths of my soul.

Hours passed until Hazel came home. I had difficulty passing the time. I couldn't sleep. Quilting would not hold my concentration. I tried a gentle stroll through the fields of Cromwell's Passage. Nothing helped ease my mind. As had been my habit since Christmas, I reached for the ivory butterfly that hung from my neck. It provided a source of strength. I was aghast to find it missing. Another festering sore in a day gone to hell. I remembered having the necklace at the hospital. It could have fallen off during my walk home or during my stroll through the fields. Maybe it was somewhere in the cottage? I threw a book against the wall. Once more, my life was plummeting toward rock bottom.

Hazel embraced me and said nothing. She readied our evening meal and guided me to sit. We broke bread when a knock befell our door. A visitor? I deduced it must be Pastor Vinson. May as well let him in. I certainly had no appetite for supper. It was a surprise to find Charles Greene at our door. He didn't look happy.

"May I come in?"

"Certainly," I replied. "May we offer you something to eat?"

"No, thank you. I am afraid I am the bearer of bad news. Please sit."

The three of us sat at the table, and Mr. Greene looked about as stern as I'd ever seen him. "The governor came to my house. He told me what transpired today. As you know, Governor Templeton and I have a long arm relationship of sorts, and with Aquila gone for some time, I oversee his affairs, and, well . . ."

"Oh my lord," cried Hazel. "Out with it already."

"Very well. The governor has asked, and I agreed, that your positions at the hospital be terminated. As the overseer of Cromwell's Passage, I think it best for the two of you to move on. You have to the end of the week to vacate these premises and the town of Cromwell."

I had no words. Cast out again. At least this time, I had my freedom and a little money.

Hazel was not so reserved in her response. "What's the matter with you people? The governor and his missus have lost several children at childbirth. You know it's common for older women to die giving birth. And this is somehow Essie's fault? Or mine by association? You should be ashamed of yourself, Mr. Greene."

"You have till the end of the week. My coachman will take you and your belongings to Baltimore." With that, he turned his back and left.

With the sound of the slamming door went all my hopes and dreams.

# CHAPTER THIRTY-SIX

## *Baltimore*

## the Maryland Colony

### 1 MAY 1774

Hazel and I were fortunate in that we did not need to wait for Mr. Greene's coachmen to take us to Baltimore. Thanks to the graces of Isaiah, we left two days before the deadline. Traveling with a friend made an undesirable exile far more pleasant. We had no notion of where to go once we arrived. Isaiah once again came to our aid. His cousin, who ran a boardinghouse by the port, offered us two rooms for three shillings a week. Isaiah's cousin arranged for us to begin work at the Waterfront Inn. Hazel became the cook, and I assumed the duties of a maid.

We promptly went to work, and when I finished my chores for the day, I returned to the boardinghouse and unpacked my few belongings. Although my life was in tatters, my nature would not permit my living quarters to be. Once that task was complete, the sun settled in where the water met the sky. I took the occasion of my first night in Baltimore to walk along the waterfront piers. Isaiah informed me that Baltimore was one of America's most prominent ports, given the ongoing British blockade of Boston Harbor following the tea dumping incident.

The smell of seawater filled my nostrils. It was a scent I found abhorrent since my journey in the hold of a ship like the many I now looked upon. To me, these ships were symbols of treacherous travel, seasickness, and unbathed men who reeked of the experience. I had little desire to travel on a ship again. When I was a girl, I didn't enjoy my father's rowboat, but the stillness of the pond, with me on the land, was a comfort. That feeling, pray tell, is now gone. My future would not be in Baltimore working as a maid. I'd come too far for that life. I wanted something more, to be something more. This would be a temporary hiatus from a dream fulfilled.

# CHAPTER THIRTY-SEVEN

## *Baltimore*

## the Maryland Colony

## 15 SEPTEMBER 1774

Five long months had gone by. The inn grew busier with the greater volume of ships coming and going from the port. I was working seven days a week from sunrise to dusk. Time to write in my diary had been scarce. Hazel and I were on different schedules and saw each other only in passing. I was hauling fresh linen into a third-floor room of the inn when a friendly voice stopped me in my tracks.

"Now tell me, young lady. What exactly must I do to get my best harpist to return to Cromwell?"

The sight of Pastor Vinson all but brought tears to my eyes. I was so weary from work that I thought his presence might just be a conjuring of my mind. But it was him! We embraced warmly. It was like being reunited with my own father. Pastor Vinson's words and warmth never failed to restore my wallowing spirit.

"How are you, Pastor?"

He let go of a garrulous laugh. "Fine, fine. It's so good to see you. I am here on a mission."

"You are seeking to add to your congregation?"

"Most certainly. By a quantity of one."

I blushed. "How did you even know I was here?"

"After months of prodding, I finally wrangled it out of Isaiah." Then he laughed again and said, "I told him he'd rot in hell if he didn't tell me where you were."

"You could have written me a letter."

"I suppose that's true, but with a carriage, I can bring you back where you belong."

I sighed. "I think it's safe to say my days in Cromwell are over for good. Mr. Greene banished me and Hazel. Governor Templeton and Mayor Bartholomew hate me. Mr. Wright views me as the devil, and even the hospital has no need for me."

"There, there. I know that's what you believe."

"Is it not reality?" I asked with conviction.

"Time heals all wounds," he replied.

"And what has changed, exactly?"

"The mayor, for one. Charles Greene temporarily supplanted Arthur Bartholomew. Mr. Greene is seeking a new sheriff and . . ." He reached into his cloak for a letter. "I have a letter addressed to Governor Templeton, signed by Drs. Clarke and Van Der Beek, seeking your reinstatement as hospital administrator. And need I say, my church has a beautiful harp that sits dormant week after week."

I stood silently in the corridor of the Waterfront Inn. I needed to collect my thoughts. Pastor Vinson was reintroducing a life I thought I left behind. "I have no place to live in Cromwell."

The pastor was silent for a moment. "I haven't been completely forthright with you. You have a suitor who approached me about the appropriateness of a marriage proposal."

"A suitor? Appropriateness?" I couldn't, for the life of me, make sense of his comments.

"Why, yes. You are a widow. Your husband passed away over a year ago, unofficially ending your period of mourning. Therefore, I told Dr. Clarke, he should express his feelings directly to you."

"Timothy wants to marry me?"

"Yes, I'm afraid the doctor has been pining for you, and until recently, your whereabouts were unknown."

My mind raced like a scared jackrabbit in the forest. Indeed, the forest was the place where Timothy and I shared a special moment. I recalled the feelings that bubbled up inside when he pulled me close before the encounter with Haverford and McCarron. Until now, that feeling eluded me. Long dissipated like a moving storm. Had it not been the same for Timothy? I wondered.

"I need time to think about all this." Then my thoughts returned to the letter he held. "Has Governor Templeton received that letter?"

"No, this is the original. After I leave here, I continue on to Annapolis to hand deliver it. I can retrieve you and Hazel on my way back."

I shrugged. "At the mere sound of my name, Governor Templeton may order me to appear in the town square to be hanged."

"Time heals all wounds," he repeated.

That nervous sweat broke out across my nose. It was too much to process. A marriage proposal and a letter seeking my reinstatement? I never contemplated returning to Cromwell. My future was to be in another colony. I'd meet a new suitor and establish roots in a community where I was wanted and needed. The thought of returning to Cromwell tugged at my heart. I wished forgiveness from Aquila, and I adored Penny. Timothy was a friend. Could I make a life with him? Was true love important? Perhaps not, but I wasn't ready to rush into any life-changing decisions.

Pastor Vinson interrupted my private thoughts. "Essie, shall I journey to Annapolis and deliver this letter?"

I sighed. Finally, I replied, in a soft whisper laced with indecision, "Yes, please do."

Pastor Vinson said he would stop by on the way home, and he left me a copy of the letter. It was three pages and signed by both Timothy and Henrik. The closing summary of the letter struck me. The doctors were expressing a logical stance based on medical facts. They attempted to acknowledge and remove the governor's pain and suffering from the equation. It read:

*While we empathize greatly with the magnitude of your astounding loss, we urge you, in retrospect, to consider the circumstances under which this unavoidable tragedy occurred. Mrs. Templeton lost four children at birth in the years preceding her visit to our new hospital. Her most recent pregnancy was a breech, a condition that might have been reversed if cared for properly earlier in the term. There was little else that might have been attempted to save your child beyond the actions undertaken by the midwife, Mrs. Lassiter. We, as experienced medical doctors, and any practiced man of medicine facing the same circumstances, would have acted in kind. The unfortunate death of Mrs. Templeton, while tragic, was not uncommon, for as we are sure you know, a woman's heart often expires under the strain of a difficult birth. As for the condition of the hospital upon your arrival, we agree that it was deplorable, at best. Your coach arrived on the heels of a bank robbery, yielding many shooting victims and deaths. The unsightly conditions were unavoidable. As you experienced personally the following day, it was Mrs. Lassiter who organized and led the process to restore the hospital to its normal high standard of order and cleanliness. In the time since Mrs. Lassiter's dismissal, the new hospital continues preparations to open, with your continued gracious support, and from a medical standpoint, all is sound. We have, however, been unable to find someone with the skills to assuage patients, their families, and the nursing staff to the betterment of the Maryland Colony and its citizens. Mrs. Lassiter provides the needed temperament and ability to help make the Maryland Hospital the shining star of American medicine.*

*We are grateful for your consideration of our request for reinstatement.*

*Respectfully submitted on this 12th day of September in the year 1774.*

*Doctor Timothy Clarke*

*Doctor Henrik Van Der Beek*

I read the letter over and over. Their words exhibited an overwhelming kindness. If I were honest with myself, I missed being at the hospital. I missed working with Timothy and Henrik. I yearned for my informal visits with Pastor Vinson and playing the harp in church on Sunday mornings. As I searched my soul, and deep down in my heart, what I truly missed was Aquila and Penny and the prospect of being an even more important part of their lives. As I drew breath into my body, I knew I might regain all that I missed about Cromwell . . . except a life with Aquila and Penny. That would never come to pass.

# CHAPTER THIRTY-EIGHT

## *Baltimore*

## the Maryland Colony

## 18 SEPTEMBER 1774

Three days later, Pastor Vinson found me again. I'd just completed my duties at the inn, and we elected to walk along the docks. The fall air intertwined with the scent of the busy harbor. It reminded me of the odor in the ship's hold where I spent one of the worst months of my life. I much prefer the countrysides of Wickhamshire and Cromwell. The air was turning cold, and I pulled my wool cloak up around my neck. I awaited the pastor's news from Annapolis, although I tried hard not to get my hopes up.

"The doctors' letter hardly moved the governor," he proclaimed flatly. "I was eager to deliver better news."

I hung my head. My ability to conceal my emotions was never very good. Inherently, I worried this reinstatement would not come to pass. I suppose it's why I made scant effort to pack a single stitch of clothing for a return to Cromwell. "Thanks for trying," I mustered.

"It is not all bad. The governor didn't say no. He simply said, 'Not now.'"

I didn't take his meaning and asked him to clarify his odd remark.

"Governor Templeton stated he would defer a decision on reinstatement until he may confer with Aquila."

"Aquila? No one even knows when he might return."

"Charles and Celia received a letter citing a potential return before year's end."

That news left me encouraged. Perhaps Pastor Vinson was right, and time did heal all wounds. "Was there word of Penny? Was the surgery a success?"

Pastor Vinson shook his head. His eyes squinted above the glasses parked on the tip of his nose. He cleared his throat and said, "I wish there were. We shall have to wait and see."

Pastor Vinson said he would spend the night at the inn and resume his journey to Cromwell in the morning. I had no faith in Governor Templeton. In his mind, I was the culprit, and perhaps for good, his heart had hardened. I couldn't imagine how conferring with Aquila might aid my plight. He also blamed me for Penny's disfigurement. I hugged Pastor Vinson and held on as long as I reasonably could. Given the news of the day, I feared I would never see him again.

# CHAPTER THIRTY-NINE

## Baltimore

## the Maryland Colony

### 30 OCTOBER 1774

Gunshots rang out in the early morn of late October. I had heard nothing so scary since that fateful day in the boardinghouse hospital. I jumped from my bed and ran next door, rapping furiously on Hazel's door. The commotion awakened her as well, and we huddled together at her window overlooking the docks.

"Well, I'll be damned! If it ain't Haverford and McCarron, causing a ruckus once more." Hazel didn't mince words.

"I wonder what they are doing here in Baltimore. I figured they'd be out west somewhere by now."

"By the looks of it, they're shootin' up the port."

My stomach fluttered. They could be seeking me. Scoundrels like Haverford never assumed accountability for their actions. There was always someone else to blame. He raped and brutalized Antonia. He lost his businesses and his standing in the town. Since I treated Antonia in the aftermath of her attack, it would stand to reason he would think me complicit in the call for his capture. Aquila was out of reach, and the Bond family was far north. I was the easy target. My mind raced. I expressed these fears to Hazel.

She embraced me and tried to calm my frayed nerves. "These animals aren't concerned with vengeance. They are desperate. Desperate men do stupid things. When I was working for Mr. Greene, I recall him saying that Haverford inherited all he had. Now it's gone, and he's resorted to thievery to survive."

"You don't believe he's after me?"

"I think it's pure coincidence he and his one-armed skunk of a sidekick showed up where you are. Besides, look down there. They got more than they can handle at the moment."

Hazel was correct. Two men lay dead on the dock across from the inn. A crowd gathered but stood back. No one possessed the courage to confront Haverford, who looked like a rabid wolf. Through the open window, we heard him yell, "Lay your money and valuables on the ground. If you refuse, Mr. McCarron will be glad to place a bullet between your eyes."

One by one, people placed valuables by their feet. In no time, the street became filled with coins, wallets, and gold pocket watches. The sight was absolutely horrifying. Just as it seemed they might get away with it, a single shot rang out from the distance. The shot came from one of the ships. It struck McCarron in the back of the head, and he crumpled to the ground. Shock seemed to run through Haverford. He spun around as a man approached, holding a musket.

It was a familiar face. I would forever remember that potbelly and bushy mustache. Captain Quarles came across the dock, the musket on his hip and a pistol aimed directly at Amos Haverford's head.

"Don't you move a lick, young fella. Not unless you want to meet the same fate as your friend here," Quarles gestured to McCarron's corpse.

Undismayed, Haverford replied most bitterly, "Where do you get off interfering in America's business?"

"Well, the way I see it, I'm a British sea captain. We are in a port where I conduct business, and last time I checked, Maryland was still a British colony. And if that ain't enough, how about this? I just don't like varmints like you taking advantage of innocent people."

Haverford snarled back, "Rot in hell!"

And without a word, Captain Quarles put a bullet in Amos Haverford's head, ending the fugitive's reign of terror.

Hazel and I clung to each other. For me, there would be no more looking over my shoulder. For the rest of Maryland, it was a respite from a worrisome time. I had no moral dilemma with what I saw. No one would miss these men.

# CHAPTER FORTY

## *Baltimore*

## the Maryland Colony

### 14 DECEMBER 1774

I'd scarcely heard from Pastor Vinson since his visit to Baltimore nearly three months earlier. There was but one letter expressing vague pleasantries but no news of substance. Certainly no word of Aquila and Penny and thankfully no further mention of Timothy's desire to propose. It completely surprised me, then, to see Aquila and Timothy stepping out of Aquila's fine carriage at the Waterfront Inn.

I was called away from my duties and asked to come to the front lobby. And there they were, both beaming like drunken sailors. I greeted them cautiously. Despite his warm smile, I believed Aquila to be angry with me—and where Timothy was concerned, it was just awkward.

"I cannot speak for long. I can ill afford to lose my position as a maid," I stated.

Aquila looked at me in a way I never imagined he again would. "That is of no concern. We are here to bring you back to Cromwell."

"I don't understand, Mr. Wright," I replied.

"I owe you an apology. And let's forget about our last encounter. You may call me by my given name once more."

"How is Penny?"

"She is fine. The skin graft surgery was a rousing success! Timothy and Henrik examined Penny upon her return and feel confident that with proper aftercare, her injury will barely be discernable."

"Oh, what a relief. I cannot tell you how many sleepless nights I've known worrying about her future. The guilt was overpowering."

"You do not need to feel guilty. Penny explained you walked up to the garden while she was foolishly feeding the cub." He placed his hands on my shoulders and lovingly stated, "I know you tried to save her. Please accept my sincerest apologies. I shall be forever in your debt."

*Ironic*, I thought. Our relationship began with me as an indentured servant, being forever in his debt.

"And the letter to Governor Templeton worked? He has approved my reinstatement?"

Timothy looked down at the floor. Aquila was the one who spoke. "No, not exactly. I met with Governor Templeton upon my return. He remains hardened at the prospect."

"Timothy and I would like to bring you and Hazel back to Cromwell. You will resume your position as hospital administrator, and Hazel will occupy the cottage at Cromwell's Passage."

"But without the governor's blessing? How is this possible?"

Aquila smirked and waved his hand in the air, almost knocking off his tricorn hat. "To hell with him. He is nothing more than a puppet for the king. America will be free before long, and Governor Templeton will be on a boat back to England."

"How can you be so cavalier? The governor provides the funds for the hospital. How will it remain viable?"

"Fear not. I will pledge the funds if need be. So will Charles and a host of other wealthy men throughout Maryland. Benjamin has solicited the backing of the Continental Congress. Once the revolution begins, the hospital will play a pivotal role in keeping our troops on their feet."

*Revolution.* Aquila spoke as if it were imminent. Being in a city like Baltimore, news was plentiful, and dustups between the British soldiers and the American militias were becoming all too common. Redcoats had even burned down

American towns and enlisted the Indians to rebel against colonists. Recalling my pledge to help America fight the England that abandoned me, I wholeheartedly welcomed my new opportunity.

Everything was falling into place. My dreams were coming true. I was about to regain my former position. Penny was all right, and Aquila was finally ready to have me as his wife. I could be a mother to Penny in earnest. It felt like someone had lifted ten anvils from my shoulders. It had to be! This must be the reason Aquila stated Hazel could take over the cottage we used to share. I braced myself against the lobby wall, waiting to hear the affirmation out loud.

Timothy, who had yet to utter a single word since their arrival, broke the silence. "And you, Essie, if you will have me, will come live with me, as my wife. Pastor Vinson can marry us on Sunday."

The blood must have drained from my face. My knees went weak. Harming Timothy was the last thing I wanted to do. He'd shown me nothing but kindness since his arrival in Cromwell. But all I could think to say was, "I am still in mourning for my late husband, you understand."

Timothy looked crushed. "Perhaps you might consider my proposal at a later date?"

"I'd be honored," I foolishly replied, as if he had requested that I deliver a baby.

Aquila stood by and waited for the awkward conversation to end. "I do hope you will still return to Cromwell with us?"

"Yes. If it's all right with you, may I share the cottage with Hazel?"

He nodded. "Of course."

Trying frantically to discuss anything other than marriage, I asked, "Has anyone kept up the cottage garden?"

"No," replied Timothy. "Unfortunately, it's one of the many things that have been sorely lacking since your departure. We have had to purchase most of our medicinal plants and herbs at a substantial cost increase and significant delay."

"Hazel and I will bring the garden back to life at the first sign of spring."

To Aquila, I added, "Penny can help only with an adult present, preferably equipped with a gun for protection."

The proud father beamed. "In England, while she was recuperating, I taught her to shoot. Her aim is quite good for a budding young lady."

"Are you suggesting that a woman cannot shoot as well as any man?" I surprised myself with the forward nature of my comment. Hazel's brash demeanor was rubbing off on me.

Aquila was taken aback. Timothy giggled. I think he enjoyed seeing Aquila squirm under the weight of the challenge.

Aquila responded thoughtfully and appeared to weigh his words. "I think, with proper teaching and an abundance of practice, a woman could potentially learn to shoot like a man."

"Potentially?" I had little experience in the matter but was sure I could be as proficient as a man. The possession of a penis did not, in my humble opinion, bestow any special skills upon a person in aim and ability to pull a trigger.

"Well, that is . . . I mean to say . . ." Aquila stammered.

"I shall be glad to teach you, Essie," offered Timothy. "It will afford us time together, which I would welcome."

I accepted Timothy's offer. Men like Haverford and McCarron were everywhere. So were predatory animals living among us. I never again aspired to be in a position of depending upon a man to defend my life if I could do so on my own.

I held my head high and walked to the broom closet to return my apron and mop. Once Hazel finished working the dinner service, she was free to accompany us back to Cromwell.

Right after sundown, rain greeted the city, prompting our decision to wait until morning.

# CHAPTER FORTY-ONE

## *Cromwell*

## the Maryland Colony

### 5 JANUARY 1775

Another new year was upon us, and with it came the opening of the new Maryland Hospital. The smell of fresh construction was exhilarating. We had fifty beds, two operating rooms, and proper storage for a month of supplies. The facility included an apothecary, kitchen, and a maid's area where linens could be washed and dried on lines behind the building. I even had my own small workspace. It wasn't a traditional office, resembling more of a small bedchamber, yet it provided enough space for a desk and storage for essential records. And although I was in Baltimore during much of the construction, I prevailed upon Aquila to allow a small parcel of the hospital's land to be allocated for our medicinal garden. All was well until the British soldiers entered the building.

"We demand to see the man in charge," barked the senior officer.

"I am the administrator. How may I be of service?"

"You? Surely you jest," the pompous redcoat replied.

"I assure you I have full authority over the Maryland Hospital."

He sighed while his three underlings stood erect behind him. He produced a scroll secured with a red ribbon and unfurled it.

"I have a writ from Governor Templeton of the British Colony of Maryland proclaiming that this hospital and all its contents belong to King George III and that citizens and loyalists of the Crown will receive favor before all others."

"Why, that's preposterous," I exclaimed without forethought.

"Are you defying the governor's order, ma'am?"

I needed to be careful. I had to speak with Aquila, Timothy, and Henrik. An impetuous response might land me back in incarceration. I couldn't risk that.

"No, I understand the order."

"Very well. My men shall affix the sign ordered by the governor and be on our way."

"Sign? But we already have a sign. It was just hung yesterday. It displays our name, the Maryland Hospital."

"We will dispose of it for you."

And with that, they retreated through the lobby and went to their wagon, replacing the large wooden sign made for us by Isaiah.

The noise from the hammer banging was irritating. When they'd departed, I walked outside and stared blankly at the unfathomable sign.

### THE ROBERT & OLIVIA TEMPLETON HOSPITAL
*For British Citizens and Loyalists*
EST. 1775

Anger flushed my cheeks. This was nothing more than retribution. Governor Templeton was responding to Aquila's refusal to abide by my banishment from the hospital. Instead of being a place of refuge and healing for all in need, this hospital was to be restricted to loyalists only. And it was all because of me! I couldn't bear standing by while my own ambition clouded my judgment. I decided to leave Cromwell. There was no other option.

—⁂—

That evening, I sat in the dining room of the main house at Cromwell's Passage. Hazel accompanied me to the dinner hosted by Aquila, which included Timothy, Henrik, Fleur, and Charles and Celia Greene. Aquila insisted we enjoy a meal of braised mutton and cabbage before getting down to business. After I ate the last of the dessert, a delicious peach cobbler, I could wait no longer.

"I must resign. It's the only way," I proclaimed.

"Even if you were to do so, what makes you think Governor Templeton would rescind the order to treat only British loyalists?" answered Aquila. "Your resignation therefore serves no purpose."

"The winds of revolution are upon us. A new hospital is part of the governor's larger strategy to defend against the patriots," decried Mr. Greene.

"I want no part in this. Perhaps Fleur and I will return to Europe," added Henrik.

"If Essie resigns, so do I. See how well their new hospital runs without doctors," said Timothy.

"You don't think the British will bring in their own doctors?" asked an incredulous Mrs. Greene. "Don't be naive. I say you burn their sign and the order that authorized it, and tell the governor he has no authority over the matter."

Mr. Greene smiled with admiration. "Why Celia, have you been secretly attending my chapter meetings for the Sons of Liberty?"

"I don't need a room full of men and their whiskey to tell me what common sense is," she replied to her husband.

"Aquila, what do you think?" I asked.

"I agree with Celia. Isaiah is completing a new sign this evening and will hang it tomorrow."

"Won't the governor argue he funded the hospital and has every right?" I inquired.

Mr. Greene, the new mayor, laughed out loud. "Thinking you have authority and successfully exercising it are two very different matters."

"What do you know we do not?" Aquila asked Mr. Greene.

"Just that the Continental Congress is moving ever closer toward a resolution enabling American independence."

"In what manner? Are they espousing a full declaration of independence?"

"That's my preference. They have asked Benjamin Franklin to draft a proposal for consideration."

And while Aquila and Charles debated the merits of declaring independence and the prospect of war, I worried that my continued presence would indeed still cause a problem for the people I cared for most. Men like Elias Carmichael, Amos Haverford, Zeke McCarron, and Arthur Bartholomew were plentiful in these parts. The governor could enlist any of them to mistreat me, just like they savagely attacked Antonia. That would be one way for Governor Templeton to keep the blood off his hands. Another would be to resort to the other favored strategy of the Crown, inciting the Indians against the colonists. But having met the governor, I would not doubt his capability to send the Redcoats straight to the cottage and drag me away. I went to bed that evening, still contemplating my departure from Cromwell.

# CHAPTER FORTY-TWO

## *Cromwell*

## the Maryland Colony

## 7 JANUARY 1775

The winter sun melted into the horizon, descending gradually, like my mood of the day. I threw myself into the work of the hospital but remained conflicted. Hazel warned me about making a rash decision. She was right. I resolved to meet with Pastor Vinson. He always had a calming effect on my frayed nerves. With the sunset, the air became far chillier, and I wrapped my cloak tightly for the walk back to the cottage. Though it was typically quiet during this time of day, I unexpectedly heard a cacophony of voices, not just a few but a whole mob. I stood and looked down the main street of the town. The torches were carried by a herd of upset people.

The mob reached the town hall building which housed the mayor, the sheriff, the judge, and the small jail. Arthur Bartholomew and three other men were at the head of the pack. The angry mob was urging him to take action. "Burn it down, burn it down!"

The idea appalled me. There was no time to call for help. I had to do something. "Mr. Bartholomew. Don't you dare! What do you hope to accomplish?"

"Stand down, Mrs. Lassiter. This is no business of yours."

"I am a member of this community, so I beg to differ."

"If you must know, I am correcting an injustice. This building and the town of Cromwell were mine to control. I was elected mayor, not Charles Greene."

"Burning down the town hall won't solve your problems. They will just build another."

"Perhaps you are right. But I will make my point nonetheless."

And with that, Bartholomew threw his torch into the town hall building. Several of his followers did likewise. Flames licked the lower portion of the building and, with the heavy black smoke, rose to envelop the structure. The smoke from the burning lumber stung my eyes. Thinking that was the worst of it, I turned in the opposite direction. My immediate thought was to retreat to the hospital. Timothy was still there. He could assemble men to quell the fire before it spread through town. I hadn't taken more than three steps when Bartholomew's surly voice yelled, "Don't let her go."

I couldn't outrun the frenzied men. A set of beefy arms wrapped around my waist, and then the butt end of a log smashed across the back of my head. Tripping over my own feet, I fell face-first into the dirt.

As I faded into a state of oblivion, Bartholomew yelled, "Burn the whole goddamned town!"

My eyes closed but not before a gunshot rang out above me.

# CHAPTER FORTY-THREE

# *Cromwell*

# the Maryland Colony

## 8 JANUARY 1775

I awoke the next morning in the largest of our hospital rooms, the one normally reserved for dignitaries. A knot had formed on the back of my head. Searing pain greeted my blurry vision. Before I could grasp the scene, I turned my head and vomited on the floor.

"Now, don't go makin' a bloody mess for me to clean up," Hazel said cheerily. "I'm glad you are awake. How are you feeling, love?"

I spoke slowly. "What happened? How did I get here?"

"You don't remember?"

I shook my head and then regretted the action as it exacerbated the pain.

"That rascal Bartholomew led an angry mob that burned down the town hall and beat the stuffing from your poor hide. Were it not for the good Dr. Clarke and his musket, you might be a goner."

"Timothy?"

"Showed up in the nick of time. Fired a warning shot and carried you all the way back here. He's barely left your side since last night."

I tried to smile at the heroics. The truth was I recalled nothing after confronting Bartholomew. "Did he get away?"

"Bartholomew? Yeah, he ran like the coward he is. Mr. Greene and Mr. Wright showed up at his tannery last night and arrested him. Since Bartholomew burned down the jail, they have him locked up in one of Mr. Greene's barns until they can arrange for a trial."

"Was anyone else hurt?"

"Just you. The jail and town hall were empty. Bartholomew ordered the whole town torched."

"I guess he's angry at being replaced as mayor."

"Mr. Greene said the town conducted a fair recall on his election. Everything was on the up and up."

"Hazel, some water, if you please."

"Of course. Let me get you some laudanum for the pain. You rest. I'll be back in momentarily."

Before Hazel returned, I must have nodded off. My eyelids were like heavy curtains descending after the last act. When I awakened, Timothy was by my side.

"You rescued me," I said in a sleep-laden voice.

He caressed my hair without reply, and then he took my hand and beamed.

"I need to get back to work," I said. "There's so much to do."

Timothy shook his head. "You are under doctor's orders to remain in bed. We'll see how you are tomorrow. Nothing can't wait or be undertaken by someone else."

"But I must complete my supply requisitions," I protested.

"I'll take care of it. We won't run out of anything. I'll journey all the way to Scott's Old Fields for supplies if it'll keep you in bed."

His kindness was appreciated and his touch a comfort.

"My proposal still stands," he declared. "Marry me, Essie. I will love and protect you as long as we both shall live."

This man's love flattered me. Truly, a part of me yearned to say yes. Something just kept the words from escaping my lips. I squeezed his hand and returned his smile. "That's a topic for another time."

There was a knock at the doorframe. I was pleased to see Pastor Vinson. He saved me from the uncomfortable question of marriage. Timothy excused himself to check on other patients, and Pastor Vinson sat down in the wooden side chair next to the bed. He hadn't yet settled in the chair before I broke down.

"Are you in pain? Shall I get help?"

"No, no, no. All the town's troubles . . ." I sniffled and blew my nose in a handkerchief he offered. "It's all because of me. I should have never come back from Baltimore."

"Why would you say such a thing?"

"Isn't it obvious?"

"Enlighten me."

"The governor placed the hospital under his purview to protest my perceived inaction in the loss of his wife and child, and Arthur Bartholomew incited a riot because I tried to stop him."

"Now, now. Let logic govern your emotions. You know as well as I that Governor Templeton's tragedy would have occurred no matter the medical personnel and Bartholomew was intent on causing trouble before he saw you. Your presence was merely a coincidence."

"I need to leave Cromwell for good. Everyone will be better off."

He arched an eyebrow. "Even Aquila and Penny?"

Pastor Vinson had obviously not forgotten my secret. My feelings for Aquila never waned. I tried to hold it back. Letting it out was fruitless.

"You are right," I replied. "At least for Penny's sake. Prudence is a capable nanny, but Penny and I, well, she needs me more than that."

"She needs a mother, Essie. She sees you as such."

"And Aquila?"

"Do you not think he sees you as a future wife?"

"It is my most heartfelt desire. I just don't know how to tell him—or Timothy, for that matter. He continues to make overtures to marriage. How do I let him down gently?"

Before Pastor Vinson could reply, Timothy's voice echoed from the doorway.

"You just did."

## CHAPTER FORTY-FOUR

# *Cromwell*

# the Maryland Hospital

## 9 JANUARY 1775

In the early hours of the morning, I lay in a hospital room so pitch black, I could just make out the page of this diary. The candle flickered, and my hand trembled as I weakly attempted to record my conflicted outlook on the terrible injustice I'd inadvertently committed with Timothy. In all my thoughts regarding how to carefully handle the situation, one thing was certain. I never wished to hurt the man's feelings. Now, I was wracked with guilt, searching for some desperate measure to try to make it right.

Another amber flame flickered in the doorway. I presumed it was the night nurse who came to check on me every few hours. Instead, it was a tall shadowy figure bearing a small bunch of posies in a mason jar. I couldn't make out the face. The light was too dim. The voice, however, was unmistakable.

"I thought I'd check on you before the day got too busy," Aquila said in a breathy whispered tone.

"It is barely sunrise," I replied, happy to see him.

His face, now clear as he approached my bedside, was fresh and vibrant, ready to tackle the day's new challenges. "These are for you," he said, placing the flowers on the bedside table.

"Thank you, Aquila. They are lovely." I drew pleasure from the flowers' sweet aroma.

"Are you going home soon?"

"Perhaps today. Once Timothy clears me, I shall walk home and prepare to return to work."

Before I uttered a single word, Aquila's face revealed a problem. "Henrik will be in to evaluate you this morning."

"What of Timothy? Is he ill?"

"No, he suffers only from a broken heart. I don't know the details, but I gather you must have refused his recent proposal. Timothy resigned and intends to leave Cromwell immediately."

With both hands, I covered my mouth to muffle the gasp that welled up from my chest. I never in my life imagined myself so strong an object of desire that it would drive a man to leave a prominent position due to his inability to have me.

"I understand how Timothy must feel," Aquila stated plainly. Then, he reached into his pocket and extracted the pendant that once belonged to his wife. The beautiful ivory-raised butterfly he'd given to me last Christmas. "Charles found this on the floor of the cottage after you departed for Baltimore."

I let him affix the pendant around my neck. His touch made my skin tingle. Not since my Thomas had I felt such a strong desire to be held by a man.

"You look ravishing," he said.

"I am a frightful mess with unkept hair and a big knot on the back of my head."

"When you are well, I'd like us to spend some time together. Perhaps you and I and Penny could go horseback riding in the open fields of Cromwell's Passage, and then, afterward, the two of us could enjoy an intimate dinner."

When I hesitated to reply, Aquila said, "Unless I am being presumptuous, like Timothy, and you don't want to be courted. I don't wish to make you uncomfortable."

"Courted?" I gathered my confidence. "By all means, if it's by the right suitor."

"Might I be that suitor?"

I gave him a devilish grin and replied, "We will just have to see, won't we?"

# CHAPTER FORTY-FIVE

## *Cromwell's Passage*
## the Maryland Colony

## 11 JANUARY 1775

Only two days had passed since I came home from the hospital. I was not yet ready to resume my duties. Hazel thoughtfully planned a tea with Penny and Prudence. Hazel's freshly baked apple fritters smelled heavenly. She hummed an old English folk song as she prepared the tea. The girls and I waited at the dining table and welcomed in the opportunity to catch up. I hadn't spent real time with Penny since my return from Baltimore. I wanted to make sure she understood that my silence toward her was not of my choosing.

I took her small hand in mine. "When you were here last, in the garden, feeding the bear, well, I—" I stopped myself, afraid that my words might upset her. Her wounded face looked almost normal, and she appeared well-healed in the incident's aftermath, but I understood how emotions lingered within one's soul.

"It's all right, Essie," Penny gently replied. She appeared so much more a young lady than before the bear attack. When I arrived from England, Penny was a few months shy of her twelfth birthday. Now she was turning fourteen. Her youthful girl look had given way to a pronounced jawline, resembling her father's, and her body was showing early signs of maturity. Penny's reply signaled a change in our relationship.

I pressed forward. "The circumstances around the attack caused your father to assume I was responsible, and he prohibited me from speaking with you. He wouldn't listen to reason. I wanted you to know how distressed I was." I took her hand and affectionately squeezed. "I missed you so much."

Penny's face lit up. "I missed you too!"

Hazel brought the tea and fritters and joined us at the table.

Penny lifted her teacup with the elegance of a young lady who had emerged in society. She spoke with a grace I hadn't encountered before. "While we were in England and I was recuperating from my surgery, Father introduced me to many people and places in London. It was quite an experience. Wouldn't you say so, Prudence?"

The young nanny nodded as crumbs from the fritter fell from the corner of her mouth.

"In fact, Father and I became quite close, in a different sort of way," Penny continued.

"Pray tell, how do you mean?" Hazel inquired.

"When I was a mere girl, our communication was Father asking me what he could do to please me or to offer instruction on chores. Since our journey across the ocean, we now converse as adults. We shared intimate thoughts on life, our hopes, and our dreams."

"That's so nice," I replied. "My father died before we achieved that type of relationship. I went right from being a teenager to wife and homemaker."

"Well," Penny said, "I told Father that you were in the garden that day by happenstance and your only role was an attempt to be the heroine."

"And he accepted your word?" I asked.

"Oh, yes. Then, he told me how guilty he felt about his treatment toward you and how he wished for something more."

Hazel, never one to shy from gossip, found herself intrigued. She sat up straight in her chair and seductively asked, "Might we have details?"

Penny burst out in a garrulous giggle, abandoning all pretense of sophisticated airs, and said, "I really shouldn't say, but yes, Essie, he is sweet on you."

I clutched the ivory butterfly around my neck and felt its warmth travel through my body, like the feel of Aquila's touch as he fastened the pendant around my neck in the hospital. "I don't know what to say," I murmured as my cheeks turned crimson.

"If Mr. Wright asked for your hand, would you know what to say?" Hazel pried.

Before I answered, Penny chimed in. "I know what I'd like you to say."

At that moment, our eyes and hearts connected in a way they never had before. I loved Penny like she was my own. Despite her reticence toward strangers when we met and the heartbreak of losing her mother, it was clear to me that through words and deeds, I had won her love.

"I think I would say yes," I finally uttered.

"You think?" cackled Hazel. "Are you daft? Of course you'd say yes."

We all laughed, and again, I reached for the pendant around my neck. Somehow, it tied us all together, Aquila, Penny, and me. I viewed it as a symbol of my love for them both and theirs for me. I vowed never to take it off.

—⁂—

Hours passed since the girls departed, and my headache subsided. Feeling stronger, I bundled up and embarked on the walk to town. The church was dark, and so I assumed Pastor Vinson was visiting parishioners. I observed a group of men loading the remains of the town hall building onto wagons. The burned-out hull that lingered was depressing. The building had served as a beacon for the town, a place for reckoning, and a symbol of the growth of our community. It would take months to rebuild. Curiously, near the wreckage, three men, led by Isaiah, were busy constructing a platform with an overhead beam reaching twelve feet or more in the air.

"Hello, Isaiah. What are you building?"

"Good day, Essie. Aquila and Charles have asked me to oversee the construction of the gallows."

"Gallows? I'm not aware that Cromwell has ever hung a man for his crimes—have they?"

"Not to my knowledge. Without a jail, Bartholomew is being held in Mr. Greene's barn, along with his accomplices. Mr. Greene said that a trial is to be held tomorrow."

"With no courthouse, where will they hold it?"

Isaiah shook his head. "I'm not sure. Charles said something about setting up right here on the street. He wants everyone in town to see and hear what went on."

The construction of the gallows presumed guilt, which, of course, there was. Still, everyone deserved the presumption of innocence and an opportunity to defend oneself. Even as the victim of one of Bartholomew's crimes, I still wasn't sure how I felt about the gallows. An eye for an eye? Was this justice in the eyes of God? I wondered. It was a topic I would have to explore with Pastor Vinson. The philosophy of the issue was stifling. A part of me, however, wouldn't mind seeing Arthur Bartholomew and his rogue friends hanging in the gallows. I pictured this in my mind, and the face of Bartholomew changed to Elias Carmichael, then Amos Haverford, and Zeke McCarron, and every other man who disregarded me and women in general. Let them all hang! And as soon as the thought raced across my mind, guilty feelings emerged. How could I be so heartless?

I meandered down the road until I arrived at the hospital. My thought was to look in on my desk and just see how bad a state things were in. I found Timothy behind the desk, sorting through mounds of stacked parchment, trying to make sense of it all. He looked flustered as he ran his hand through his hair.

"I can help with that," I prodded.

"Essie, you should be home resting."

"My condition has improved significantly." Nervously, I paused and felt my foot moving to and fro like it always did. "I'm glad I bumped into you. I heard you are planning to leave."

He laughed half-heartedly. "Leave? With this mess and you out? Henrik would have a stroke. I shall get things in proper order before making my exit."

"Don't go," I pleaded. "Look what you've built here. This hospital needs you. This town needs you. I need you."

He scrutinized me. "Do you? You made your feelings quite clear."

"Just because I don't want to marry you doesn't mean I don't treasure our relationship." A tear fell unexpectedly from my eye. "I want the best for you. I want you to have a woman who will love you unconditionally, with all her heart. You deserve that. I am your friend and wish to remain so."

He took in my words. His eyes revealed the penetration of my plea.

Before he replied, I said again, "Don't go."

"I—I don't really wish to leave. I have fallen in love with Cromwell. It is my home. I only resigned out of love and respect for you. I want you to be happy."

"And I wish the same for you. Please stay, and let us remain friends."

To my great relief, he gently nodded.

# CHAPTER FORTY-SIX

## Cromwell

## the Maryland Colony

### 13 JANUARY 1775

My first impression of the town's lone judge was concerning. He was a tall, gaunt man with sallow cheeks and a small swath of beard below steely gray eyes and bushy eyebrows. He stood in the town square in front of the site where his courthouse once stood. The townspeople shivered in the gently falling snow and listened as Charles Greene addressed the judge. Bartholomew and his three primary cohorts sat on the ground, chained together at the ankles as two men with muskets stood over them. They received nothing warm to wear and trembled from the cold.

"Your Honor, the town of Cromwell, at present, has no prosecutor. As mayor, I shall present the charges and the evidence, and the accused will each have an opportunity to speak on their behalf," stated Mr. Greene.

"Very well, please proceed," stated the judge stoically.

"On the evening of 7 January, in the Lord's year 1775, Mr. Arthur Bartholomew led a pack of angry citizens into town with malicious intentions. They burned down the town hall building. After which, he ordered the attack on Mrs. Esther Lassiter, our hospital administrator, restraining her while one of his men struck her on the back of the head with a log."

"What evidence do you have to support these claims, Mr. Greene?" The judge was perfunctory in his actions. The ending to this story had already been written.

"Your Honor, look behind you and behold the remnants of Mr. Bartholomew's crime. We have two witnesses, both of whom are here today and willing to testify, Mrs. Esther Lassiter and Dr. Timothy Clarke. Dr. Clarke rescued Mrs. Lassiter and fired a warning shot toward Mr. Bartholomew and his crew. May I present the witnesses for their testimony?"

"Given this wretched outdoor trial, the snow, and the wintry winds, I don't think we need to take the time. Everyone in this town already knows what transpired and who was responsible," the angry judge extolled. "Do the accused have anything they wish to say in their defense?"

"Your Honor, I have been appointed to speak for all of us," Arthur Bartholomew said.

"So be it," the judge stated.

Bartholomew cleared his throat and spoke hesitantly at first and then more confidently. "This town, you people . . . you know little of justice. America should think of a republic, not a monolithic demagogue at its helm." He paused and cleared his throat again. "When the people elect a man and someone unfairly usurps power, it endangers the idea of a republic. This happened to me, and these men helped lead the rebellion to support what is fair and just."

Mr. Greene interrupted Bartholomew. "Your Honor, I believe we just heard Mr. Bartholomew admit guilt. I suggest we move to immediate sentencing."

The judge glared at the prisoners and then declared, "This court sentences you each to be hanged by the neck until life shall forever leave your body. Damn you all to hell."

Surprisingly, the crowd responded with a mix of cheers and dismay. The snow came down harder as Bartholomew and his men were taken to the gallows.

"This is a crime. What you have done to me, what you are now doing to me. This is a crime," shouted Bartholomew.

The guard silenced him with a club. Bartholomew's knees buckled, and all four men crumpled to the ground.

"Get up, you filthy degenerates," the lead guard snarled.

The men rose slowly and stumbled toward the gallows. The guards cast aside the leg irons and, one by one, threw a black sack over each man's head and placed a noose around his neck. A moment later, they removed the sandbags holding the slack ropes, and the four men swung perilously in the cold wind.

# CHAPTER FORTY-SEVEN

## *Cromwell*

## the Maryland Colony

## 22 MARCH 1775

Mr. Greene did yeoman's work as the mayor of Cromwell. The construction of the new town hall was advancing smoothly in view of the mild conclusion of winter. The framed-lumber structure was similar in size to the building Bartholomew destroyed, but according to Aquila, the interior would be far nicer. I admired the tenacity with which the men of the town worked to restore Cromwell to its prior status.

I was on my way to the hospital to work until midday. Aquila and I finally planned the long-awaited horseback adventure with Penny. Once he attended to his chores and Penny's school day concluded, we would be off. I was a little apprehensive, as I'd scarcely ridden a horse in recent years. Penny promised I would recoup my prior skill with ease. I wasn't so sure.

As I made my way toward the hospital, I noticed more redcoats than usual. The pompous soldier who installed the governor's new sign was about, and he didn't look happy. He approached me on Main Street. I did my best to avert eye contact in the vague attempt to ignore him. Alas, this effort failed.

"Mrs. Lassiter, I have noticed that you removed the governor's sign denoting the new name for the hospital."

I sighed, not wishing to engage in a confrontation. The prospect of being unjustly incarcerated still caused me a great deal of anxiety. "You would need to discuss the matter with Mr. Aquila Wright," I replied.

He guffawed condescendingly. "But I thought you were the hospital administrator."

"Yes, this is true. However, Mr. Wright is my employer." Although it felt awkward, Aquila explicitly instructed me to defer when confronted by British soldiers.

"Where can I find Mr. Wright?" inquired the soldier.

"I am not sure. You might check down at the grist mill."

"I shall. Governor Templeton will not take this news too kindly."

I hoped Aquila could ward off his advances.

—⚹—

That afternoon, I met Penny at the stable, and we saddled up our horses. She would ride a white steed of seventeen hands, and I a gray mare past her prime. Penny promised the mare would be gentler. Aquila's horse was a black beauty with a white spot between his eyes. He was a majestic animal but held a look of mischief to him. Aquila enjoyed the challenge of breaking a horse, and with this one, I was confident his hands would be full. As Penny and I prepared to mount our horses, Aquila strolled up to the stable and gave the prized horse a love pat on his face.

After greeting us both and inquiring of Penny how her school day went, Aquila brought up the subject of which I was most curious. "A nice British soldier came to see me at the mill today."

Penny and I noted the sarcasm in his voice.

"He took issue with the removal of the governor's sign and the policy to favor British soldiers and those loyal to the Crown."

"Did they threaten the hospital? Or us?" I asked anxiously.

"Of course," Aquila replied. "The British like to pound their chests and exert their perceived power."

"What did you say to him, Father?" Penny asked.

Aquila laughed. "I told him that the hospital will remain the Maryland Hospital and will treat all patients in need equally."

"I am sure he didn't take too kindly to your reply," I said.

"No, his response was macabre. He told me I needed to pledge fealty to Governor Templeton and King George III." He laughed again while mounting his horse. "I explained in no uncertain terms that I was now a member of the Second Continental Congress and had brought the matter up before the entire body. The Congress viewed the governor and King George III, for that matter, as ruling on borrowed time and that their orders were of no consequence to us."

"And he accepted this explanation?" Penny asked.

"No, not in the least. He threatened a regiment would soon be upon us to restore British rule and that I would never forget the coming Battle of Cromwell."

"Does that news not bother you?" I asked in a cracked voice.

"The Congress has appointed George Washington as the leader of the Continental Army. I have already sent word to General Washington of what is transpiring in Cromwell. Help is on the way."

"War is upon us, isn't it?" I asked.

"Yes, it was always a matter of when and not if." Aquila hesitated before guiding his horse toward the open fields of Cromwell's Passage. "I have enlisted in the Continental Army, as have Charles and Timothy."

"Enlisted? Father, won't that put you in danger? Can't you get wounded or killed?" Penny cried.

"War is dangerous, my sweet. A man must fight for what he believes, and I know with every fiber of my being that America must be free, totally free."

"What of Benjamin's draft declaration for peace with the British?" I asked, hoping that might prevent Aquila and the other leaders of our community from taking up arms against the British.

"Rejected by Congress, I'm afraid. Benjamin proposed a sovereign state with formal ties to England. Something short of true independence."

We trotted in silence. The gray mare was much slower than the other two horses, and I found myself many paces behind Aquila and Penny. It didn't bother me. It gave me time to consider what was about to come. War. What did this mean for the hospital? With Timothy enlisted, could Henrik and the small staff of nurses oversee the inevitable volume of wounded soldiers? And what was to become of the man I loved? Would Aquila live to fulfill his quest to marry me? Would his loyalty to the American Revolution leave his only daughter without a parent?

These were uncertain times. The horses ahead of me kicked up dirt from the beaten paths of the open field. Like the cloud of dust trailing Aquila and Penny, my view of the future was murky. I honestly didn't know whether to be excited for American independence or scared silly for the safety and well-being of those I loved.

# CHAPTER FORTY-EIGHT

## *Cromwell*

## the Maryland Colony

### 3 APRIL 1775

The so-called Battle of Cromwell began in earnest on this day.
I moved back into my old room at the main house so I could care for Penny while Aquila went off to war. General Washington commissioned him as a colonel, just like Mr. Greene. Timothy also received an appointment to the rank of colonel and would serve as a roving medical officer.

General Washington arrived in Cromwell the night before and set up command at Cromwell's Passage. The main house provided quarters for him, along with several other Continental Army officers, while the rest of the regiment pitched tents in the same field in which we had ridden horses just a few weeks earlier. Life now seemed so unbalanced and chaotic. The redcoats, we were told by a patriot reconnaissance mission, were establishing camp on the former property of Arthur Bartholomew. Although Bartholomew was not a British loyalist, the British Army usurped his land before General Washington arrived. The spring air held a chill with the struggle for control of Cromwell and the larger prize of Harford County. Which side would strike first? And how? Those were the only questions remaining. Aquila said General Washington was apt to wait until provoked by the British. In my estimation, it wouldn't take long.

General Washington was a regal man. His disposition was firm but fair. My first impression was of a natural born leader, one who commanded respect but never took it for granted. Men serving under General Washington, I was sure, felt valued and served with pride. This was unlike the totalitarian military order employed by the British.

I was at the hospital discussing these sentiments with Hazel and the nursing staff as we attempted to prepare ourselves for what was to come. Henrik urgently sent couriers to Philadelphia, New York, and Boston, asking for another doctor to dispatch to Cromwell. With conflicts occurring throughout America, I held out little hope of another doctor arriving anytime soon. Fleur volunteered to help, and we began teaching her how to tend to our medicinal garden and dispense remedies from the apothecary. Other women from Cromwell would learn to nurse, Mrs. Greene among them. Mr. Greene temporarily suspended school, and many of the older girls were taught easier chores like tending bedpans, changing linens, and bringing meals to the wounded. Penny wished to help, but Aquila, knowledgeable in the horrors of wartime injuries, forbade her. He was adamant that she work with the staff at Cromwell's Passage to maintain the estate in his absence and avoid the devastation of war. My biggest concern in preparing the hospital was Timothy's absence. If Henrik didn't have another doctor to assist him, we would be overrun by wounded and he would be overworked. I informed the staff that I might have to serve as the second doctor, even though I had no formal training. My time assisting Thomas, as the medic on the voyage to America, and serving as the first to help Aquila after the bridge collapse in Harford Town gave me confidence that I could help, if needed. At least this was what I conveyed to the women in my charge. Privately, I was worried sick.

As I predicted, we didn't wait long to learn how the battle for Cromwell began. The British soldier who brought the proclamation and its new sign demanded to inventory the patients in residence at the hospital. As he walked from room to room, he saw the few patients we treated and assessed all of them to be traitors to the Crown.

"These people should not curry favor in the Templeton Hospital," he proclaimed.

"Favor?" I replied. "We are well below capacity, and at no time was there a choice between treating a British loyalist and anyone else."

Undismayed, he pressed forward with his judgment, as if seeking a reason to begin the military conflict that weighted the air about town. "That's not the way I see it. According to one of my troops, he had to wait while traitors to the Crown were treated first."

I could not restrain my anger, despite knowing better the consequences of speaking my mind. "That's a lie. No such incident occurred."

Straightening his back and drawing his long pistol, he pointed the barrel at my head and firmly stated, "You dare to question the honor of a British soldier, a servant of King George III?"

At that moment, Henrik came onto the scene and asked what the matter was.

"This . . . this woman has insulted me, my regiment, and the entirety of England. We should strip her of her authority and take her to the gallows."

I reared back in reply. "It's balderdash. This soldier has created an illusion as a pretense for war."

Henrik, ever the pacifist, was at a loss for words. Although he was an excellent physician, he lacked courage in the face of conflict. And this soldier cut an imposing figure with his condescending demeanor.

"I am sure this is some sort of misunderstanding," Henrik pleaded.

"I am perfectly clear on the events and will act accordingly to bring justice to bear," the haughty British soldier replied. To his troops, he commanded, "Remove this woman from the premises. Doctor, I presume you will serve this hospital in accordance with Governor Templeton's edict."

Events rapidly spun out of hand. Henrik, not knowing what else to do, looked at me and yelled, "Essie, run!"

Before I contemplated my next move, the main doors to the hospital burst open, and a musket blast ended the life of the commanding British soldier. A band of Continental Army soldiers came through the door and took the subordinate British troops into custody. Blood pooled on the floor from their fallen leader.

General Washington entered the hospital and, in his wry assessment, stated, "This is just the beginning."

# CHAPTER FORTY-NINE

## *Cromwell*
## the Maryland Colony

## 7 APRIL 1775

After the inciting incident at the hospital, I believed General Washington would quell any larger conflict. The local British regiment lost its leader. The patriots quickly erected a prison camp on the outskirts of town. Four days in, I felt fortunate that the conflict hadn't caused any additional casualties. General Washington clarified that the Maryland Hospital was to treat only patriots. Any British soldier or loyalist was to be turned away despite the severity of their injuries. I harkened back to the conversation at the dinner table at Cromwell's Passage—the one where it was stated that the hospital would be viewed by both sides as a key strategic outpost in the larger battle for control of Harford County and, for that matter, Baltimore and the surrounding region. As the only hospital in the colony, the side who controlled it would stand the best chance of getting its troops healed and back onto the battlefield. General Washington understood this, and I agreed to abide by his decree. After all, England had cast me aside. I was an American now and would work tirelessly to defend the honor of the country that gave me every opportunity to prove my mettle and to matter.

The tranquility I cherished was not to last. The British, believing that their man at the hospital had been cold-bloodedly murdered, became energized under the leadership of a newly assigned general who led a battle raging all the way to the edge of the camp at Cromwell's Passage. A young soldier in his blue uniform came into the room and handed General Washington a courier's dispatch.

"What is it, General?" I inquired.

"We must go. Our camp at Cromwell's Passage has suffered an attack with cannon and muskets. Expect an influx of wounded, Mrs. Lassiter."

And with that, he and his troops departed. Two soldiers remained behind to guard the hospital entrance and ensure no British soldiers or loyalists were offered refuge.

As the troops marched with their leader, I wanted to run to Cromwell's Passage to protect Penny. Where was she? We discussed this possibility. Penny knew to hide in a secret underground cellar in the main stable. Aquila had devised this plan. If Penny heard cannon or gunfire, she was to dash to her hiding place. I had to trust that she would follow through. I needed to be at the hospital, and walking to Cromwell's Passage was not safe.

Before I could fret about Penny's well-being, she suddenly appeared before me, gasping for breath and perspiring heavily.

"Why aren't you in your hiding place? Did you not hear the cannon and gunfire?"

"I did. It felt safer to get farther away, and I knew you'd need help at the hospital. I can stitch wounds and apply bandages, among other things."

Part of me wanted to admonish her, but I embraced her with all my might. "I am glad you are all right. Now, go find Hazel and tell her I said you are to assist her wherever needed."

She skipped off cheerfully, and I readied the entrance for the influx of wounded. Not thirty minutes later, the first of the fallen patriots arrived. They were all soaking wet. A sudden spring rainfall materialized. Some men were shot, others pounded by the force of a cannonball. One soldier said the British used catapults to launch fireballs into the Continental Army camp. That was most concerning. I now had to be prepared for burn victims besides the worry of the main house and my cottage being reduced to ash. Thank heavens for the rain. It might have saved the day.

Twenty or more men streamed through the hospital entrance. Soon, we would be at capacity and would begin the emergency procedure of erecting triage tents on the now muddy main road. Pastor Vinson, too old to enlist, volunteered to undertake this duty with help from some schoolboys who were on temporary hiatus from their lessons. I went to the operating suite where Henrik was already in it up to his elbows. Wounded men who required procedures lined up through the corridors. I ran over to the wash basin to clean my hands, placed a surgical smock over my dress, and yelled over to Henrik, "I am going to work on some of these patients."

"Essie, you do not have the training for surgery. I cannot allow you to proceed."

"I know enough, and one man could never keep up. I will call over with questions."

I must have been out of my mind. But, in times of crisis, one can surprise oneself by performing extraordinary feats. I had two men bring the next patient over to the second operating table, and I assessed the damage. It was a burn victim. The soldier's wet blue uniform bore a ragged hole in the left shoulder. Fire singed the cloth and his skin. The best I could do was to cut away the charred flesh and apply a salve of animal fat to promote healing. A nurse would take over providing retreatment of the salve and administer laudanum for pain. They brought the next patient before me. A young man, who appeared to be about seventeen, had suffered a gunshot wound to the stomach. I had never removed a bullet or musket ball before. I called over to Henrik for instructions.

"Treat the wound with alcohol, grab a scalpel, and carefully excise the bullet without cutting into any organs. Once you have the bullet out, stitch the wound."

None of that seemed especially distressful except, of course, for the part about digging around in a man's innards with a sharp object. I took a deep breath, used my sleeve to wipe the sweat from my brow, and began the procedure. I went slowly. The young man was unconscious, affording me time to do things properly. Yet the groans of wounded men waiting outside the operating room were deafening. I couldn't concentrate.

Henrik saw my distress and left his patient to assist me. He took my hand, the one with the scalpel, and confidently directed it to where the bullet ought to be. "Do you feel that?" he asked.

I nodded.

"When you feel something hard, unless it's a rib, you have found the bullet, and you can gently extract it. Now, do it."

He let go of my hand, and I guided the instrument under the hard surface of the foreign object until I felt it rising with my subtle pressure. Placing the bullet within the grasp of a pair of forceps, I exhaled. I had done it! I saved this soldier's life. I stitched him up and called for the next patient.

While the next patient was placed on the operating table, I paused to get a glass of water. When I turned and saw Aquila's face, I almost fainted.

"Essie," he said through a strained and barely audible voice. "The attack. Brutal. Is Penny . . ."

And with that, he fell unconscious. I placed my face to his to evaluate the depth of his breathing. It was below expectations but stable. Along with a nurse, we undressed him, still in search of a wound. Remarkably, I found no sign of a gunshot and no burns. Now, I was worried about more serious internal injuries. Something way beyond my limited capabilities. If need be, I would pull Henrik from the patient on his table. I couldn't lose Aquila.

"Does anyone know what happened to Colonel Wright?" I called out to the cadre of the wounded.

A man responded from the back of the line of wounded men awaiting medical attention. "Colonel Wright took a secondary cannon impact."

I raced to the man and urgently asked, "What does that mean?"

The wounded man, barely conscious, said, "It means he was hit by a man who was hit by a cannonball."

I'd never heard of such a thing. I did not know what to do for Aquila. I ran back to Henrik's operating table and told him what I heard.

"Place your fingers here," he said, pointing to the open wound of the patient he'd been operating on. "Don't move until I get back."

Henrik walked over to Aquila and examined him, pressing here and there with his hands, performing some sort of diagnostic dance over the body that I failed to comprehend. "He's fine. A broken rib on the left side. He'll heal in time," Henrik proclaimed. "Take him to the top floor and let him rest."

I desperately wanted to go with Aquila and sit by his side, but the wounded kept pouring in. I couldn't leave Henrik. I directed my instructions to the men transporting Aquila. "Go find Nurse Giddings and tell her to bring Colonel Wright's daughter to his room."

# CHAPTER FIFTY

## Cromwell

## the Maryland Colony

### 8 APRIL 1775

If someone suggested that I would be married in a hospital room in the throes of war, I might have laughed. But that's precisely what occurred. After getting the Continental Army wounded settled in for the night, I went to an overstuffed side chair in the lobby and slept restlessly for three hours. I awoke to Pastor Vinson making his sunrise entrance, and I bristled when he approached to embrace me. His reaction was evident in his immediate retreat.

"I am a frightful sight, and I smell worse," I stated emphatically. "I have blood all over me and no clothes to change into. It's not safe to go home."

"I understand. Do not be alarmed. Aquila sent for me."

Suddenly, I felt guilty for sleeping. I hadn't checked on Aquila during the night. Was he sending for Pastor Vinson in search of spirituality in his final moments? "I shall accompany you upstairs," I said firmly.

When we entered his room, Penny was by Aquila's side. He was lying flat on his back but awake and alert. Penny gently sponged his forehead.

"Just the two people I wanted to see," he said with a vibrancy I hadn't heard from him in weeks.

Looking at me, he smiled. His eyes danced magically, and he said, "I have asked Pastor Vinson here to marry us, right here and now."

I was aghast. The blood must have drained from my face. I didn't immediately respond.

"Essie, will you not have me as your husband?"

Through moist eyes, I replied, "Oh, yes. Of course. I do love you and Penny so. But here? Now? Look at me."

When people are in love, they look past the obvious. Aquila didn't see my haggard appearance in bloodstained clothes. He saw the woman with whom he wished to spend the rest of his life.

"This war. My injury. It has made me acutely aware of my mortality. I wish to marry you today. Should anything happen to me, Penny will still have you, and the two of you will have Cromwell's Passage and my entire estate."

Before I could reply, Pastor Vinson came to my rescue. "Aquila, perhaps we could do this later today? Essie, I am sure, would like to go to the inn and take a bath."

Then he assured me, "I'm certain there are appropriate clothes for you at the church."

"Thank you, Pastor Vinson. That sounds splendid," I said.

I went over to Penny and asked, "Is this all right with you?"

Penny responded with a hug. When the embrace concluded, she gazed at me with affection. "I can't imagine anything better."

"Then, noon, if it's all right with you, Aquila," I said.

"My daughter and I agree. I can't imagine anything better."

I set off to the church first and then planned to indulge in a hot bath at the inn. All my dreams of marrying Aquila contained lavish festivities with a wedding gown handmade by the local seamstress and the entire town in attendance. We would honeymoon in Europe, Paris perhaps, and return to the stately manor of Cromwell's Passage. Now, I would be married, wearing a discarded dress from a box of donated garments, to a man flat on his back in a hospital. When this was over, I told myself, we would have a proper wedding, and the envisioned harmony would be magical. But America was at war, and who knew what the future held?

# CHAPTER FIFTY-ONE

## Cromwell's Passage
## the Maryland Colony

### 1 JUNE 1775

Aquila came home on a weekend furlough. Against advice from Henrik, Aquila had insisted on returning to his regiment. The rib would heal, he argued, whether he was lying flat on his back at Cromwell's Passage or on a cot in the field. Turning back the redcoats was his understandable priority, although it was somewhat foolish given the state of his body. As his wife, I offered an impassioned plea that any number of things might drastically curtail his recovery. It was easy to envision. After all, this man survived impalement from a bridge collapse and the secondary force of a cannonball. What else might happen? It was war. He might get shot, he could suffer blows in hand-to-hand combat, he might slip on a muddy embankment. I went on and on, but Aquila would hear none of it. In my heart, I knew he loved me, but I wondered whether my care of Penny in the event of his demise played a stronger role in his decision to marry me so suddenly.

In the time Aquila was gone, Penny and I grew closer. School had not yet reopened, and summer was almost upon us. We were careful in our movements. Along with Hazel, we agreed that none of us would walk alone to town. Redcoats were lurking about everywhere. Before he left, Aquila warned that the British soldiers would not bypass any opportunity to gain an advantage, including the capture of wives and children. Redcoats might take refuge in or even forcefully occupy homes. Aquila instructed us to carry a weapon. He provided each of us with a long-barreled pistol, and we practiced shooting in the fields abandoned by the Continental Army. Among the three of us, Penny was the best shot. She developed a sure eye for aim and a hand as steady as her father's. Hazel and I were less comfortable with a pistol, but at close range, each of us was confident we could hit our target.

I was more comfortable when the Continental Army occupied the fields of Cromwell's Passage, but General Washington chose to relocate the troops to where they were needed. General Washington dispatched Charles Greene's regiment south to Williamsburg, while Aquila and his men valiantly fought up north in the Brandywine Valley. A handful of soldiers remained to guard the hospital and fend off British attempts to occupy Cromwell. Even Pastor Vinson took up arms, claiming it was God's will that he defend the church and the town to the best of his abilities. It was a noble gesture, but I couldn't see this kind-spirited man engaging in the horrors of warfare.

As the head of the house in Aquila's absence, I instructed the staff to prepare a regal meal fit for a king. Aquila's return merited nothing less. With the burgeoning prelude to a full-scale war, food and supplies were in short supply. Even our own grist mill slowed to a crawl while Isaiah and most of the employees went off to fight. Still, the cook informed me he could offer a meal of seasoned squab, a rabbit stew, and cherry cobbler for dessert. I was pleased but still felt awkward in my new role. Planning and preparing such a special meal on my own was my natural inclination.

As she had done upon my arrival as an indentured servant, Celia guided me in the transition and the ways of managing a large home and its staff. She said it was the woman's responsibility to manage the affairs of the estate, even when the man of the manor was home. We just needed to let them think they were in charge. Her savvy for life and marriage was inspiring, and I hoped I would live up to the example she set. My only experience in running a home was the small house I had shared with Thomas in Wickhamshire. It barely surpassed the size of the cottage Hazel currently lived in. The main house of Cromwell's Passage was ten times the size, and the grounds of the estate were almost the same as the whole of Wickhamshire. My job was daunting at times, especially when one considered I was now a mother to a fourteen-year-old girl.

The preparations for Aquila's furlough were nearly complete. I'd been living in his chamber alone and trying to become comfortable with the luxury it afforded. We had not yet consummated our marriage. I presumed that might happen on this very evening in the enormous canopy bed that Aquila once shared with Rebecca. I tried to wipe that thought from my mind. I reasoned that if I'd been Aquila's first wife, I would want him to remarry and provide a mother figure for our daughter and a traditional family structure. I therefore assured myself that Rebecca's spirit would not haunt me or this room when it finally came time for Aquila and me to make love in the very same bed.

The aroma of baked cherry cobbler wafted in from the kitchen when Aquila entered the house in the late afternoon. His virility was not diminished by the tattered uniform I would need to mend. His smile was infectious as he, trailed by Isaiah, extended his arms and lifted his beloved daughter high in the air. He spun her around in the gleeful way a father might with a girl half her age. His joy was evident, but I detected the wince from the still sore rib. He was trying to hide it. Men have their pride. After he put Penny down, he embraced me tenderly before gazing into my eyes and kissing me on the lips. That warm, bubbly feeling brewed up from my toes. I had missed him so.

I gave Isaiah a hug and welcomed him into our home. I hadn't realized he'd been serving under Aquila, but it made perfect sense. General Washington preferred his regiment leaders to have men with whom they were familiar. Isaiah had faithfully served Aquila's mill for decades. When the dinner bell rang, we were all seated at the dining room table, and the first course was served.

"It's good to be home," Aquila stated triumphantly.

"I wish you didn't have to leave again, Father," Penny said.

"How long do you think the conflict will rage on?" I inquired.

"It's hard to say. America seeks true independence while the British insist on keeping some formal tie to the Crown. It appears we are at an impasse."

"Do you think Congress will officially declare war?" I asked.

"I think it's inevitable," Aquila said. Then he took a spoonful of the stew and remarked, "This is a treat. Field rations make a man hunger for a proper meal."

"Declaration or not, we are already embroiled in a war," Hazel stated. "Wounded soldiers never stop appearing at the hospital."

"I fear you are correct, Hazel. Isolated skirmishes have become full-scale battles. Both sides have sent more and more soldiers into the field." He bowed his head and became somber for a moment. "It is tragic how many young men have already died seeking our independence." He paused again, this time to collect himself. "Unfortunately, things will likely get worse before they get better."

"Can we win, Father?" inquired Penny.

"I must believe that we can. We will need help. Benjamin is trying his best to enlist aid from France. The French do not care to see England retain any more world influence than they already have."

"Do you think the French will enter the battle?" I asked.

"I wish I knew. Their government is divided on the matter. At a minimum, we hope they will provide arms and supplies."

The table became quiet. We finished the meal with a cup of tea, and then Isaiah offered to walk Hazel to her cottage on the way back to his home. Penny said goodnight, and Aquila and I sat there as the staff cleared the table. He looked at me the way lovers do when emotions carry two people into a blissful union of bodily pleasure. Our eyes locked. It was time to go upstairs. I was anxious. I had dreamed of making love to Aquila almost from the day I arrived in Annapolis. Now, we were husband and wife, and the time was at hand. Years passed since Thomas died. I was afraid that the long stretch without sharing a bed with a man would render me unable to please him. Butterflies filled my stomach.

Sensing my frayed nerves, Aquila rose from the table and slowly walked toward me. Like the gentleman he was, he approached from behind and tenderly kissed me on the cheek. Then he pulled the chair back for me to join him. As I rose, he delicately spun me around, and we shared the most passionate kiss.

"Essie, it will be all right." Gazing directly into my eyes, he said, "The good Lord sent you to me, and I love you with all my heart."

His touch, his kiss, and his kind words made my inhibitions slip away. I took his hand, and we walked up the grand staircase in silence. When we entered the chamber, I closed the door, and we undressed. Although we had been married for weeks, Aquila had not yet seen me without clothes. I was too thin, and although I had not yet seen my thirtieth birthday, the experiences of the past few years aged my body precariously. Consequently, I undressed as quickly as was reasonable and slipped under the covers.

Aquila winced while undressing. His rib was still sore. His body was splendid. The strength of his physique was remarkable. But I already knew this from the times we embraced and the occasions when he required medical attention.

When he was in the bed and snuggled up next to me, the fear vanished, and I felt safe, warm, and, most important, loved. God graced me with Aquila and Penny, and I would be forever grateful. We held each other tight and kissed as his hand explored my body. He was so gentle, it tickled me, and I let go a small laugh.

His head rose from the pillow. He grinned and said with a mischievous tone, "Is something funny?"

"No, your touch was so subtle, it sent a tickle across my bones. It was magical. Please, by all means, continue."

Aquila kissed me softly and made my body quiver in a way it never had before, not even with Thomas. When he entered me, I was surprised by how naturally my body responded to our union, as if we had been passionately entwined for a lifetime.

When we both lay exhausted, soaked in the pleasure of matrimonial harmony, Aquila fell into a deep sleep. I stepped out of the soft feather bed, kneeled beside it, and prayed to God to keep this man safe during the war. I prayed like never before. For the first time in years, God was wholeheartedly on my side. I prayed the same was true for America.

# CHAPTER FIFTY-TWO

## *Cromwell*

## the Maryland Colony

## 3 SEPTEMBER 1775

Henrik was beside himself. Months of relentless searching yielded nothing in the quest for a second doctor. It seems, he said, that no American city could spare a doctor. Passage from Europe was more challenging than when Henrik and Fleur crossed the Atlantic Ocean. Even his colleagues in Holland had turned Henrik down. I tried to console him. The man was exhausted. I was not sure when he rested. He was always at the hospital. Fleur brought him meals, and I was doing my best to assist with whatever medical procedures were practical. Along with keeping order at Cromwell's Passage, my duties as the hospital's administrator, and raising a teenaged girl, I was feeling Henrik's strain. Hazel was working seven days a week, and when she had a little time, she began managing the requisition of supplies. This task had become significantly more difficult. Everything was in short supply. More and more, we were relying on imported goods, but even this path was fraught with delay. When one considered the time and higher than normal cargo costs, keeping a busy hospital properly supplied was no easy task. Thank God I'd insisted on planting a medicinal garden. Penny assumed responsibility for its care and harvest.

At midmorning, I needed a break and went to the trough outside for drinking water.

Pastor Vinson enthusiastically greeted me as he brushed by a stoic redcoat. "Hello, Essie." He inhaled deeply. "The early morning air smells so fresh. God has graced us with another beautiful day."

I wished I could savor the simple pleasure of life in the face of so much adversity. Pastor Vinson had a gift for lifting others.

"'Good morning, Pastor Vinson. What is on your agenda today?"

He smiled and his rosy cheeks puffed. "I am having a linen drive. Hazel tells me you are in short supply. I am enlisting the ladies of Cromwell and surrounding towns to donate or make fresh linen for your beds. They will also make surgical cloths for wound care. I will round them up as they become available and deliver them to you."

I nearly broke down in tears. I cherished this man. His kind manner helped me in so many ways. Namely, to reconnect with the Lord, but just as important, to believe in myself and the goodness of people. After Thomas died, I foundered in those areas.

"Oh, and I almost forgot," he said, reaching into his inner breast pocket. "I was at the general store earlier, and this post arrived for you from Pennsylvania."

He handed me the folded parchment with the Cromwell family seal.

The only person who had access to that seal was Aquila. I'd heard nary a word from my beloved since his furlough. Only prayers kept me from a full-scale panic.

"I'll leave you in peace to read your letter."

I thanked him and sat down on the front steps of the hospital.

*My Dearest Essie,*

*I beg your forgiveness for not writing sooner. Skirmishes turned to battle have occupied my full attention as we continue to ward off British attempts to seize control of territory through the valley and along the river. I have been involved in conflicts from the north of Maryland all the way to Philadelphia. General Washington tells of similar battles in New Jersey, New York, and Massachusetts. The British have cut off principal supply routes by sea and land, and my men are in short supply of everything from uniforms to rations. Consequently, I must carefully manage every aspect of my regiment. Needless to say, it is exhausting.*

*I think of you and Penny constantly and dream of the day when we can lead a normal family life in a free and independent America. To win this war, however, we will need help. Congress is urgently working on the problem, and I continue to receive updates and actively contribute opinions and votes on key matters. Taking part in Congress while engaging in battle is a slow and arduous endeavor, to say the least. We are still hopeful the French will send troops, munitions, and supplies. To date, they have sent much-needed funds, but we need more.*

*The memory of your touch, your beautiful smile, and your flame within keeps me going. General Washington is sending our regiment on a reconnaissance mission to a place in Pennsylvania called Valley Forge. He wishes to see if it might serve as a future stronghold for the Continental Army. Valley Forge is near to Philadelphia, and General Washington is sure that the British will wage war there in the effort to take our capitol.*

*I pray you and Penny are well. I will write again as soon as I am able.*

*All my love,*

*Aquila*

As I grasped the raised butterfly pendant, I drew a deep breath and once again prayed for Aquila's safety. I thought to write and let him know about the challenges at the hospital, but I didn't wish to burden his mind with problems that he could do nothing about. Folding his letter, I returned to the hospital. I tucked the letter into the secret compartment of my rolltop desk and returned to the line of wounded needing medical attention.

# CHAPTER FIFTY-THREE

## *Cromwell*

## the Maryland Colony

### 15 OCTOBER 1775

We received most of our news of the war from the patients. The latest stories were told of a battle outside Baltimore. The fighting was so fierce, men from both sides fell in alarming numbers. I assisted Henrik in surgery. So many did not make it, and numerous others lost limbs. Despite Pastor Vinson's intentions, bandages and cloth remained scarce. We made do by boiling the clothes of the deceased and turning the garments into medical supplies. Henrik was wearing down. He appeared to have aged ten years in the previous six months. His nerves were so frayed, he lashed out at anyone he encountered. Fleur tried her best to boost his mood but to no avail. After all, how much could one man absorb?

Most of us worked through the night. I made up a cot for Penny, who slept in my office. Prudence was squeamish around patients, so I sent her to be with her Aunt Celia. Pastor Vinson accompanied her. When I finished treating the last patient from the recent fighting, I took off my bloody apron. The nonstop medical procedures had also dirtied my dress. Because of the heavy fighting and long hours, I started keeping extra clothes on the premises so that I wouldn't have to raid the church's surplus. I went to my office to change into a fresh garment and noticed that Penny was gone. Perhaps she woke early and was tending to nurse rounds. She'd become adept at catering to the needs of the wounded men. This entire affair forced her to grow up too fast. I silently wished I could shield her from the travails of these terrible times.

After changing, I poured tea from last night's kettle. While cold, the flavor soothed me. I sat in my office chair and let out a long breath. Sometimes, I thought, one arrives at a point of being so incredibly tired that a numbness takes over and, oddly, allows a push forward.

I lay down in Penny's cot and let myself relax. *Just five minutes,* I promised myself. Then, I would resume my other duties. My eyes were closed, but my mind was very much alert. I thought of myself as the hunter camping in the deep forest during a long night. One could rest but not soundly slumber. Danger was always on the prowl. This protective sheath became a godsend, never clearer than when an unmistakable scream emboldened my senses. It was Penny! She was in trouble. I grabbed the musket I kept behind the door and walked slowly toward the hospital entrance. A swath of redcoats stood defiantly on the road. The leader kept Penny in a left-handed stranglehold while he held a pistol to her temple.

"Mrs. Wright, lay down your weapon and remain on the hospital step with your hands in the air," commanded the lead soldier.

My first instinct was to fight. I had to protect Penny. But I, one woman with a musket, was no match for a regiment of soldiers armed to the teeth. I obeyed the order and stood there, waiting for further instruction. The silence of the moment kept building. The redcoats brought dozens of their wounded to our doorstep. The injured outnumbered the armed men. I struggled to see through the thick of the gathering. A moment later, the sea of redcoats parted, and a familiar but unwelcome rider appeared atop an imposing steed.

"We meet again, Mrs. Lassiter. Oh, pardon me, I believe it's now Mrs. Wright, is it not? You have done well for yourself," stated Governor Templeton. "You should know that the paltry array of men guarding your hospital are dead." He paused as his horse brought him up to the stairs upon which I stood. "The blood of my Olivia and our baby is on your hands," he huffed. "If you do not relinquish control of this hospital, you will also feel the pain from the loss of a child."

I gazed at Penny. To emphasize the threat uttered by the governor, the soldier holding Penny shoved the pistol into her head. Penny's knees buckled, and tears streamed down her face. The innocence of youth was being annihilated by the evils of war.

I gathered my remaining strength. I had no choice. I had to surrender.

Before I said a word, Hazel and Henrik appeared behind me. Hazel held a pistol and Henrik a musket. They had drawn their weapons and were ready to fire.

"Release the girl, or I'll put a shot right between the eyes of the governor," Henrik proclaimed.

"Do not be foolish, Dr. Van Der Beek," the governor replied. "These men will take you out before you fire the first round." Then pointing to Penny, he said, "And you wouldn't want to risk the life of poor Miss Wright?"

Hazel, known for her sharp-tongued rebukes toward authority, was the next to speak. "Doctor, we have no choice. We must lie down our arms . . . if for no other reason than for the life of the girl."

Henrik lowered his weapon and held it by his side.

"That's more like it," stated Governor Templeton. "These men need medical attention. You shall immediately tend to them with favor over all others. If you refuse, we will kill the rebel wounded in each bed where they lie." Then he dismounted the horse and walked toward the soldier holding Penny. He stroked her brown hair and said, "And as insurance, we shall keep this young lady in our company. No harm will come to her if everyone does as I say."

Defiantly, Henrik replied, "You can take over this hospital, but without a doctor, it will be little more than a place of refuge."

"I thought you might take that stance, Doctor. You will continue working. If you refuse to abide by my orders, I will consider it an act of treason, punishable by death. Public hangings will begin immediately upon my order." He stared at me with fire in his eyes and said, "Give me a reason to sentence you. I welcome it."

The quiet of the next moment defined the doom hanging over us. Our predicament was perilous. I was so tired that I couldn't think fast enough.

"Essie, do something," cried Penny. The desperation in her voice was heartbreaking. If I thought it would help Penny, I would have laid down my life in that very moment, but weary as my mind was, it would be a frivolous act. I looked at Penny reassuringly and mouthed the words, *Be brave.*

She mouthed back, *I'll try.*

With that, the three of us relinquished our weapons, and the British stood victoriously in the street.

"Bring the prisoner to the front," Governor Templeton commanded. And then, a tall, gaunt man in shackles moved forward with a redcoat on either side. It was Timothy! He was alive.

Governor Templeton said to us, "I believe Dr. Clarke is assigned to this hospital." Then, to the British soldiers, "Release him."

"Dr. Clarke will resume his work. These men will begin carrying the wounded into the hospital. This facility and all of Cromwell will be heavily guarded. Do not entertain any thoughts of rebellion. Do we understand one another?"

We all nodded, and Timothy staggered up the steps. He had bruises and was extremely weak. I embraced him. "Come, let's get you cleaned up. Henrik will look you over, and I will get you a proper meal."

Before we entered the building, the lecherous governor snarled one more edict. "Oh, Mrs. Wright, don't plan on returning home anytime soon. These men and I will assume title and occupancy of Cromwell's Passage. After losing my family, it is the least I am owed in reparation."

I said nothing but was overcome with the realization that once again, I was a prisoner. I was homeless, and, worst of all, evil and treacherous men had my stepdaughter, and I couldn't trust them to honor their word.

The redcoats dragged Penny down the dusty road toward the town center and its recently built jail, and I watched in horror.

# CHAPTER FIFTY-FOUR

## Cromwell

## the Maryland Colony

### 30 OCTOBER 1775

It had been two weeks since the British took over the Maryland Hospital. Celia provided rooms for Hazel and me. I was grateful but worried the enemy might also overtake her home. Celia assured me that between her slaves and employed laborers who were too old to join the army, we were safe. Penny remained a captive, and no amount of reasoning with the governor would change the situation. I tried to visit her on several occasions, but each time, I was refused. The guards assured me she was being well cared for. I wanted to believe that.

The hospital staff routinely refused admission to Continental Army troops. There was nowhere else to go. Medics were few and far between, and the next closest hospital was in Philadelphia, a two-day journey from Cromwell. People left men to die in the street.

The commanding officer burst into my office as I was rereading my last letter from Aquila. He snatched the parchment from my hand and demanded, "What is this?"

"Just a letter from my husband. It is none of your concern."

He held up a hand, indicating he wished for silence while he read the letter.

"I should have known France was aiding the rebellion. And Valley Forge, eh? This is most useful." Before I realized the implications went beyond my privacy, he left with my letter in hand.

I chased after him. "Return the letter at once!" I demanded. But my words rang hollow, and my actions were meaningless. The damage had been done. Aquila had shared a portion of General Washington's war strategy, and I accidentally betrayed his trust. For that matter, I unknowingly betrayed America. A powerful wave of guilt consumed me.

The British commander said nothing. He just went on his way.

Distraught, I ran to find Henrik and Timothy. I needed to tell them what I'd done. Their counsel was vital. The three of us walked out back, beyond the medicinal garden, and found a place where we whispered to one another without fear of being overheard.

"How could you be so careless?" Henrik admonished.

"It's not like she did so intentionally," said Timothy. He gallantly defended my honor.

I didn't view Henrik's question with malice. He was at his wit's end. He did not sign up for the hazards of war when he came from Holland.

"We must get word to the Continental Army. They must know what is happening here," Henrik declared.

"With our soldiers being turned away for two weeks, word must have reached General Washington up north. I tell you this—if Aquila knew his daughter was being held in captivity, he'd have been here by now," I proclaimed.

"I agree with Essie. Word has likely reached our troops. But even so, we will take no chances. Who can we trust to ride north and make sure?" Timothy asked.

There was only one logical candidate. "Pastor Vinson," I blurted out. "He routinely travels to visit parishioners. The British will think nothing of it."

"Excellent," replied Henrik. "Can he leave today?"

Before we made it back into the hospital, the sound of thundering hooves and loud soldiers barreled into town. At the head of the pack was none other than Colonel Charles Greene. From the north, another band of patriots galloped in and was led by General Washington himself. Behind him was Isaiah. The two regiments met in the street in front of the hospital. Isaiah was part of Aquila's regiment. Where was he? Had he been killed?

I ran to Isaiah. The fear in my eyes must have been evident. I didn't need to ask the obvious question. Isaiah understood. "Mrs. Greene sent a courier to Virgina to alert Colonel Greene as to the status of Cromwell. Colonel Greene sent a courier to Aquila. They agreed to meet here to retake Cromwell. Aquila is at the jail with five other men freeing Penny. He will be along shortly." I thanked him, and he slipped me his pistol. "Hide this under your cloak. The fighting will get ugly. If a redcoat confronts you, shoot first and ask questions later."

Ten minutes later, Aquila rode down the street with Penny behind him. She clutched her father's waist and held on for dear life. I could only imagine the relief she must have felt at the sight of her father coming to her rescue. Aquila blew me a kiss and helped Penny dismount.

"Take Penny inside. Keep her safe. We will meet up later."

And with that, he led his troops to Cromwell's Passage to ferret out the governor and remove his men from our home. Aquila and his men took the main road to Cromwell's Passage. The forest route would have been difficult for the large contingent of soldiers.

Witnessing their disappearance in the cold fall air, I hastily took Penny inside. Isaiah's pistol rested inside my cloak. I prayed I would not need to use it. I had one foot inside the hospital when that evil voice rattled my resolve.

"Mrs. Wright. It appears that you have orchestrated a coup. Need I remind you this is an act of treason. For that, I hereby sentence you to be hanged at sunset tonight." The expression on Governor Templeton's face was macabre. His pronouncement of my guilt galled me. No evidence existed to support the claim.

"Seize her!" Governor Templeton commanded.

Two redcoats approached. Without thinking, I yelled to Penny, "Run, hide!"

Once she was out of range, I pulled the pistol from under my cloak and fired at Governor Templeton. My shot hit him squarely in the chest, and his ruffled white shirt filled with blood. The governor's eyes grew wide with shock. He tilted sideways and fell off the horse. The two soldiers attempting to apprehend me ran to the governor's aid. But the man was dead. I saw from where I stood. I killed the governor of Maryland. I took a life. As horrible of a human being as he was, God did not abide murder. I was no better than the man I just killed. The pistol dangled in my cold, sweat-laden hand, and then it fell to the ground. Shots rang out from behind. The scent of gunpowder stung my nose, and my eyes rolled backward. The last thing I remembered before blacking out was Charles's voice yelling, "Take that, you bastards," and the townspeople cheering in triumph.

—⚍—

A few hours later, I awoke in the hospital. Hazel stood above me with an open bottle of smelling salts. I sprang from the bed frantically, saying, "Is Penny all right? What about Aquila?" And then I remembered. I killed Governor Templeton. "They are going to hang me, aren't they?"

Hazel laughed. "Hang you? Why they are more likely to erect a statue of you. People in the street are celebrating your bravery. Once Templeton fell, our men swept Cromwell clean of redcoats, including the patients in the hospital."

I breathed a sigh of relief. I had acted on instinct and now felt somewhat astounded. My memory flashed back to my first days in the London Debtor's Prison and my inability to defend young Marie. I was now a different person. Perhaps the passing of years granted this newfound courage. Or maybe I was like a wolf who guards her pack to keep the ones she loves safe. Lost in these thoughts, I didn't notice my husband enter the room with Penny.

He approached the bedside, kissed my forehead, and stroked my hair. "You are nothing short of extraordinary. A hero worthy of commendation," he said.

Given my thoughts just prior to his arrival, I couldn't fathom such praise. I had followed my instincts, and the direction given to me by Isaiah: Shoot first and ask questions later. In response, I said nothing to Aquila. I smiled and accepted praise for which I felt unworthy.

Penny came to the other side of the bed and took my hand. Overnight, in the throes of war, she blossomed into a strong young lady. The ordeal she endured! At her age, I might have melted in the face of such adversity. I told her as much.

"I found strength I didn't know I possessed. My mother is a brave woman."

It didn't register at first. I thought Penny referred to Rebecca, whom I'd never met. But her eyes revealed her admiration and reverence . . . *for me*. My heart's melody rang true, like the beauty of a harp's song. The moment lingered until an unfamiliar voice made its presence known.

"Mrs. Wright, it is my honor and privilege to make your acquaintance. You have done a great service for America."

I was staring up at the face of General George Washington. For a man who had just emerged victorious from battle, his appearance was as if he were about to attend a ball. The powdered hair remained in place, and his dark blue uniform held only a modest amount of grime. His voice was strong yet compassionate, and his eyes revealed a man of genuine nature.

"General Washington, the honor is all mine. You are too kind to pay me a visit."

"I shall write Congress to speak of your heroics. I have requested that they extend to you the same honor for which we grant the bravest of our men. You will be the first woman ever to receive such recognition."

I blushed. My face felt hot. "I don't know what to say. I am unworthy of such an honor."

"Nonsense," he replied. "In fact, I don't feel a commendation is sufficient. I have recommended to Aquila that we rechristen this hospital as the Esther Wright Hospital. We shall construct a plaque that memorializes today's events and place it on the face of the building as a shining example of your bravery and dedication to your country."

Aquila beamed. "As a member of Congress, I will be voting in favor of these measures."

"As will I," said an exuberant Charles Greene, who had just entered with Celia.

There I lay, collecting my strength and my wits. Those I loved surrounded me. Yes, I killed an evil man who wrought death upon us, but something good arose from something bad. God had empowered me to extinguish those who might defy Him and bring harm to people. I would explore these thoughts in private conversation with Pastor Vinson. But in my heart, I believed I was forthright in my deliberations.

# CHAPTER FIFTY-FIVE

## Cromwell's Passage
## the Maryland Colony

### 14 DECEMBER 1775

Fortunately, the short occupation of our estate by the British Army did minimal damage. Once they were driven out, the house staff had done astonishing work getting everything back in order. I required all the beds stripped and the linens washed with great care. The staff scrubbed the floors and restored Cromwell's Passage to its former glory. Now, I could plan the ornamentation of the house for the holidays. I prayed Aquila would be home for Christmas, but with conflicts still occurring, the prospects appeared dim. His regiment traveled even further north and was now somewhere in New York. Keeping track was a challenge. By the time a letter might arrive, weeks had passed, and the troops had likely moved on. Penny and I spoke often of a conclusion to the war. An ending was nowhere in sight.

The hospital was still busy with an endless flow of wounded, and with no other doctors around, I was pressed into service as the Cromwell midwife. Penny accompanied me, and I made her my apprentice. She was a few years younger than I had been when I apprenticed back in London. With the expectant mothers, she showed a compassionate manner. She was nearing the point where she might attend these calls on her own.

Today, however, all was calm, and I had time to plan Christmas dinner. Our guests would include Celia, Hazel, Timothy, Henrik, and Fleur, and God willing, our men fighting for America's independence. I pictured our dining table, covered in the finest white linen and lined with red and green lace. Aquila would be at the head accompanied by the jubilant smile of Charles and the stoic demeanor worn by Isaiah. I hoped my contemplation would prove true. I pondered goose or turkey for the main course and couldn't make up my mind.

A knock on the front door disturbed my thoughts. Our butler answered, and I returned to my chore, paying the visitor no mind. The butler entered the library where I was sitting and handed me two dispatches. The first bore the seal of the Continental Congress and was very official looking. It read:

> *The Second Continental Congress requests Mrs. Esther Wright's presence in Philadelphia on the seventh day of June in the year 1776 to receive an official commendation for acts of bravery in service to her country.*

A chill ran down my spine. This invitation was not unexpected, but in the aftermath of the events of 30 October, I had dismissed it from my mind.

The second dispatch was from Aquila. It read:

> *My Dearest Essie,*
>
> *By now, you have likely received the dispatch from Congress inviting you to Philadelphia to receive a commendation. General Washington has granted me a brief leave of absence in order that I may be by your side. We will share one night together, and then I must return to battle. I ask that you travel on main roads only, driven by Clement and accompanied by Penny. As a precaution, I have arranged for four Harford County militiamen to accompany you. I cannot disclose military positions or strategy, but suffice it to say that I believe the main road route to Philadelphia should be safe to travel come spring. If this changes, I will advise forthwith and delay your appearance in the capital.*

*I pray I will see you and Penny for Christmas, but at the moment, I do not hold out much hope. I will see you no later than 7 June in Philadelphia. Until then, I am your devoted husband.*

*Love,*

*Aquila*

## CHAPTER FIFTY-SIX

---

### *Philadelphia*
### the Pennsylvania Colony

---

### 7 JUNE 1776

The journey to Philadelphia was without incident. Clement felt it best to continue through the night and not risk stopping anywhere without cause. Summer was upon us, and already the air was heavy with moisture. We emerged from the carriage and stepped onto the cobblestone street. I gazed up at the Pennsylvania State House, the home of the Second Continental Congress, and found myself in awe. An architectural marvel, the structure was two stories and had a single level wing built on either side. The steeple was breathtaking, and in its cupola hung the largest and shiniest bell one might imagine.

Aquila emerged from the main entrance to greet us. More than six months passed since we last saw one another. He bear-hugged both Penny and me. I didn't want him to let go. But he did, and he stood back and looked up with us.

"This structure is both grand and unyielding," proclaimed Aquila.

Before we entered the building, I spied Benjamin leaving with another gentleman. He noticed us and approached with open arms.

"Benjamin!" I embraced him tightly. "You are a sight for sore eyes."

"It is good to see you looking so well, Essie. And I hear you and Aquila have married. And you are appearing before Congress today. You have been quite busy since we last met."

I blushed and smiled broadly.

"Where are my manners?" Benjamin asked. "Allow me to introduce my colleague, Mr. John Hancock of Massachusetts."

Mr. Hancock already knew Aquila. They shook hands, and then he took mine and brought it to his lips, softly kissing it. "Mrs. Wright, welcome to Philadelphia. I shall be among the legions singing your praises at today's ceremony."

"You flatter me, Mr. Hancock. I am but a humble servant of the Lord."

"I hear you are much more than that, Mrs. Wright. In fact, I would sign my name in attestation."

"You are much too kind," I replied.

Benjamin walked off with Mr. Hancock, and Aquila escorted us into the State House. Despite its size, the main hall lacked the grandeur one would expect for a building of such importance. The chairs and tables were old, distressed, and mismatched. It looked like someone had taken the curtains from a prison. I was sure that no woman engaged in the building's finishing touches. For the life of me, I could not see erecting a beautiful building on the outside and not practicing the same diligence in the interior.

Aquila informed me that Benjamin and Deborah insisted we stay in their home while we were there. Benjamin felt obliged since he had spent so much time at Cromwell's Passage.

"And he likes us," I added with a smile.

"Congress will be in recess until two o'clock. Come, we will go drop our things and have lunch. Then we will return to the State House for the afternoon session."

We ate lunch at a local tavern on Chestnut Street as passersby traveled to and fro. Unlike the slower town life in Cromwell, everyone in Philadelphia was in a hurry. The city bustled with the growing excitement of the long-endured hope for independence, and it showed in the faces of its citizens. I finished a bowl of chicken soup and a sourdough roll. It was all the food I could stomach. The appearance before Congress caused me anxiety, and my innards paid the price.

"Are you ready, my love?" asked Aquila.

I gulped a swig of water and nodded. We walked a few blocks to the State House, and my knees quivered as Aquila held the door for Penny and me. Aquila sat in the designated spot for representatives, and we settled in the front row, a special place reserved for honored guests. I sat facing the master of ceremonies—the president of this august body, the man I met earlier from Massachusetts, Mr. John Hancock.

He smiled to acknowledge my presence, but other more pressing matters diverted his attention. He peered out among the throng of representatives from the colonies and addressed the group.

"Honored Colleagues. The afternoon session of the Second Continental Congress shall come to order. I have just received word that King George III has refused to hear our Olive Branch Petition and thus has declared the American colonies rebellious and unworthy of deliberation or negotiation."

A man raised his hand.

"The gentleman from Virginia, Henry Lee, is recognized."

"Thank you, Mr. Hancock. Given this news, be it resolved, America makes its own declaration. A declaration of independence."

"Is there a second to this motion?" Hancock asked.

A delegate raised his hand and was promptly acknowledged by John Hancock.

"Motion carried," stated Hancock. "Are there volunteers willing to work in committee to draft this declaration?"

Hands went up again.

"We hereby commission the following delegates to draft a declaration of independence.

The chair recognizes Mr. John Adams of Massachusetts, Dr. Benjamin Franklin of Pennsylvania, Mr. Thomas Jefferson of Virginia, Mr. Robert Livingston of New York, and Mr. Roger Sherman of Connecticut. Mr. Jefferson, being the chair of said committee, will present a draft for consideration by Congress as soon as possible."

John Hancock threw down a gavel and turned his attention to me.

"This Congress has held many men in esteem and officially acknowledged each for matters of bravery and ingenuity. Today, for the first time, we shall do so for a woman."

A hush fell over the room, followed by the gasping sound of men in total disbelief. I imagined their thoughts. *What could a woman have done to earn the recognition of Congress?*

Mr. Hancock held up both arms with palms out to quiet the delegates. "Now, now. When you hear the tale of Mrs. Esther Wright, the wife of Aquila Wright, our delegate from Maryland, I assure you we will ease your concerns."

Mr. Hancock paused and then continued with his planned remarks.

"Mrs. Wright helped found the Maryland Hospital and serves as its administrator, surgical nurse, and town midwife, not to mention the hard work of being a mother to a teenaged girl and a homemaker in one of Harford County's largest estates. On 30 October 1775, Mrs. Wright was caught in the crosshairs of the British governor of Maryland, Robert Templeton. Unknown to Mrs. Wright, the Continental Army had regiments entering Cromwell from two directions. Delegate Colonel Charles Greene of Cromwell came from the south, and General George Washington accompanied by Delegate Aquila Wright, Mrs. Wright's husband, led the northern regiment. Governor Templeton was aware of the troops and falsely blamed Mrs. Wright for staging a coup. He proclaimed her guilt without evidence or benefit of a trial and sentenced her to be hung in the town square that very evening at sundown. Mrs. Wright, using a pistol she hid beneath her cloak, took aim at the governor and shot him in the chest, killing him instantly. Because of Mrs. Wright's bravery, our troops could quickly overtake the British and evict them from our hospital and the town of Cromwell. Mrs. Wright, this Congress extends its most heartfelt gratitude for your courageous actions on behalf of our country."

I didn't know what to expect. The room was silent. These men, America's leaders, seemed uncertain about applauding a woman.

Then my dear husband stood and clapped his hands once, resoundingly, and then again with the same cadence. Charles joined him, and then Benjamin rose and did the same. Mr. Hancock joined in, and before I knew it, I was the recipient of raucous applause.

When the chamber settled, Mr. Hancock called me forward and presented me with a piece of rolled parchment commemorating my achievement. Aquila and Penny joined me at the head of the room, and not knowing what was appropriate in such a circumstance, I curtsied. Later that evening, we finished supper at Benjamin's house, and when we had consumed the last of the tea and apple pie, Penny went up to her room.

"We'll look after her and make sure she has a hearty breakfast in the morning for the journey home," stated Deborah.

I was lost, uncertain about the meaning of her remarks. Then, Aquila came behind me and delicately pulled out my chair. I stood, and he took my hand. "I have a surprise for you, my love."

"A surprise? Why, Mr. Wright, whatever could it be?" I said teasingly in the way we'd become accustomed.

"Come with me. We shall return for Penny in the morning."

"Well, it seems everyone here knows the nature of this secret but me."

When we were outside, Aquila said, "We shall take a short carriage ride to the river separating Pennsylvania and New Jersey. There, we will board a large boat, where I have hired a captain to navigate the gentle river. We will have our private quarters and will remain undisturbed."

"Oh, Aquila, it sounds so romantic. But you know I hate being on the water."

"I do recall that your past experiences at sea have been somewhat unpleasant." He brought me close and embraced me passionately. He looked into my eyes and said, "Trust me. Your opinion of being on the water will be different in the morning."

# EPILOGUE

## *Cromwell's Passage*
## the State of Maryland

## 4 JULY 1776

It had taken a month. Thomas Jefferson did a superb job drafting a declaration of independence embodying the ideology of America. With input from the committee and a few other adjustments, all the delegates ratified the declaration, giving birth to the United States of America. And I was born again with it.

When I began this diary, I was a midwife married to the town doctor in a quaint English village, believing I had reached the pinnacle of my existence. I was content with that notion. I loved Thomas and the life we had. Were it not for smallpox taking the lives of so many in Wickhamshire, Thomas and I might still live contentedly in England. When I came to America and met Pastor Vinson, he told me that sometimes bad things happen to good people. God teaches us to respond in the face of that adversity. I didn't believe Pastor Vinson at the time, but I do now. With all my heart and soul. Being thrown into the London Debtor's Prison was the worst thing that ever happened to me, short of losing Thomas. But then, in a twist of fate, a wonderful, kind man purchased my indentured servitude. Aquila helped me to love myself once again and to be free to love others in kind. He provided me with the opportunity to love him and Penny, and to start a hospital! My fondest hope was that the war would soon end and he would return home to us—Penny, me, and our unborn child. I wished for this with all my might, but I never escaped the words of George Washington from when we first met. As I learned, General Washington was usually correct in his assessments. This was just the beginning.

# AUTHOR'S NOTE

My earliest recollection of reading adult fiction dates to the beginning of the 1970s. My father was an avid reader. In a series of paper bags in a basement closet, I discovered dozens of his old paperbacks. Chief amongst these were Ian Fleming's James Bond novels, which I fell in love with. Later, Dad introduced me to Arthur Haley, who so famously chose an industry and created amazing stories from each. Gems like *Hotel, Airport, The Moneychangers,* and *The Final Diagnosis* kept me wanting more. Later, I followed my father's love of Robert Ludlum, of *The Bourne Identity* fame. As much as these successful authors enabled me to escape the loneliness of growing up as the youngest child of a broken home, my true reading passion came from historical fiction. My favorite author was James Clavell, who whisked me away to the early days of Hong Kong trading, feudal warriors, and Asian business tycoons. I later discovered other authors who successfully transported me to other places and times where I could bathe in history while escaping reality.

As I embarked on my writing journey, I immersed myself in thrillers that made the completely impossible feel semi-plausible. And while I enjoyed this protracted stretch of my imagination, I had always yearned to write historical fiction. *The Diary of Essie Lassiter* was an attempt to challenge myself from many standpoints, namely writing as an eighteenth-century midwife and in a first-person diary format.

I should point out that while this book was loosely based on actual events, I have chosen not to stick to historical timelines in all cases. As a novelist, I feel strongly that my final output is for entertainment value and not necessarily for historical accuracy. With that said, I tried to stay true to history where it suited the storyline.

While doing research for this novel, several people helped steer me in good directions. Carol Deibel, a notable Harford County historian, provided the tale of women in London's debtor's prison being shipped off to the colonies to rid England of overflowing facilities. The following people referred me to helpful books and research materials: Peter Friesen and Dr. Jennifer Ogborne of Historic St. Mary's City, and David Armenti of the Maryland Center for History and Culture. Thanks to each for sharing your time and expertise.

As always, my first reader and sounding board is my wife. I cannot express enough how much I appreciate Denise's love and support of my writing habit and crazy ideas.

I would also like to offer my sincere gratitude to a wonderful group of friends and family who volunteered to be my beta reader group. Tom Brunner, Leah Contino, Greg Harmis, Anne Hicks, Dave Jennings, Debbie Jennings, Becca Mitchell, Jay Polakoff, Ryan Polakoff, Bruce Savadkin, Greg Tutino, and Liz Tutino. You each have my undying gratitude.

The arduous task of scrutinizing a manuscript for errors fell to two wonderful ladies: Jeanne Brooks and Sheila Weinstock. Their exceptional effort ensures a flawless reading experience. I thank you. My tired eyes thank you.

I would like to thank Gwyn Flowers of GKS Creative for outdoing herself on the book cover and interior design. This makes number five! Your talents and skill are appreciated. Similarly, this book would not be the quality product it is without my longtime copyeditor, Kim Bookless. Kim is the unsung hero of book publishing.

Shelly Allen was the winner of a contest to have a character named after her. Shelly's character appears in the early chapters when Essie first lands in Annapolis.

And now, it's on to the research phase for Book 2 in the Essie Lassiter Trilogy. The book will cover Essie and Aquila throughout the war years and should prove to be an exciting second installment. Book 2 will be titled *Freedom's Lonely Cry*.

Finally, I wish to express my appreciation to you, the reader. Your dedication to my stories is humbling. I will endeavor to keep the pages turning!

Sam Polakoff
October 8, 2024

# PLEASE LEAVE A REVIEW

THANK YOU FOR READING

## The Diary of Essie Lassiter.

Your honest reviews on Amazon and Goodreads
are greatly appreciated.

Tell a friend!

# COMING SOON

# FREEDOM'S LONELY CRY

BOOK 2 *of the* ESSIE LASSITER TRILOGY

## SAM POLAKOFF

sampolakoff.com

# STAY IN TOUCH

Join our mailing list for updates on future releases.

## FOLLOW

Facebook @sampolakoffauthor

Instagram @sampolakoffauthor

X @spolakoffauthor

YouTube @sampolakoff4320

**KOMODO DRAGON BOOKS**

Komodo Dragon Books, LLC

Forest Hill, Maryland
https://komododragonbooks.com